DEAD ON TARGET

Red began counting out loud, having already calculated how long he thought the missile would take to cover the distance to them. Red let the missile get as close as he dared, then launched the final flares.

"It's veering," Dizie called out, relieved.

The missile indeed appeared to veer as its infrared counter-counter measures kicked in. In actuality, the missile was leading the plane, waiting for the flare to fall away before re-engaging the target.

Once the last flare fell away, the missile tried to turn back into the plane. Red watched in horror as the missile screamed over the right wing, his eyes growing wide as the proximity fuse detonated the warhead just outside the cockpit window. . . .

JOE GRIBBLE

SILENT LIGHTNING

AN ONYX BOOK

ONYX
Published by the Penguin Group
Penguin Putnam Inc., 375 Hudson Street,
New York, New York 10014, U.S.A.
Penguin Books Ltd, 27 Wrights Lane,
London W8 5TZ, England
Penguin Books Australia Ltd, Ringwood,
Victoria, Australia
Penguin Books Canada Ltd, 10 Alcorn Avenue,
Toronto, Ontario, Canada M4V 3B2
Penguin Books (N.Z.) Ltd, 182–190 Wairau Road,
Auckland 10, New Zealand

Penguin Books Ltd, Registered Offices:
Harmondsworth, Middlesex, England

First published by Onyx, an imprint of Dutton NAL,
a member of Penguin Putnam Inc.

First Printing, November, 1998
10 9 8 7 6 5 4 3 2 1

 REGISTERED TRADEMARK—MARCA REGISTRADA

Printed in the United States of America

"War is an ugly thing but not the ugliest of things; the decayed and degraded state of moral and patriotic feelings which thinks that nothing is worth fighting for is much worse. A man who has nothing for which he is willing to fight, nothing he cares about more than his personal safety, is a miserable creature who has no chance of being free unless made and kept so by the exertions of better men than himself."

—JOHN STUART MILL, 1868

To our fallen comrades.

ACKNOWLEDGMENTS

This story could not have been possible without the Airborne Laser Lab. The team that developed it—military, civilian, and contractor—pioneered the next generation weapons which will ensure our nation's continued freedom. Future generations will likely remember them by the Airborne Laser Lab creed: Peace Through Light.

I owe a great deal of thanks to the fine folks at Dutton/Signet who provided me the opportunity to create my first book: Joseph Pittman for opening the door, Todd Keithley for pointing out what was wrong and how it could be repaired, Kari Paschall and Aili Dalton for ushering the project along, and Michaela Hamilton and Elaine Koster for their continued interest and support.

There was much needed assistance in other quarters, and I wish to thank Bob Diforio and Alan Kaufman for steering me in the right direction.

But above all, my heartfelt thanks go to my wife, Nedra, for her unwavering support and encouragement.

PROLOGUE

1983—Somewhere over the California desert

"Agar three three, this is Range Control."

Major Kirk, the test director, listened intently to the voice over his headset, barely audible above the radio static.

"You are approaching maneuver point 'X-ray,'" Range Control continued. "On my mark begin left turn to heading two seven zero."

"Three . . . two . . . one . . . Mark!"

Kirk felt a gentle roll as the big Airborne Laser Laboratory, the ALL, pulled into a twenty-degree left bank, the final maneuver before the A-7 attack jet, five kilometers to their rear, would unleash its deadly air-to-air missile. Kirk was monitoring Range Control's instructions from his specially designed test director's console in the rear of the airplane. The controllers had done a good job this time; all the players were in perfect position. Kirk checked the angle of bank on the attitude indicator. This was a duplicate of the one the pilot relied on in the forward crew compartment of the NKC-135, the militarized version of the Boeing 707. Everything looked good. He leaned slightly to his left, looking past his console to the darkened rear of the plane, making one last check on the engineers and scientists that made up his test crew.

They were busy. Under his leadership they all had special tasks to perform, and every move had to be flawless. Each member of the team knew only seconds remained before the laser operator would light off the dual rocket engines in the laser device compartment, located between themselves and the aircrew. They also knew how dangerous that could be. Only a thin aluminum bulkhead, designed to maintain air pressure in the aft portion of the airplane, separated them from the dangers inherent in the rocket-powered laser device.

Kirk keyed his interphone and went through a quick status check. "Safety?"

"Nitrous oxide increasing in the device compartment; all other fuel levels nominal," replied the engineer.

"Copy. Crew go to one hundred percent oxygen." Kirk watched as the men around him reached up to toggle the switches on their individual aircraft oxygen-distribution panels. From now on they would all be breathing pure oxygen through their helmet-mounted masks, a guard against asphyxiation.

"Instrumentation?" Kirk continued the checks.

"Nominal, solid telemetry link to Agar Three Five."

Good. The other NKC-135, full of instrumentation equipment and scientists, would provide them with quick-reaction diagnostic capability if anything went wrong. They would also be able to perform postmortem analysis if the ALL suffered a catastrophic failure.

"OAD?"

"Ready. No target in sight yet."

It would be soon, and the lieutenant operating the optical acquisition device, the OAD, would be the first to see it. His zoom-capable binoculars faced the only uncovered window in the aft end of the airplane.

"Device?"

"Nominal."

The pointer/tracker operator and the laser-device operator positions were on Kirk's immediate left. He glanced over at the device operator's console first. The operator was leaning back, arms crossed, watching the dozens of multicolored lights and indicators on the console before him. The device-control computer was doing all the work now. At this late stage of the mission there was little for the operator to do but monitor the system, scanning the readouts for any problems. In a few seconds the computer would do what no operator could: send hundreds of commands, separated by mere thousandths of a second, to the laser device. The commands would direct valves to open or close, query pressure sensors and flow meters for current operating levels, then send further commands to other valves, adjusting them to compensate for any inadequate readings the sensors might report. The computer was already checking the status of the ten high-pressure laser fuel bottles in the device compartment, ready to abort the test automatically if any of the previously set safety limits were breached.

"Beam Control?" Kirk queried the newly promoted captain on the crew, Lance Brandon.

"Ready."

It was dark in the back of the plane, the only light came from the glow of the video monitors and the small work lights at each of the consoles. Even in the darkness Kirk could see Brandon's brown hair hanging slightly below the back of his helmet, out of regulations again. That was the only problem Kirk had ever had with the beam control operator, constantly having to remind him to get his hair cut. If he weren't so damn good . . .

Brandon's right hand rested lightly on the joystick. Originally it had been the control stick of a fighter aircraft, with buttons protruding near his thumb and a trigger beneath his index finger. Now it performed a different function, though just as deadly. The joystick had been modified, enabling him to point the beam director manually, to steer the high-power laser beam at the target in case the computer system locked up. Right now the huge pointer/tracker, a large telescope mounted in a special fairing on top of the plane, was running freely. It was receiving electrical signals from the optical acquisition device and pointing in the appropriate direction. Lance was waiting for the missile to fire, watching for the flash on the infrared video monitor that would signal the deadly missile's launch. It would be up to him to hit the switch on the joystick and let the computer take control of the system. The trigger beneath his index finger would open pneumatic shutters, freeing the high-energy laser beam from the laser device, allowing it to travel up and through the pointer telescope and through the atmosphere to the target. If the computer lost the target for any reason, it was Lance's job to regain control and put the laser beam back on the missile.

Lance was a little nervous. The straps of the restraint harness pinned him forcefully into his seat. The oxygen mask pressed tightly against his face, and the laser protective glasses turned everything a shade of green. Eerie. Lance knew he was about to perform the most important task of his four years in the Air Force. He had spent his entire time in the Air Force working on the optical system for this project and he was confident it would work, yet he'd heard this test was being carefully monitored at the highest levels in the Pentagon and by several congressional committees. He wasn't used to such oversight.

Kirk released his seat restraint and stood up. Dragging his oxygen hose and interphone cable with him, he made his way down the cramped aisle to stand behind Lance.

Lance could feel the test director looking over

his shoulder, monitoring the infrared video. They could clearly see the Navy A-7 attack jet pull into the screen, could tell there were missiles mounted on three of the four wing stations. Both men knew, as did the entire crew, that the test was about to begin.

"Open the diffuser doors," Kirk ordered, his voice echoing hollowly in Lance's headset.

The device operator unfolded his arms and leaned forward to toggle a switch on his console. The red light beneath the switch glowed yellow, then after two full seconds faded to green.

Beneath the airplane, just below the rocket engines, two sets of doors opened into the airstream. They resembled bomb-bay hatches, but on the Airborne Laser Lab there were no bombs. Instead, these hatches allowed the laser fuels to escape into the atmosphere after being burned in the rocket engines, venting the waste heat before it could melt the laser.

"Doors open and locked," the device engineer reported, monitoring the system display panel over the device operator's shoulder.

Everyone was quiet now. All the tasks were complete. It was time.

"*Tallyho!*" came the nervous warning from the optical acquisition device operator, reporting over the interphone system. "Missile off the number two rail!"

Kirk and Lance saw the bright flash in the infrared monitor clearly when the missile motor ignited. Al-

14

most simultaneously there was a loud, high-pitched squeal in their ears.

"Missile Launch Detect." The other beam control engineer reached over to switch off the audio tone from the warning system.

Though only a few of the other engineers inside the darkened airplane could see the video display, they all knew the air-to-air missile was rapidly accelerating to Mach 3, flying undeterred to its target. Things were tense. The "pucker factor" went up a notch.

Ten years of technology development were about to be put to the ultimate test. The aircrew up front knew they were at the mercy of the scientists and engineers in the back. Except for the experimental high-energy laser, the lumbering, overloaded NKC-135 was completely defenseless in the face of the inbound threat.

The test crew leaped into action. Months of practice couldn't totally relieve the anxiety they felt. Especially the test director. Major Kirk knew this test could make or break his career, not to mention the inherent danger of the test itself. He pulled the straps of his parachute tight against his lanky frame. In the back of his mind, he remembered the survival instructor's warning. "Jumping out of a KC-135 is nearly suicidal, even using the specially constructed escape hatch in this plane."

Kirk checked the display again. He saw the smoke from the missile launch in the infrared video monitor. In spite of the low resolution infrared image of the missile, he felt he had an almost perfect view of what was going on. He ignored the checklist in his hand, months of practice allowing him to go through the sequence from memory. Looking back to check the system status board, he saw no indication of the problems that had haunted them in the previous weeks. All systems were go!

"Beam Control, do you have a track?" he asked, releasing the microphone button.

"Negative" came the terse reply from Lance. His crosshairs were wobbling near the center of the missile's nose cone. Lance waited impatiently, his forehead wrinkled, all his muscles tense as he willed the computer on, urging it to close the track loop on the target's position. Finally the crosshairs concluded their dance, stabilizing directly in the middle of the missile seeker's nose cone. "Positive Track!" he yelled.

"Device on." Kirk keyed his microphone, squeezing the switch on the black plastic box, attached to the interphone cord, tighter than necessary.

The device operator reached forward, flipped up the red plastic safety cover over the button labeled "DEVICE ARM," and pushed the button home. Everyone, including the crew up front, felt the rumble as the rocket engines lit off and began to pump massive amounts of gas into the laser device. It took nine tenths of a second for the "device" to stabilize.

"Device on," the operator stated calmly after his instruments verified the rockets were running smoothly.

"Beam on!" Lance anticipated the order from the test director, squeezing the trigger on the joystick. The pneumatic shutters in the laser cavity exploded outward, releasing the lethal light energy from the confinement of the rocket engines.

Instantaneously the high-energy laser beam traversed the mirrors inside the airplane, leaped up through the beam pointer, and penetrated the three kilometers of air to the target. The laser beam was moving at the speed of light, and there was no need to lead the missile. Even traveling at Mach 3, the missile moved a mere millimeter in the time it took the laser beam to reach it.

Microscopic misalignments in the mirrors were the only obstacles left to overcome. Lance had modified a radar-tracking algorithm he had studied as an undergraduate student at MIT to compensate for the errors. In less than a tenth of a second the computer placed the beam on the nose of the missile, exactly where the tracker's crosshairs sat, and held the lethal stick of light steady. Everyone who had a view of the infrared monitor watched the high-speed missile's nose start to glow as the laser struck the target. Thousands of watts of laser energy cooked the glass and metal in the missile's seeker.

"Damn it!" Kirk screamed into the mike as the image in the monitor began to oscillate violently.

"Break lock!" Lance reacted quickly, clicking a switch on the joystick to stabilize the beam director. In a split second he centered the crosshairs on the nose of the missile and released the switch, allowing the computer to take control again.

"Tracking." Lance held his breath, reflecting the mood of the entire crew. A few more seconds and there would have been little left of the ALL, or the crew. Hours and hours of practice had paid off. He exhaled slowly as the missile seeker began to glow again, this time without interruption.

Because of the distances involved they couldn't see what was happening to the missile, now less than two kilometers away, streaking toward them. Earlier ground tests had shown that in the first second the lens of the missile seeker would crack. The air pressure might hold the broken lens in place, but even that wouldn't save the missile from destruction. In the next second the metal around the lens would begin to melt away, eventually causing the missile to lose its aerodynamic stability. It would then fall from the sky, tumbling out of control.

The laser had been cooking the missile for over two full seconds when one of the leads to the missile warhead detonator was severed by the heat, shorting out the circuit. The infrared screen flashed white as the missile exploded, still over a kilometer from the Airborne Laser Laboratory.

"Look at that son of a bitch burn!" Kirk screamed

into his mask, voicing the elation the entire crew felt. Then he realized he was still squeezing the microphone switch, and that he was still tied into the aircraft radio as well. His expletive had been broadcast to anyone and everyone who had a radio tuned to that frequency. He'd probably have to answer to someone for that screwup, but he didn't care.

"Closing shutters!" The device operator flipped a switch to begin shutting down the rocket engines, bringing Kirk back to the business at hand. Several crucial steps remained to be executed before the volatile laser device could be brought back to a safely stored mode.

Kirk was content to watch as the device operator secured the fuel switches and recirculated the water used to cool the mirrors, returning the heated fluid to the high-pressure storage tank.

Lance was also busy. He secured the beam control system and turned off the high-pressure gas used to cool the infrared sensor, saving it in case they needed to make another run. He was taking his time now. There was no doubt in his mind the test was a success. He would have to look at the missile data later to write the report, but the video had said it all. Even the break lock had been handled, though its cause wasn't at all clear. Probably something in the tracking algorithm, he decided. He would be certain to check it out and fix the problem before the next test.

Four years. It had taken him four years to get

ready for those last few seconds. And others had been working even longer. Back while he was still in college, they were trying to make this operation a success, trying to make the laser small enough to fit inside the plane, working to reduce the jitter and vibrations the air flowing around the huge telescope impressed on the laser beam. They spent long hours striving to resolve a myriad of other technical and operational problems.

As Lance finished going through the shutdown procedure, he came to a decision, one that would affect both him and his family. Over the last few months he had been wrestling with a problem, trying to decide whether to continue in the Air Force or get out. He already had a very good job offer from a firm in California, Santa Barbara Electro-Optics. If he stayed in the Air Force he would be forced to move into management, to monitor contractors while they did all the exciting work. That wasn't what he had gone to school for. Besides, the rated guys—the pilots and navigators—they made up the real Air Force. And they weren't slow to let you know it.

Like the guys up front. The pilot was older, a major, but the copilot was his age. Same amount of time in the Air Force, same rank. But the copilot took home flight pay. A significant amount of money in itself, and that didn't count the bonus money he would get if he signed up for another tour.

It wasn't really the money that upset him. If it weren't for his left eye, which had 20/40 vision, he could have been a pilot himself. Already had his own private license. No, it was the whole Air Force mentality, the way they treated the rated guys versus the non-rated. They were always considered separately; the base clinic even had a special group of doctors to take care of the pilots and their families. The rest were left to the care of the nurses and physician's aides. Lance's wife, Mandy, had visited the clinic three times before they assigned a real doctor to her problem and found out she had an ulcer and a small ovarian cyst. The cyst wasn't cancerous, thank God, but probably the reason she hadn't been able to get pregnant.

Lance switched off the final system and leaned back in his seat. He released the left bayonet connector holding his oxygen mask on, letting it hang by the other, and crossed his arms. Lance shook his head in disgust. He had joined the Air Force to make a career, to serve his country as his father had. But it didn't make sense anymore. In addition to Mandy's recent illness, she had been showing a great deal of concern over the dangers of the test flights. Or maybe that was part of the cause of her sickness, her ulcer. Lance came to a decision. It was time to move on to something new, to give his wife the life she deserved, the life he'd promised her when he asked for her hand.

Jungle School, Eglin Air Force Base, Florida

Staff Sergeant Jay Conner staggered backward in the darkness, his face stinging from the branch that had just raked across his face. His first thought was to sit down, to rest, to take off the heavy rucksack. He couldn't, wouldn't be able to live it down. He sucked the blood from his swollen lip, tasted the waxy flavor of the camouflage paint melting in the heat, and pushed forward, stumbling straight over the thorn-laden bush that blocked his way instead of taking the extra step to go around it. His mind wandered. For about the thousandth time he asked himself what the hell he was doing here. He had joined the Air Force to work on planes, to get an education, not to dress in camouflaged battle uniforms and hump an M-16 through the forest with a bunch of soldiers.

Why had he allowed his first sergeant to talk him into applying for this assignment? If only he hadn't asked the first sergeant how he got the Ranger tab, hadn't let him buy the beer that night after they got through lifting weights at the base gym. It was a good thing he'd been training with the free weights since high school, good thing he'd been in such good shape before he got here. Or else these Ranger instructors would have killed him. He thought briefly of his younger brother, the reason he'd started lifting in the first place, to keep the big lug from pounding his head in. Conner wondered if the troublemaker could survive a real challenge like this one. Probably, if he could stay out of jail long enough.

Conner led his "Ranger buddy," an Army private, into a waist-deep mud hole, then helped pull him out of the muck onto the other side. How much farther did they have to go?

Southern Lebanon

Gurion checked his watch, pulling the camouflage material away from the special digital timepiece. It was 0715. Thirty minutes to the planned strike. The KFIR strike package should already be preparing to launch. The distance to the target would be covered in less than twenty minutes, too quickly for spies to alert the enemy.

Gurion's six men, an elite group of Special Night Fighters, were deployed in two separate hidden positions. Each team had brought one of the new devices, bulky lasers that had yet to be officially introduced into Israeli army inventory. This would be the first application of the new laser target designators. Gurion had originally been concerned with introducing such high-technology equipment into a light force such as his night squad, but after their initial training he had already come to appreciate their utility.

Gurion heard voices penetrate the cool, early morning air. He used his binoculars to carefully push back the netting that disguised their position and looked eastward toward their target.

There were three small buildings: homes, less than two hundred yards away. They had been told the center and left buildings were where the terrorists were hiding, preparing bombs to be infiltrated south into Israel, and that a family lived in the house on the right. Until now all external indications had seemed to verify that information. What he saw now didn't. In the light of the early morning hours, he saw two men, each carrying a small, automatic weapon, leaving the house on the right. He watched as the men relieved two guards already on duty nearby. Gurion checked his watch; it was now 0725. Twenty minutes till the strike.

"We have a problem." Gurion spoke quietly into the small microphone attached to his lapel. "On my mark drop the guard on the left."

Gurion slid his silenced rifle through a small hole in the camouflage net, knowing Sergeant Reitman, in charge of the other hidden outpost north of Gurion's position, was doing the same.

He whispered into the microphone: "Three, two, one, Mark."

A small flash accompanied the quiet "puff" that signaled the undistinguished end of a terrorist's career. Removing the rifle, Gurion retrieved his binoculars and checked on the other guard. His lifeless body was barely visible in the tall grass. Gurion was concerned the noise, minimal though it was, might have aroused their enemy. So far he could see no indication of alarm.

"Reconnoiter and meet me at the center house."
Gurion spoke in a whisper. "Gunners, continue to
designate the current targets."

Gurion had hoped they wouldn't have to leave
their hidden sanctuary, but it had become necessary.
If the guards were deployed in the house on the
right, it could well be that one of the designated targets was actually a home, a family dwelling. And
families were never targets.

Gurion eased out of the hole, careful to limit noise
and to use existing cover to mask his movements.
He moved slowly, confident there was enough time
to positively identify the target and return to cover
before the sleek KFIR aircraft would scream overhead
and unleash their deadly, laser-directed bombs.

The route to the house took Gurion past the guard
he had shot. Instinctively, he reached out and checked
for a pulse. None. It had been an accurate shot. Gurion continued forward until he was beneath one partially covered window. He carefully looked inside.
He could hear several men in the house, at least three
were visible inside this room. They were cleaning
weapons.

His information was obviously inaccurate.

Carefully, Gurion crept to the adjacent dwelling
and peered through a broken window. In the room he
could see two men sleeping. On a table were over two
dozen boxes. One of the boxes was open, filled with
nails about two inches long. Perfect shrapnel for an
antipersonnel bomb, the kind so loved by terrorists.

He continued to the rear of the house, where he met up with Reitman. They spoke in the language of the deaf. Reitman used hand signals to inform him there was a family sleeping in the other house, the one they had targeted for destruction. There were children. He had also checked the rear room of the house they were hiding beside. There was another problem. A prisoner was being held here.

Reitman led Gurion to the window where he had spotted the prisoner. Gurion looked through while Reitman kept watch. Inside there were two guards, relaxing on a worn-out sofa, casually smoking cigarettes. The man they guarded was in the center of the room tied to a chair, his hands bound to the armrests. He was asleep, or unconscious, Gurion wasn't sure. In a small ashtray on the table near the prisoner was a finger. Gurion inspected the bound man's hands. His right hand was covered with blood, his index finger was missing. Gurion tried to get a look at his face, but the man was slumped over, his face hidden.

He retreated from the window, then again used hand signals to give Reitman his orders. The sergeant protested, but only briefly. Gurion's fingers spoke the words, but his eyes gave the orders. There were less than ten minutes left. Reitman slid into the shadows, moving away from the house so he could safely relay the orders he had been given. The gunners, still hidden in their holes, were to change targets.

Gurion quietly slid his rifle to the ground and pulled the 9mm automatic from his holster. He adjusted the silencer and began to move to the front of the home, checking each window he went past. The house was small, and the prisoner was held in the rear room. Windows gave him access to three other rooms. Two men were sleeping in one of them, the other two were empty. The window to the fourth room was completely covered, but Gurion thought he heard voices inside.

There was only one entrance to the house. He slipped in the front and moved carefully to the room where the men slept. The door opened outward, and Gurion wedged a chair beneath the handle. That would keep them inside, at least temporarily. The door to the room where he had heard the voices was also closed, but it opened inward. There was no way to keep it shut. He would have to keep an eye on it.

Gurion continued to the rear of the house, his pistol held ready. He could hear the two guards talking. His first bullet hit one guard in the right eye, and he slumped back on the sofa. The second guard began to stand, the rifle laying across his lap sliding toward the hard wooden floor. Gurion's second bullet hit this man in the chest, blood spattering the wall behind him.

Gurion dived to catch the rifle as his target fell back onto the couch. He barely scooped it up before it fell to the floor. Gurion checked his watch. Only minutes left.

The prisoner stirred. He stared up at Gurion, and a look of salvation crossed his face. He started to speak.

Gurion held his finger to his lips, urging silence. He pulled a knife and quickly slit the bonds holding the man, taking care not to cause further pain to the prisoner's wounded hand. The prisoner pulled his bleeding hand to his chest and held it there tightly. With his other hand he retrieved the severed finger, stuffing it in his pocket.

Gurion thought it strange, but was glad the man had sufficient strength to get around on his own. They moved toward the hallway when the door opened unexpectedly. The first man strolled out, unaware of the intruder. Gurion mowed him down with a pair of muffled shots. Warned, the men behind him fell back. Gurion and the prisoner rushed past the door, just as shots erupted from within the room. The men stopped, trapped between the open door and the one Gurion had previously jammed shut. They hugged the wall. Gurion leaned around the opening and fired three quick shots into the room.

The prisoner was standing next to the closed door when the men inside kicked it open. He grabbed the knife from Gurion's scabbard with his good hand and in one quick motion severed the first man's throat. The second man retreated as his comrade spun back around, spurting blood from the open wound. Gurion moved around the prisoner and finished the other terrorist with a bullet.

The two men rushed from the house, just as a bomb detonated in the building next to them, followed closely by the scream of jet engines. Gurion and the prisoner raced from the house as the remaining terrorists filled the doorway and fired their weapons. Gurion glanced back as the house erupted, highlighting the terrorists in a flash of light moments before the force of the five-hundred-pound bomb obliterated them.

Gurion and his charge were thrown to the ground, briefly stunned by the carnage around them.

"We must go. You need medical attention." Gurion rose slowly to his feet.

The prisoner looked around. "I cannot. My work here is not finished."

"Who are you?"

"A brother."

"They will kill you."

The men studied each other.

"All that knew who I am died in this house. I had the pleasure of killing the one who cut off my finger." He wiped the blood from Gurion's knife on his pants, then held it up.

"Keep it." Gurion opened a small package on his belt and offered his medical kit to the man.

"Until we meet again," the man said, then made his way through the shadows to mingle with the crowd that was now beginning to form on the other side of the burning houses.

Gurion turned and headed for the coordinated recovery point. He would meet his men there, then they would move south, to safety. He glanced back, wondering if he would ever find out who this man was.

1

Dimashq (Damascus), Syria

Ha'im shuffled down the hallway, slowly pushing the heavy cleaning cart in front of him. He dragged his left leg behind, pulling the lame member across the highly polished tile floor. Two officers walked past, discussing the weather. No one even noticed him anymore, which was exactly what he intended. Ha'im had gone to great lengths to make himself appear anything but threatening. With the proper makeup his skin appeared parched and wrinkled, as if from many years in the desert sun. His hair was graying, unfortunately without the help of makeup, and disheveled. "Old Fingerless One" they called him.

He walked with his head bowed, giving the impression he was interested in nothing. But Ha'im's eyes never rested, continuously searching for anything out of the ordinary. Another group of Syrian army officers approached, and he lowered his head further, absentmindedly mumbling to himself. This group passed without a word, halting their conversation as they approached, continuing only after they had gone by. They were serious about security here at Syrian army headquarters. Even minor breaches were dealt with harshly.

Ha'im saw a soldier standing guard outside the conference room he was supposed to clean. That was strange. They didn't normally station guards at that room. Had they found it? Ha'im began to perspire. If they had found the hidden recorder he was finished, condemned to a certain, painful execution. He stopped the cart and used one of the dirty cleaning rags to dab the moisture from his face, careful not to smudge his makeup.

There was only one way to find out. Ha'im continued on, stopping when he neared the guard.

The guard looked at him with the usual disdain. "What do you want, old one?"

"I am to clean this room," Ha'im answered, bowing his head in mock respect.

The guard looked him over again, more thoroughly this time. Then he checked the cart, even pulling back the dirty brown drapes on the side to inspect the shelves.

"All right, but be quick about it. There is a meeting soon."

Ha'im maneuvered his cart through the ornately decorated portal, grateful the guard hadn't made a thorough search. It would have been suspicious if they found him with one of the expensive ashtrays. He would be prosecuted as a thief, might even lose a hand. Worse, he would be shot if they discovered the miniature recording device hidden inside the ashtray.

The guard closed the door after Ha'im went in. Ha'im breathed easier, thankful the guard didn't accompany him inside. It would have been much more difficult to make the switch with him watching. Still, next time he would have to prepare for such a possibility, security was apparently getting tighter. But why?

Ha'im stopped at the end of the hall, just outside the storage room. He looked down to check the tiny, nearly invisible wax seal he had placed in the doorjamb. It was still intact. He opened the door without concern, certain no one had been in the room since he left it earlier in the afternoon. He spent several minutes negotiating the doorway, working the cart back and forth to get it inside. Anyone watching him would probably laugh at his troubles, but that would only add credence to his cover. When he finally got the door closed behind him, he stood fully erect, stretching the tired muscles in his back. It was physically demanding for him to impersonate a man who was small of stature, and the greatest toll was taken on his lower spine.

He turned and locked the door so he could work undisturbed. First he pulled the crystal ashtray from beneath the cleaning rags on the bottom of the cart. While cleaning the main briefing room on the second floor, the room where the headquarters staff received their daily updates, he had removed the tray, replacing it with an exact duplicate. Ha'im smiled, the nervous tension was now gone, replaced by a sense of exhilaration that was difficult to explain. It was a feeling he always had after winning the game, a game with the highest stakes of all.

The Israeli spy turned the ashtray over in his hands, admiring it with an appreciation only he and the designers at the Technical Center could understand. It was an elegant piece of work, not only for its aesthetic qualities, but for its hidden capabilities as well. An intricate array of mirrors and prisms combined within the apparently clear ashtray to effectively conceal a small recording device. He turned the crystal ashtray over and manipulated several small panels to expose a battery and a microcassette tape, hidden within the glass.

Laying the ashtray on the floor, he removed the microcassette, taking care not to touch the delicate tape. Ha'im sat on an ancient, broken chair and pulled off his old, worn-out boot. He carefully hid the microcassette in the hollowed-out heel of his boot. Ha'im caught his breath, hearing a key being inserted in the door.

A man, a soldier, stepped in. Ha'im faked a snore and then pretended to jerk awake, using his foot to push the ashtray, its compartment exposed, beneath the cleaning cart.

"What? What is it," he said, rubbing his eye with one hand, pulling his boot back on with the other to hide the evidence.

"Ah," the soldier said, "I didn't know you were in here. There is no paper in the commander's toilet. They sent me to get some."

"That area is not my responsibility," Ha'im complained, maintaining the persona of someone who did not actively seek out extra work.

"I know, but this is the closest supply closet." The guard moved closer. "Now, give me some toilet paper before I make you regret I found you sleeping here."

Ha'im handed the guard some paper, hoping he would leave. He did, but not before backhanding him.

"Don't let me catch you sleeping in here again, or maybe I'll cut off another one of your fingers." The guard grabbed his hand and made a motion as if to cut off the middle finger of his right hand, next to the already missing index finger. Finally he left.

Ha'im rubbed his cheek, stinging from the force of the soldier's vicious blow. It was one of the most difficult parts of the masquerade, taking the abuse from the Syrians, knowing he had the ability to kill most of them with his bare hands. As a Palestinian, he was treated with contempt. He smiled again as the stinging abated. What if they knew he was really an Israeli . . .

He silently completed his work, retrieving the ashtray and replacing the battery, inserting a fresh tape from a box hidden beneath the sink. Finished, Ha'im reassumed his false persona and stepped out of the closet. He locked the door from the outside. Training mandated he reseal the wax at the bottom of the door as a simple check against intrusion.

Ha'im hobbled down the hallway, heading for the exit. The hallway was crowded now, men in military uniforms rushed past him to get to the exits before the lines became too long. Most wore army uniforms, officers from the command staff. A man in an air force uniform rushed past, shoving Ha'im to the side. There had been an increasing number of air force uniforms in the building lately; he decided that was something worth reporting.

He limped along, avoiding as many of the officers as possible. The civilians weren't as bad, although they certainly didn't go out of their way to make room for him, not for a crippled Palestinian. If there was one thing that turned his stomach about the Syrians, it was their hypocrisy. They claimed to be representing Palestinian rights in negotiations with Israel, yet they were brutal to the Palestinians in Syria. They were treated as lower-class citizens able to perform only the most menial of duties; those too dangerous or demeaning for the Syrians to do themselves.

Finally Ha'im saw the lines of people waiting to

get through the exits. He had no choice but to get into the longest line; the others were reserved for the people with the permanent passes. His pass was only temporary, the type issued to the janitorial and administrative workers.

The line moved slowly. Ha'im wobbled on his feet, pretending to be on the verge of collapsing. When he finally approached the front of the line, Ha'im could see the guards interrogating a woman. She was young, frightened. He felt sorry for her. It wasn't a good idea to show fear in front of these men, they would take advantage of it.

The woman was wearing a veil and robe. Ha'im could see enough of her face to tell she wasn't particularly attractive. Her body, however, pushed at the fabric of her robe in some particularly interesting places. The guards were aware of this as well, brushing against her time and again, threatening to have her searched if she didn't answer their questions, if she didn't cooperate.

Ha'im stepped around the old woman in front of him and glared at the guards.

"Leave her alone," he called out, trying to appear as menacing as such a little old man could. "You have no right to treat her this way."

The three guards glared at him. The old woman in front of him began to mumble to herself as the guards passed the young girl through the gate, taking her badge and storing it in a box. The guards then passed the old woman through with little more than a cursory glance. They were impatient to deal with the man that had yelled at them. Ha'im wasn't worried. If the guards were busy roughing him up, they would be less intent on searching him thoroughly.

One guard cracked his knuckles, inviting Ha'im to step forward. The people waiting behind him in line grew silent.

"So, you think to question our authority?" one guard asked as Ha'im shuffled forward.

Ha'im kept silent, his cold stare in itself a rebuke to the overbearing guard. Ha'im knew he could kill the man with a single thrust of his hand, but he reminded himself to play the part. He bent his head low and tried to get past the guards without a confrontation, but it was not to be.

One guard grabbed his arm and another stood in his path.

"I mean no trouble," Ha'im said, keeping his head bowed.

"I'm sure you don't." The guard laughed with his friends. "But you have questioned our authority. We certainly can't let you leave without teaching you a lesson."

The guard moved forward, placing his boot above Ha'im's right foot. Ha'im grimaced. The guard leaned forward, putting his full weight on Ha'im's supposedly lame foot. Ha'im did what any crippled man would do in such an instance: he screamed in pain.

It was a good scream, it pierced the air around the

exit, floating down the hall to reverberate off the walls. The guard retreated, not expecting such an outburst. Ha'im had hoped for just such a reaction. As soon as the guard released the pressure from his foot, Ha'im stumbled forward. He grabbed at the guard to keep from falling.

"Let go of me, you filthy bastard," the guard yelled, shoving him away.

If there was one thing the guards disliked, it was being touched by the lowly Palestinian workers. As if they carried some kind of disease.

Ha'im released the guard and limped forward. His foot barely hurt, but he pretended to be in great pain. The other guards didn't try to stop him so he kept moving, eventually making his way through the exit and into the street.

Once out of sight of the entrance, Ha'im straightened slightly, relieving the strain on his back. His limp all but disappeared. He smiled and made his way to the bus stop.

Ha'im sat on a box in the closet, the only closet in his small hovel. An oversize bar was jammed across the front door. It served as a rudimentary, but effective, lock. He eyes showed no emotion as he listened intently, gleaning as much information as he could from the tape, the microcassette he had recovered from the military headquarters of the Syrian General Staff. Usually this was the most difficult part of the job, trying to decide if the information on the microcassette was important enough to transmit to his superiors in Tel Aviv, or if it could wait until several of the microcassettes could be delivered at the same time. It was a trade-off. His tendency was always to save the microcassettes, limiting the risk of exposing his intricate, yet delicate communications network. But that also made the perishable information less valuable. It was usually a difficult decision.

Ha'im's ears twitched, his eyes intently focused on some invisible demon. "So that's what the military buildup has been for," he mumbled to himself. He knew this information could not wait. It would have to be passed as quickly as possible. He pulled the earphones from his head and took a small box from beneath a loose board in the floor. He connected the box to the small cassette player and copied the tape onto a slightly larger one, a tape that already held duplicates of the previous two recordings.

He placed the new tape in his boot and the equipment back into the hole. It would be a short walk to the market, where he would deliver the tape to another agent, another brother of the Mossad. From there it would make a circuitous journey to another part of the city, where a hidden radio would transmit the message over a satellite communication link to Israel; Intelligence Headquarters. Then it would be up to the army, or the air force. Ha'im hoped it wouldn't come to that, hoped a preemptive strike could be avoided. Yet somehow he knew it couldn't.

Syria's intentions were clear. Ha'im had just heard

the defense minister report to his staff that they had the approval and blessing of the king himself. According to the tape, Syria intended to use a new weapon, a laser radar, to somehow thwart Israel's air force. With Israel's aerial weapons disabled, Syria was then going to use its armor superiority to retake the Golan Heights, and then unleash something code-named DARSHAM. What they hadn't achieved through negotiations, Syria intended to take through force. Ha'im knew little about the technology he had heard described, but he did know that if the Israeli air force were disabled, it would be impossible to stop the Syrian tanks. One way or another, Syria and Israel would soon be at war.

2

D-Day minus Forty
A secret airfield in eastern Kuwait

"Damn it, Pervert. Watch where you're going. You don't have to hit every stinking hole," Lieutenant Colonel Robert "Snake" Gabriel chastised his driver, holding one hand against the roof of the car to keep from smashing his head against the top.

Major Johnny "Pervert" Armstrong yanked the wheel of the rented Mercedes to the right to avoid a large bomb crater on the left, sacrificing the right tire to a smaller, unavoidable, pit.

"Sorry, sir." Pervert grinned at his commander, his flight cap tilted slightly back on his head.

Lieutenant Colonel Gabriel hid his own smile. He was glad to have the Pervert in country. In spite of being barely tall enough to pass the flight physical, Pervert was probably the best fighter pilot he'd ever flown with. Snake was his sponsor into the new 117th Squadron, the Nighthawks. Pervert had rotated back to the States after the cease-fire with Iraq, with sixty-five F-117A attack missions under his belt. Now he was back. Snake had picked Pervert to be his new wingman.

Pervert spun the steering wheel to the right and slammed on his brakes, sending gravel flying from the parking lot. The car slid to a stop, noticeably bumping the steel pipe set in the ground to keep cars from encroaching too close to the hangar.

"Damn it, Pervert." Snake unbuckled his seat belt and climbed out of the car. "If you've screwed up the bumper, it's going to cost us an arm and a leg to have it fixed."

"Aw, come on, sir. I know this machine." Pervert patted the steering wheel. "There's no way I hit the pipe hard enough to dent the bumper. I got a six-pack that says it's not even scratched."

Snake knew not to take the bet. He'd never known Pervert to bet on anything that wasn't a sure thing, even if he was only risking a six-pack of soda this time. He met Pervert at the front of the car. As promised, there wasn't even a scratch on the bumper's hard plastic cover, at least not one he could see in the fading light of the evening.

Snake followed the short major around to the front of the hangar, on the runway side. The main hangar doors were open a couple of feet, so they entered there.

Snake took off his sunglasses and glanced at the six RF-117s and two TR-1s that made up the One Seventeen Tactical Reconnaissance Wing (Provisional). The formation of the Wing was one of the big tactical lessons from the war with Iraq. The TR-1s provided the otherwise "strategic" intelligence information directly to the tactical commanders. The RF-117s were outfitted with modified film pods originally used on the RF-4Cs, the old tactical reconnaissance birds. The RF-117s were able to get much closer to the target due to their low-radar signature, qualities that had been incorporated into the film pods.

"Looks like we're loaded for a long ride." Pervert nodded at their two airplanes, each with two wing-mounted fuel "drop" tanks installed. "Got any idea what's up, sir?"

"No. I guess we'll find out in a minute, though." Snake pulled off his flight cap and used his hand to wipe a thick layer of sweat from the top of his balding head. "Let's get our helmets out of life support before we check in for the mission brief."

It was only half an hour after sunset, but it might as well have been midnight. The sky was black, the stars obscured by the billowy clouds at twelve thousand feet. No moon. Perfect. It was the kind of night Snake loved to fly in, the kind of night his RF-117 was designed to exploit. With very little radar signature, the only indication of its presence would be the small thermal glow from the engines, and that had been suppressed until it was minimal. He would be practically undetectable, a characteristic he was definitely going to need for this mission. Even the extra fuel tanks were specially designed with steeply angled sides to reduce their radar return. The areas that couldn't be angled, like where the tanks attached to the pylons, were coated with SPray on radar Absorbent Material, affectionately called "SPAM in a can" by the ground crews.

Sitting in the cockpit, Snake went through the pre-takeoff checklist from memory, just as he knew his wingman was doing in the airplane to his right. He looked over as he keyed the radio, still uncomfortable knowing his name—normally stenciled below the canopy—had been painted over.

"Radio check" was all he said, annoyed at the obtrusive hiss in his ears when he released the switch, an artifact of the millimeter wave "secure" radio, which allowed him to communicate with the other RF-117 as long as they remained within one-half mile of each other. Beyond that distance the atmosphere absorbed the signal, adding to their invisibility.

"Read you five by five," Pervert responded, confirming that he, too, had finished his own checklist.

They were ready. Snake contacted the tower on the normal radio: "Tower, this is Kuwaiti Air flight 635 ready for takeoff."

"Kuwaiti Air 635, you are cleared onto the active, winds zero three zero at ten."

He gently pushed the throttle forward. Pervert followed him onto the runway and lined up on his right side. Snake thumbed the secure radio button and immediately shoved the throttle forward. Out of the corner of his eye, he saw his wingman follow in quiet unison. They would be climbing out slower than they were capable, their unusual flight path and deployed radar reflectors mimicking the signature of a Boeing 737. Anyone who didn't know better would think a commercial airliner was launching from the airfield.

Snake glanced down to where he normally kept a picture of his wife taped below the window. It was gone, too. The maintenance crew had been instructed to remove any indication of who the airplane belonged to, in case they were shot down. Not a comforting thought. They had even been ordered to leave all their personal identification at the hangar. This was a spooky mission, but what the hell, he'd never been to Syria before. Too bad he wouldn't be able to get his passport stamped.

Snake contacted the tower and requested permission to depart the pattern. His request was approved, with further instructions to contact departure control. He ignored the tower's instructions and turned off the transponder, which had been blinking an identifying radio signal to the ground controllers, then flipped another switch to retract the radar reflectors. He keyed the millimeter radio briefly, and Pervert pulled in tight. It was time to be quiet, another hour before they met up with the tanker.

*   *   *

Both aircraft were full of gas and ready to go. Snake took a bite from the candy bar he'd brought with him, then made the call on the secure radio.

"Start descent to one thousand feet."

"Wilco," Pervert replied.

"Let's keep it tight now, Pervert. No room for error this time." The dimly glowing instruments showed their airspeed at three hundred fifty knots, increasing as they descended. They were already less than fifty miles from the Syrian border. The Iraqi surface to air weapons weren't a threat; they still hadn't recovered from the devastating air campaign that leveled almost all their border defenses. The Syrians were another story. They were already suspicious of Iraq's intentions, and their air defenses were top of the line, second only to U.S. systems.

Their mission, straight from the SECDEF and briefed only to the two pilots and their commander, was to fly directly across Syria's southern border, then use their cameras to survey the western half of the country. They would recover through Lebanon, where another tanker was waiting for them. That would be the easy part. The hard part was coming up now.

Snake checked the digital map display, then looked back outside. The lights of Busra ash Sham were visible to the north, but he could barely see the twin mountain peaks to the south. They were slightly north of the planned flight path. Normally this much variation wouldn't be a problem, but in this instance it could be critical. The radar masking plots had designated a route that would use the existing terrain to further hide their otherwise minimal radar signature. A slight pressure on the stick, and the airplane obediently moved to the left.

"I'm picking up an air search radar from the As Suwayda complex. It's intermittent," Pervert warned.

"Copy." Snake silently chastised himself for not having kept a closer eye on the radar warning display. The radar was still pretty far away, and he doubted it could have picked them up. Most of the radar beam was either absorbed by the special materials in the RF-117's skin or deflected away from the radar receiver by the sharply canted surfaces. Nevertheless, he dipped lower, down to five hundred feet. The narrow beam of his radar altimeter, undetected by anyone or anything in their flight path, kept them from digging a hole in the Syrian sand.

It was cool in the air-conditioned cockpit, but sweat ran down Snake's back, soaking his flight suit. They were out of the relative safety of the Iraqi desert, with no possibility of search and rescue if something went wrong—if one of the planes malfunctioned or if they took a lucky shot from a Syrian gunner. Their only way to survive was to remain invisible.

"Approaching first survey point."

"Roger. You take the lead," Snake replied. Pervert was to take the first photo run down the Syrian Jordanian border, heading south.

"Beginning climb to five thousand feet."

Snake pulled back on his own stick, pulling his aircraft a hundred fifty feet behind Pervert, who was now the lead ship.

Pervert enjoyed being in the lead, relying on his own skill to stay on course over the target area. Too much wander and his cameras, already documenting everything in a two-mile swath on either side of their flight path, might miss whatever it was they were supposed to find. Six and a half minutes later they were on the northern edge of the Golan Heights. He called the break over his radio and pulled into a tight climbing left turn, bleeding airspeed to let Snake pull into the lead. They would take turns in the lead position until the photo runs were complete.

Snake cursed under his breath as he pulled hard on his stick, felt the force of six G's, six times his own weight, pull him deep into his ejection seat. He barely made the turn in time to wheel into lead position. It was almost a game with Pervert, Snake decided, to see how hard and how quickly he could force his boss to swap positions. In all fairness, Pervert never made the turn until after he called the break . . . about a millisecond after he called it.

"I've got lead," Snake called as soon as he was in position, glancing over his shoulder to see if Pervert was in place yet. He was. He always was. Snake flicked on his camera systems and started the photo run. He could see the lights of Sayqal military airfield in the distance and decided to use them as a navigation aid.

All at once a bright orange flash of light saturated the inside of his canopy. The light remained only an instant, disappearing as quickly as it came. But it took several seconds for his night vision to recover, and even then he had to turn the instruments up to full bright before he could see them clearly.

"Snake," Pervert called over the secure radio. "Are you all right? What the hell was that? Someone just set off a strobe right in front of my face."

"I'm all right. I've still got spots in my eyes, though. Wait a minute, I've got a warning indicator flashing. That was a laser hit!" Snake reached down to toggle the reset switch for the laser warning sensor.

"Copy. I've got an indication, too. Did you see which way it came from?"

"Negative, but it sure screwed up my night vision. I hope it was just some carnival light show that accidentally strayed this way. Let's continue the run, we're almost to the turn now." Snake considered calling break and taking advantage of his companion's concern with the laser to get even with him for that last hard maneuver, but the thought was only fleeting. That laser hit could have been serious. Besides, Pervert could outfly him any day of the week, he'd proven it on many occasions.

"We'll break on my mark, but take it easy this time, Pervert. I don't want to be in a hard turn if that laser hits us again. Ready . . . Break."

Snake climbed to bleed airspeed while Pervert

pulled into a tight turn below him, searching for the lead slot. Snake scanned the dark skies around them, looking for the bright orange beam. He thought he saw a low cloud light up momentarily, but couldn't be sure, the illumination was too brief.

"Cameras on," Pervert said.

Snake pulled in behind him. Closer this time at one hundred feet.

After only fifteen seconds into the photo run the orange light returned, again blasting their eyesight.

"Shit!" Snake closed his eyes to try and get rid of the afterimage, but the steady tone in his left ear forced him to open them to check the warning display.

"I've got a missile warning," Snake told his wingman. "The laser warning light is on again, too."

"Mine, too. I see the missile. It's just ahead, about two o'clock."

Snake craned his neck to look down and forward. He glimpsed the missile just as the rocket motor finished its burn, the red glow of the hot thruster rapidly fading. The passive, infrared-sensing missile-warning receiver lost signal when the missile's hot plume faded.

"I doubt if they're just shooting for target practice, Snake. I'm going active."

Both Snake and Pervert knew that engaging the active radar of the missile-warning-and-tracking system would give Pervert's position away to anyone who had the appropriate sensor, and that accounted for almost half the Syrian air defense forces. They had no choice, had to know if the missile was coming for them.

"I read one missile, vectoring for my position. It's faster than I'd expect for an SA-3, but it's definitely heading for me. Dispensing chaff and flares now."

Snake watched on as Pervert went through the drill: first punch up two rounds of chaff, to confuse any radar-targeting system, then an automatic sequence of the new infrared flares, designed to act as decoys against even the most modern infrared missile seekers. In just a few seconds, the missile should be diverted from its target.

"It's no good, Snake." Pervert pushed the plane over hard, trying to shake the missile. The G forces pushed him deep into his seat. "The missile's still locked on. End game begins in six seconds. Back off and give me some room."

Snake saw Pervert's engines glow bright red as his wingman shoved his throttles full forward to military power. Beyond the G-induced strain in his words, Pervert's voice showed no sign of emotion, no fear.

The endgame was all that was left. The high-tech countermeasures had failed. Now it was just Pervert and his RF-117 against the unthinking, uncaring warhead flying on a Mach 3 suicide mission. Snake knew Pervert was the best. If anyone could outfly the missile, he could.

He saw Pervert jink left, then right into a hard dive.

Snake lost track of him in the dark and decided to

descend to fifteen hundred feet to avoid the clutches of other missiles. Then, several hundred feet below him, Snake spotted Pervert, his airplane awash in an orange glow as it streaked through the air. Snake could now tell the laser beam illuminating his friend wasn't coming from the ground, but from an airborne platform several thousand feet above them.

When he realized the laser was guiding the missile to its target, Snake screamed over his radio: "Bail out! Bail out! Bail out! Now!"

Pervert never heard the call, the distance between the planes now too great for the secure radio to reach him. Blinded by the laser, he used his intuition to tell him when the missile was close enough to be fooled into missing him, jerking the stick at the last possible moment.

His intuition was good, but not good enough. Twenty feet from Pervert's airplane the missile exploded, detonated by the proximity fuse sensor. Shrapnel tore through the vertical stabilizer and ripped off a big chunk of the left wing. Pervert tried to regain control but it was impossible. He reached between his legs and pulled the ejection release, remembering to put his chin down and pull his arms and legs in tight.

Snake cried out when he saw the missile detonate, the violent flash adding to the bright orange glow illuminating his wingman's RF-117. Then everything went dark, the laser beam extinguished. He tried to make out the trail of the RF-117 as it started down, but could barely see it. What little he could see wasn't encouraging. The plane appeared to enter a flat spin, and he hadn't seen a chute.

The bright orange light hit him once more, blasting away his sight for a few more seconds. But he was low now, farther away from the laser. He hoped it didn't pick him up. When his eyesight recovered, he checked the warning display: the laser warning light was fading, and there was no missile-warning indication. At least that was encouraging.

There was one other thing he had to do. Snake released the safety cover on the Master Cooperative Destruct switch. Their orders in this situation were both clear and unequivocal: If one or both of the aircraft were crippled, the damaged aircraft was to be destroyed to deny the enemy an opportunity to exploit the stealth technology incorporated in the airframe and avionics. Snake keyed in the proper code, memorized before the mission, and prepared to flip the switch.

One last look out the window, praying he would see something that would make this unnecessary. He used his gloved hand to wipe the clear glass visor of his helmet, bothered by the spots floating in front of his eyes. He couldn't get rid of them, even when he rotated the visor up, out of the way. Outside there was nothing but blackness.

*   *   *

The RF-117 exploded violently. Shards of metal and minute pieces of radar-absorbing material would litter the desert and mountains below, but none of the pieces would be large enough to exploit for information.

Snake smiled beneath his oxygen mask. He hadn't flipped his own switch, yet the airplane below him had explosively self-destructed. That would only happen if the pilot ejected. Pervert was alive! Hopefully he could get to Israel before he was picked up by the Syrians, but Snake realized that was a long shot. He dropped down to two hundred feet and pointed the nose of the plane toward Lebanon. Time to get the hell out of there.

3

D-Day minus Thirty-nine
The Old Executive Office Building, Washington, D.C.

The curtains in the large conference room were drawn shut when Colonel Kirk walked in. In the dim light he could make out only about a dozen people, some mingling, most already seated around the large, oval conference table. They all wore civilian clothes, in sharp contrast to Kirk's Air Force uniform. But there was no guarantee some of the men sitting there weren't in the military as well, military appointees to the National Security Council were authorized, actually required, to wear civilian clothes. Kirk had just found his name at a seat on the far side of the conference table when he heard the door open again.

The next man to come in was an Army officer—a four-star general. Kirk recognized the officer as General Wainwright, commander of Central Command. Central Command, or CENTCOM, was responsible for the region everyone now knew as Southwest

Asia. *Newsweek* had just written an extensive article about the CENTCOM commander, a West Pointer and infantry officer. Throughout his career he had worked hard to make sure the Army's priorities were placed above the other services whenever possible. His appointment to CENTCOM was interpreted as a move by the Army to reestablish their prominence in exercises and contingency planning after the Air Force had dominated the recent desert war.

The general took his seat near the middle of the table and poured himself some coffee from one of the silver decanters. Kirk was about to sit as well when two other men walked in. Everyone in the room, including the general, stood when they recognized the secretary of state. Close behind him was an Air Force three star, Lieutenant General Morris, whom Kirk had met before. He led the Joint Directors of Laboratories, the committee that oversaw all military research efforts. Kirk realized he was the only military man present who didn't hold flag officer rank. He was beginning to feel like a very small fish.

Morris glanced around the room, then turned and locked the door.

The secretary of state took his chair at the head of the table. Everyone else had taken their seats and the secretary was about to speak, when there was a loud knock. Lieutenant General Morris went back to unlock the door.

"You're late," he said, stepping back to let the newcomer in.

"I know, I'm sorry."

Kirk recognized the new guy, too. Dr. L. N. Kashwa'ar was a wiry, nervous man whose off-the-rack suit hung loosely from his small frame. He was the director of DARPA, the Defense Advanced Research Projects Agency. As commander of the Air Force Weapons Laboratory, newly renamed the Phillips Laboratory, Kirk had fought with DARPA's leader on several occasions. The arguments were generally turf battles, fights over mission responsibilities and the funding that went with them. Especially in the area of advanced laser development. Dr. Kashwa'ar, nobody could even pronounce his first name, had been his chief foe in those arguments. Kirk smiled, he had won most of the fights.

Kashwa'ar walked briskly past the empty seat and straight up to the secretary of state.

"I'm Dr. Kashwa'ar," he said, extending his hand.

General Morris was apparently upset at the breach of protocol and didn't wait for Kashwa'ar to repeat the formality with him: "Take a seat, Kashwa'ar, let's get this meeting started."

Kashwa'ar headed for the only empty seat at the table, just across from Kirk. He stopped to speak quietly to two of the men on that side of the table, ignoring the urgency in Morris's voice. Morris drummed his fingers on the table while everyone waited for Kashwa'ar to sit.

"Not a good way to win friends or influence enemies," Kirk thought, knowing from experience to expect such behavior from Kashwa'ar. He was a little slow, the kind of guy who never got the joke until everyone else had already stopped laughing. Kirk wasn't very impressed with Kashwa'ar's abilities, either, and felt he'd made it to the top of DARPA by being near a few programs that turned out to be successful, but always far enough away to distance himself as soon as something started to go wrong.

General Morris began the introductions: "Mr. Secretary, I believe you know the commander of CENT-COM, General Wainwright. Mr. Kashwa'ar, whom you've met—" Morris glared at Kashwa'ar, who seemed not to notice—"is the Director of DARPA." General Morris quickly introduced Kirk and the three men sitting closest to him. They were all scientific advisors to heads of military laboratories, much like Kirk's own technical assistant. Kirk knew he had been invited personally because he knew almost as much about his own laboratory as his personal advisor. More in some areas.

After introducing Kirk, Morris sat down, and Dr. Kashwa'ar stood to introduce the men he'd invited to the meeting. Instead of the brief one-line introductions like General Morris had made, Kashwa'ar pulled out small cards and began to espouse on the qualifications of the men on his side of the table. Everything from the number of doctorates they held to the number of scientific papers they had published. Each of the men swelled with pride as Kashwa'ar recited their qualifications.

Morris didn't seem to appreciate it, though. Kirk watched his face go through several colors, finally turning beet red as Kashwa'ar droned on. The secretary, on the other hand, seemed interested in every word. Kirk couldn't tell if it was genuine interest or just the practiced expression of a professional diplomat.

"Gentlemen," Morris interrupted Kashwa'ar before he got a chance to introduce the last member of his group, "before we get started, I want to remind each of you, the information you are about to hear is top secret and is not to be repeated outside this room without written permission from me personally. The secretary of defense sends his regrets. As you all know, he's dealing with some extremely sensitive issues on the Hill and unfortunately couldn't attend this meeting."

Sensitive is right, thought Kirk. Trying to save his career after getting caught with his female assistant, not something that the public had been very forgiving about in the last few years.

"However," General Morris continued, "he is fully aware of the issue we're about to discuss and requests you give your full support to this problem. Mr. Secretary, if you'd care to begin?"

"Certainly. I have just returned from a trip to Israel, where I met with the prime minister." The secretary spoke quietly, but with a tone that implied a deadly seriousness to what he was about to say.

Kirk was surprised. CNN had just televised pictures of the secretary in a retreat meeting with the embattled president of the Russian Republic, in Moscow. Apparently, the meeting in Israel was a well-kept secret.

"The prime minister has confided with me some particularly sensitive information acquired by one of his Mossad sources in Syria. I'll sum it up in one sentence: Syria is preparing to invade Israel. They plan to attack in exactly thirty-nine days." The secretary paused to let the revelation sink in.

"Some of you may have a hard time believing this, may think it is simply political rhetoric. I want to assure you, I am certain the prime minister is correct in his assessment. We know the Syrian leadership has been secretly working to foment anti-Israeli sentiment in the Gulf region ever since Israel extended its Security Zone further into Lebanon. Syria has already moved over 250,000 men into positions adjacent to the occupied territories in the Golan Heights. But that isn't what has the Israelis concerned. The prime minister feels he still has the air power to overcome the numerically superior Syrians. Unfortunately, his air power is also his Achilles' heel. One of his Mossad agents has reported the Syrians have developed a new weapon, a device that will render the Israeli air force impotent. A laser weapon!"

"Ludicrous!" Kashwa'ar interrupted the secretary.

"Hold your comments." Morris glared at Kash-wa'ar, embarrassed at the scientist's outburst. He finally turned back to the secretary of state. "My apologies, Mr. Secretary. Please continue."

"Apparently, the laser is mounted in an airplane. It is used to guide surface-to-air and air-to-air missiles. I obviously don't have the expertise to evaluate the validity of the Israeli claim; however, I did accept a synopsis of the Israeli findings. Each of you can make your own decisions as to whether or not such a device is technically feasible. You'll find a copy of the synopsis in the folder in front of you."

Several of the scientists opened the folders. Kirk opened his as well, quickly reviewing the document as he listened. He doubted if the technology was indigenous. It was probably from Germany, sold to the Syrians after the war with Iraq. He'd heard the Germans gave the Syrians a line of credit after they supported the coalition. The Germans certainly had the technical capability, they remained a world leader in developing optical systems such as this.

"Actually, whatever you decide is irrelevant. The Israeli prime minister is convinced his situation is critical and has asked for our help. He realizes he would stand little chance of protecting the Israeli state with an incapacitated air force. I am convinced, and the president has agreed, that we should assist the Israelis against this potentially destabilizing force in the Middle East. If we don't, the political gains we made by defeating the Iraqis will be lost. Gentlemen,

I ask for your assistance in helping the United States preserve the State of Israel.'' The secretary of state sat back in his seat, finished with his statement.

Kirk could barely believe what he was reading. The paper claimed Syria was using a gold vapor laser, mounted in a Russian-built An-74 ''COALER'' aircraft, as a laser radar. The laser radar configuration, or LADAR, provided surveillance of the airspace throughout Syria and the adjacent border areas. When an unknown aircraft entered Syria, the LADAR would track the threat and provide targeting information to the surface-to-air missiles. As the missiles approached the threat, the LADAR took on a more important role by marking the target, allowing the missile to home in on the reflected light. This rendered most standard electronic warfare measures, like chaff and flares, useless. More importantly, the Syrians were moving more of their surface-to-air missile batteries forward, toward the Israeli border. In an offensive, the batteries could be moved forward as the ground troops pushed through the lines, creating an umbrella of protection from the Israeli aircraft. The relatively small Israeli Army would be slaughtered by the Syrians overwhelming armor, even if the Jordanians didn't join Syria as they had in the last two wars with Israel.

''Another Desert Shield?'' General Wainwright asked.

''No!'' the secretary of state answered immediately. ''Definitely not. It would be impossible to form a coalition in support of the Jewish State. The other

Arab nations would almost certainly align against the U.S. if we were to provide overt military support to Israel. No, if we are to be of help, we will have to be discreet. And quick. We have little time."

"This is ludicrous!" One of the civilians, a Ph.D. from one of the national labs, spoke up.

Kirk knew of the man's reputation. He was brilliant . . . on paper. His success in turning any of his ideas into working hardware had been extremely limited.

"I've looked at this application before," the civilian continued. "It won't work. Not from an airplane at any rate because the vibration problems are too severe to overcome. In all probability, the laser—if indeed it is a laser—is emanating from a satellite."

What an idiot, Kirk thought to himself. Not only was the scientist completely lacking in common sense, he tended to voice his opinion in spite of the fact. And the more important the audience, the louder he tended to be. Besides, he was wrong. The vibration problem could be solved, they'd proven that almost ten years ago on the Airborne Laser Lab using Captain Brandon's tracking algorithm. The proverbial lightbulb snapped on when Kirk thought of the Laser Lab. Perhaps his old airplane, now sitting in the Air Force Museum, was the solution to this problem. Kirk relished the thought of bringing the Laser Lab back for one final mission.

"It's definitely not a satellite," the secretary said.

"It's an airplane; there are photos of it in the package."

Now everyone, including those who hadn't opened their folders already, began to shuffle through the document. Kirk turned past the paper he'd been reading and found copies of the photographs, each numbered for accountability, near the back. The photographs were grainy, fuzzy. They'd obviously been taken from a long distance, the yellow tint of the image confessed the use of a filter to reduce atmospheric haze. And they had been taken at night, using high-speed film, which contributed to the graininess of the photos.

The airplane in the photograph was parked, half inside a hangar. Kirk sensed a kind of kinship with the aircraft, as if it were a near cousin to his own flying laser. This airplane was much smaller, though. It probably held no more than six people and certainly a much lower-power laser than the one he'd flown with. The LADAR concept wouldn't require nearly as much power as the one he had used to destroy the Sidewinder air-to-air missiles back in 1983.

"As you can see, gentlemen, there is some kind of laser port on top of the fuselage near the middle of the plane. You can't tell from the pictures, but the Israeli spy claims there is a similar port of the bottom of the plane."

"Exactly the way I would have done it," Kirk

thought. Two ports would provide coverage above as well as below the aircraft.

"Forgive my ignorance," General Wainwright said, looking up from the folder, "but wouldn't a laser like this wreak havoc on everything on the ground?"

"Not really, General," Lieutenant General Morris said, always willing to explain the intricacies of modern science, especially to an Army officer. "Don't confuse this application of laser technology with the Star Wars efforts. This laser is relatively low in power, much like the target designators we use to guide smart weapons, like Pave Tack, or even the G/VLLD the infantry uses. No, the laser wouldn't set anything on the ground on fire. There's a slight possibility someone might get eye damage if they happened to be looking in the right direction, but since the ranges are quite long, the possibilities are remote."

"We still can't be certain this is all true," Kashwa'ar interrupted. "The Israelis have lied to us before. What does DIA have to say about the Israeli claims?"

"The Defense Intelligence Agency doesn't know about it," the secretary responded. "Nor will they ever be told. I made a pledge to the Israelis not to tell DIA, CIA, or any other intelligence agency about this information. The Israelis are concerned about the numerous leaks that have sprung from our intelligence community in recent years. They're in an excellent position to know, as it was one of their agents who infiltrated the agency. However, I understand we have some evidence to corroborate the Israeli story."

"That's right," Morris took over. "General Wainwright sent two specially equipped reconnaissance aircraft into the Golan Heights to check this out. That's where these pictures came from. One plane was lost, the other barely made it back out. Sensors on the plane, as well as the pilot's observations, lead us to believe the Israelis are correct. Unfortunately, we won't be able to make any more flights. The pilot who made it back has severe lacerations inside his eyes, cuts from a laser."

"Why don't the Israelis just shoot the damn thing down?" Kashwa'ar asked.

"Can't do it," General Morris replied. "The same technology gives the airplane an immensely effective self-defense capability. Before any of our aircraft or ships can get within missile range, they've already been picked up by the laser radar."

"Why not use the Stealth fighters?" one of Kashwa'ar's scientists asked.

Morris looked at Wainwright. Wainwright shook his head.

"Can't risk it," Morris said, hiding the fact they had already lost one radar evading plane to the LADAR technology. "If one were shot down the technology would be lost to the Syrians, who would certainly pass it along to our enemies. No, that's not something we can afford to do. Some of the same technology has been used in our other advanced systems, including the stealth bomber. We can't risk letting anyone get their hands on something that would allow our enemies to develop countermeasures to our strategic nuclear capability."

Kirk sensed Morris was going overboard to justify his refusal to use the F-117s. But why?

"And the missile launch sites?" Kashwa'ar asked.

"Again, we can't get close enough to take them out. We know where most of the sites are, though not all of them. We wouldn't even be able to get at them with Tomahawks. The laser radar would easily identify our cruise missiles, and Syria's antimissile batteries are state-of-the-art, extremely effective."

"Then what's the answer?" the secretary of state asked, addressing the group at large.

Kirk was about to bring up his idea when Dr. Kashwa'ar jumped to his feet.

"My guess is the laser plane wouldn't notice something coming at it from directly overhead. If that is true, we can attack it from above, from space!"

"But we have no spacecraft with that kind of capability," General Morris countered.

"General, the Strategic Defense Initiative focused its efforts in its last few years on a concept developed at Lawrence Livermore National Lab. I'm sure you've heard of the 'Brilliant Pebble.' " Kashwa'ar stood and walked to stand behind the representative from Livermore. "It is a high-speed, space-to-space missile with an electronic brain, coupled to a very sophisticated tracking system. Its method of killing the target is very simple. It uses the kinetic energy that exists when two bodies approach at extremely high speeds to devastate the target. We've continued to research the concept under with the support of the Ballistic Missile Defense Office. There are three prototype models nearly complete at Livermore now."

"And how do you propose to get your Brilliant Pebble into space, then back through the atmosphere to the target?" a program manager from Los Alamos National Lab, traditional contender for funds with Livermore, challenged.

"Pegasus!"

"Pegasus? What's Pegasus?" Wainwright asked.

"It's also called a Micro-Sat, a miniature rocket used to launch small satellites. It's captively carried on a NASA B-52, then released at high altitude. Upon release, the rocket motor ignites and the satellite package is launched into low orbit. We can mate one of the Brilliant Pebbles to the Pegasus and launch it over California. The Brilliant Pebble can be programmed to reenter the atmosphere over Southwest Asia and target the Syrian plane. Reentry should be no problem, Livermore has designed hundreds of reentry vehicles."

"Sounds good to me," the secretary of state said. "I've heard a lot about these Brilliant Pebbles. What do you think, General?"

"I don't think anyone knows what the reentry would do to the tracker, Mr. Secretary," Lieutenant General Morris said. "That's never been analyzed."

"That would be no problem." Kashwa'ar rested his hands on the Livermore scientist's shoulders. "I have complete confidence it can be done."

The scientist from Livermore sank slightly in his chair.

Kirk smiled. The reentry problem was a difficult one at best, and Kirk knew Kashwa'ar had no idea how much effort had already gone into trying to solve that problem at the Army's Strategic Defense Command in Huntsville.

"Then, get on it," the secretary ordered. "Anyone else have an idea?"

Kirk started to speak up, but thought better of it. He wrote a short note on the back of one of his business cards and pushed it along the table to Lieutenant General Morris.

Morris picked up the card and read it, then looked up at Kirk, suspiciously. He remembered Kirk's impeccable reputation, then nodded.

"If not I guess we're adjourned. Dr. Kashwa'ar, I'd like to hear a little more about your plan. Can you come by the White House sometime next week?" the secretary asked as he stood.

Kashwa'ar beamed. "Of course, sir. It would be my pleasure."

"One moment, Mr. Secretary," General Wainwright said. "Sir, I must insist a military officer be placed in charge of the project. This 'Brilliant Pebble,' or whatever it's going to be called, will have to be integrated into an overall scheme of maneuver if it is going to stop the Syrians. Just taking out the laser will not be sufficient. My CENTCOM intelligence analysts have been watching Syrian troop movements as a matter of routine—we know they are moving toward the Israeli border. In addition to the usual deployment of Syrian infantry, two tank divisions are on the road, with reserves being called up in inordinate numbers. My point is that even with the laser out of commission, the Israelis will have a hell of a time dealing with the conventional Syrian forces."

"General Wainwright." The secretary of state leaned forward, placing his hands on the table, knuckles down, resting his weight on his arms. He stared directly at the CENTCOM commander. "There is no way I will allow you to put a military officer in charge of this project. It is too important and, frankly, I'm afraid one of your officers would just screw it up. You may attach a liaison officer to DARPA for this project, but he will be there only to provide force coordination. Is that understood?"

Kirk wondered if there was some kind of power play going on here. The secretary of state hadn't raised his voice, hadn't altered his tone appreciably, but there had definitely been a change.

"I understand, Mr. Secretary," Wainwright answered in his most proper, West Point-honed, military response.

The secretary backed away, turning to head for the exit. Before he went through the door, he turned back to address Wainwright and Morris. "In case any of you have missed the point, the idea here is to prevent a war. Get rid of the Syrian laser plane, and the Syrians will not attack. Without their special weapon, they have no more advantage than they've had in the last two wars with Israel. This is our chance to use the military technology we're always bragging about to stop a war, gentlemen. And if you need any assurance about how serious this is, the prime minister admitted to me the Israelis have perfected their tactical nuclear capability. He promised me he would use it before he let the Syrians overrun his country.''

The politician turned and walked out, with Kashwa'ar on his heels. The other civilians also got up to leave.

"I'd like a few more minutes of your time, General Wainwright," General Morris said. "I believe you will be interested in what Colonel Kirk has to say as well.''

As soon as the others left the room, Kirk stood to speak.

"General, I'll make this brief. Kashwa'ar's idea has only a slim chance of working. If there's anything left of the tracker after it burns through the upper atmosphere, it will be lucky to find what it's supposed to kill.''

"You should have argued that point with Kashwa'ar when he was in here," Wainwright said, disturbed. He was already angry at the secretary of state, and was now hearing what sounded like a schoolboy squabble between the Air Force colonel and the civilian scientist.

"I'm sure Kashwa'ar will get all the arguments he can handle when he tells his engineers to build the system," Kirk continued, undeterred, "but that's not the point I want to make. I just wanted you to be aware of the inherent difficulty you face when your liaison officer gets ready to lay out the attack profile. What I really want to do is offer you an alternative."

"General Morris." Wainwright raised his hand to stop Kirk. "Is there someone you can recommend to stick with these DARPA geeks to ride herd, make sure they don't build a system we can't integrate into a master attack plan?"

"Yes, sir, General. I know the perfect guy, a geek himself. Much as I hate to admit it, he's an Army officer, used to be in the infantry but crossed over into the Signal Corps. Name's Lieutenant Colonel Chris Delaney. I met him when he was assigned to DARPA. He's in Omaha now, working at the Joint Strategic Target Planning Staff. He's writing computer models for contingency strike plans, just the kind of guy we need."

"Good. Send him. And make sure he reports back to me daily. We'll have to integrate the Israelis into this. In spite of what the secretary thinks, taking out this one plane will not deter a war. There will be other planes, backups. They'll have to be considered. That politician didn't even read the whole report, in the back of it you'll see some other pictures. One in particular is of a missile launch facility. We've confirmed they're preparing chemical warheads for those weapons. Those missile systems will have to be taken out as well. Under the political restrictions we've just been given, our role will be limited to taking out the laser. We'll have to let the Israelis carry out a strike to disable the missiles. I'll coordinate that aspect of the mission myself. Now, Kirk, what's this alternative?''

Kirk smiled as he told them of his idea on how to deal with the Syrian airborne laser.

''Damn, Kirk. You've been trying to get that old bird out of the museum since she went in,'' Morris said. He was also grinning. This would be an Air Force operation. *If* the general approved.

''She never should have gone into the museum in the first place,'' Kirk admitted.

''So you think this laser plane of yours is the answer?'' Wainwright asked.

''Yes, sir, I do.''

''Well, I'll have to admit it makes sense. Throughout history the best response when an enemy develops a new weapon has usually been a weapon of the same type, the machine gun, armor, nukes . . .'' Wainwright thought for a moment. ''There's one big advantage the Brilliant Pebble has over your system. With the Pebble coming from out in space, the Syrians won't know they're being targeted until it's too late, won't have time to launch their chemical missiles. With your plane, though, they'll have a lot of warning. As soon as you hit their airspace, they'll know they're under attack. If they can, they'll start getting ready to launch the missiles and their backup aircraft, if they have any. That'll only give you an hour, at most, to take out the laser so the Israelis can get in with their bombers and hit the missiles."

"I think it can be done, sir." Kirk had already thought through many of the possible complications, though he hadn't noticed the photos of the chemical missiles in the back of the folder.

"It's going to be a pretty complex operation. Tell me, Kirk, this laser, what will it look like when you shoot it?"

"Very much like a pencil beam of light, sort of orange in color."

"Like lightning?" Wainwright asked.

"Sort of," Kirk continued to explain. "Of course, there will be no thunder. And the laser will travel in a straight line, unlike lightning, which of course is really a beam of electrons, bent into its zigzag path due to interaction with the atmos—"

"Silent lightning, huh?" Wainwright asked, a broad smile crossing his face.

Kirk nodded, knowing he had lost his audience. The general was fixated on the similarity of laser beams to lightning. It would be futile to try and explain the difference.

"What do you think, Morris?"

"It won't hurt to have a backup plan."

Wainwright nodded. "All right Kirk. Do it. Call

this project Silent Lightning. What do you need from us?''

Kirk briefly considered trying to convince Wainwright to change the nickname for the project, then rejected the idea. It wouldn't be worth the effort. As for the general's question, he realized he didn't know. He hadn't really expected to get approval this quickly, hadn't thought out exactly what he needed to make his scheme work. There was one thing he knew he'd need, though. "I'll have to call at least one civilian engineer back to active duty, maybe more. I want this project handled entirely by military personnel. Beyond that, I don't think I'll need anything other than the option to use your name if I need to.''

Wainwright looked at Morris.

"Just tell me who you want," Morris said. "We still have some limited recall authority to support what's left of the Bosnian effort.''

"As for the use of my name," Wainwright slid a small white business card across the table to Kirk. "Here. Make sure General Morris knows how to get in touch with you. And good luck, Colonel.''

"Thanks, General." Kirk stood as the Army officer left. Morris stayed behind.

"You know," Morris said, "if you pull this off, they'll hand you your star on a silver platter.''

"Yes, sir, I know. The trick is to pull it off.''

"You just can't stand the thought of her sitting in the museum, can you? I've got to admit, this is quite an opportunity. I wouldn't have allowed you to bring her out for any other reason."

"I know."

"So, what's your first move?"

"Back to the Pentagon to make a few phone calls, then I've got to go to Dayton, to the museum. I need to see what kind of shape she's in."

4

D-Day minus Thirty-nine
Santa Barbara, California

Lance Brandon sat at his desk sweating slightly, even in the cool comfort of the conditioned air. Light from the overhead fluorescent bulbs illuminated folders of paper and computer printouts stacked throughout the office. He was pouring over one of the computer printouts. The system wasn't functioning correctly, and he had precious little time to figure out what the problem was. The telescope was going to be launched on the next shuttle mission, sometime next month if nothing went wrong with the shuttle itself. Lance had designed the phase-measuring system, one of the packages required to make the entire earth mapping system work. Without it the atmospheric compensation circuit wouldn't do its job, and that was the key to the entire concept.

The radio station Lance was listening to, the only local station that broadcast classical music, was normally devoid of interruptions. That made this third news bulletin, interrupting a taped concert by the Boston Symphony, cause Lance to lose his train of thought again. He listened intently as the broadcaster read an announcement of the latest news from Madrid, where the second Arab–Israeli summit was being held. It had taken the secretary of state over six months to arrange this meeting, hoping to regain the momentum lost since the original Madrid summit. The secretary of state was confident, along with the rest of the world, that some conclusive peace accord could be achieved this time. That confidence, according to the radio report, was being rapidly eroded. And it wasn't even because of the Palestinians, at least not directly.

The Syrian representative had just proven his allegations, with an apparently dramatic videotape, that Israel was again resettling some of the newest wave of Jewish immigrants in the occupied lands north of the Golan Heights. Syria was threatening to walk away from the talks if the Israelis didn't admit what they were doing was in direct conflict with an informal agreement reached at the last summit. The Syrian delegation also wanted Israel to publicly promise to negotiate a treaty where the Golan Heights would be returned to Syria. It was an old theme: Land for Peace.

Lance had been following the news with great interest, convinced in his own mind the rift between the Arabs and the Israelis could be the fuse to ignite the next major war. He hoped he was wrong, but all this activity was proving otherwise. He reached up to turn off the small radio. The news broadcasts were interrupting his concentration, and he needed to get back to the work at hand.

He pulled one of the red marking pens out of his pocket and traced the output of one of the feedback amplifiers until he saw where the circuit started to go nonlinear. That might be the problem. He turned back to the computer. Pushing his long hair out of his eyes, he punched away at the well-worn keyboard, changing a resistor value in one part of the amplifier circuit. The computer simulation was another one of his own ideas, patented by the company he worked for—Santa Barbara Electro-Optics. The circuit he designed would be simulated on the computer, over the entire range of input values, without soldering any of the basic components together. This circuit was fairly complex, though, and it would take over two hours for the computer to generate the result. Lance finished instructing the computer to begin the simulation when his phone rang.

He started to pick it up, but changed his mind. It was almost eleven o'clock, time to go run. He needed to get out today, to loosen up the calf muscle he'd strained in the 5K fun run the previous week. He hadn't finished with a good time, but the race was well worth the effort. He'd helped sponsor the race, and it had brought in a good deal of money for the Santa Barbara Shelter for Abused Women and Children. His wife, Mandy, did a great deal of volunteer work there, and he tried to do as much as he could to support her efforts. It was the least he could do after all the support she had given him since he left the Air Force. After two more rings the voice-mail system automatically answered the phone. Lance changed his mind, grabbing the receiver when he heard Dr. Alexander, the company president, on the speaker.

"Sir, Lance Brandon here."

"Lance, I'm glad I caught you in. I know it's almost time for lunch, but I wonder if you could take a few minutes to come by my office on your way out. I've got something to talk to you about."

"Sure, I'll come over right now."

"Good, I'll be waiting for you."

Lance hung up. He didn't get calls from the front office very often, management usually left him alone. That was one of the great things about his job. It was technically challenging, the pay was great, and management seldom gave him a hard time about schedules. That's why he was so curious to find out what Alexander wanted. Could be a new contract, maybe something the boss wanted his input on before turning it over to marketing. Lance grabbed his sports coat off the rack in his office and pulled it on as he went out the door.

"Hey, Lance, aren't you going to the gym today?" one of his running partners asked from the hallway.

"I'll get over there if I have time," he called back

as he jogged down the white-tiled hallway, reaching in the empty pockets of his jacket, wondering where he'd left his tie. "I have to go see the boss first."

"Your hair's a mess, Lance." Alexander's secretary smiled when he got to her office. "Of course, we wouldn't expect any different would we?"

Lance ran both hands through his hair, shoving most of it out of his face and back over his neck. "Sorry" was all he could think of to say.

"It's okay, Lance. Dr. Alexander's on the phone, but he wants you to go right in."

"Thanks."

Lance opened the door, glancing at the small brass plate with its simple inscription: Walter Alexander, Ph.D.

Once inside, Lance could hear Alexander talking to his speaker phone. The voice on the other end sounded distantly familiar. Alexander, his badly damaged eyes grossly distorted beneath his thick, dark glasses, motioned him over to the empty chair across from the desk.

"He's just walked in, John," Alexander said, directing his comment to the small white box on his desk.

"Good. How are you, Lance?" came the reply from the same box, the voice slightly garbled. Lance wondered why it sounded that way; it kept him from making out who he was talking to.

"Fine," Lance replied, not knowing what else to say. He shrugged his shoulders, looking at his boss.

"You don't recognize your old friend's voice, do you, Lance? It's John Kirk."

"Major Kirk?" Lance asked, totally surprised. He hadn't talked to Kirk since he left the Air Force.

"Hardly," Alexander answered. "It's Colonel Kirk now."

"Colonel?" Lance looked at the little box. "Congratulations, sir."

"Thanks, Lance," came the garbled response. "Listen, we don't have a lot of time to chat, so I'll get right to the point. Walter, I need Lance back."

"Lance is tied up on an important project right now, John. Besides, you'd better be asking him, not me."

"I didn't know you two knew each other," Lance said.

"Since before you even came to work here, Lance. In fact, it was Colonel Kirk who told me about you in the first place."

"I thought you were pissed at me for getting out!"

"Damn right I was pissed," came the garbled reply. "I didn't want the Air Force to lose you."

"When Kirk realized you were going to hang up your uniform, he called me," Alexander said. "He told me you were one of the best electrical engineers at the lab. He also sent me a copy of your résumé. I wouldn't say I hired you on his recommendation, but his opinion carried a lot of weight."

Lance sat back in the chair. He had no idea Kirk had helped him land the job.

"I guess I owe you some thanks, Colonel."

"Bullshit!" Kirk replied. "You've done some good work there. We've used some of your results here at the lab. I just didn't want to see your talents go to waste."

"You're still at the Weapons Lab, sir?"

"It's the Phillips Lab now. I've been on a couple of other assignments since you left, but I'm back at the lab now, as the commander."

"And now you want to call in your favor?" Alexander asked.

"Not really, but I do need some help. I think you'll want to give me a hand when you hear my problem, Lance."

"Go ahead, sir," Lance said. All of a sudden he had a new respect for Kirk, and an unexpected indebtedness.

"I've got to remind you he doesn't have a security clearance anymore, John," Alexander interrupted again.

"Yes he does. I'm giving it to him. Besides, this thing is beyond normal security clearance procedures. What I'm about to tell you is not to be repeated—to anyone! The project is being handled on a very strict need-to-know basis."

"In that case, is it safe to be discussing this on the phone?" Lance asked, remembering the lectures on communications security from his days in the Air Force, the little red labels on all the phones reminding everyone not to conduct classified conversations over them.

"We're in secure mode, at the top secret level," Alexander assured him. "This is a STU III, a secure telephone unit. They came out a couple of years ago. There are only a few here, mostly in the special projects branch. You've probably never seen one in your section, there's not much classified work going on there. Come around here and take a look."

Lance leaned over the desk to check out the phone. It had a liquid crystal display above the keypad. The display read "TOP SECRET-AF/XO."

"That's the Pentagon, Air Force Operations," Alexander explained.

"That's where I'm calling from, D.C. I've just come from a meeting with the secretary of state and a bunch of other folks. We've got a big problem in the Mideast."

Lance listened intently as Kirk briefed them on what had transpired at the meeting, not the least bit pleased that his assumptions about the potential of war in the Mideast appeared to be correct.

"I'm bringing the Laser Lab back out," Kirk concluded. "That's why I need your help. I need you back in the Air Force for a while."

Lance sat back in his chair. He was surprised by Kirk's request. He had thought he was through with the military, but during the Desert Storm war he had felt some pangs of guilt, worried he hadn't contributed his fair share to the nation. Now he had a chance to make his contribution. Yet there were other considerations, other things in his life this decision would affect. His family and his work were the two most important. He wondered what Mandy would think if he told her he was going to be in the Air Force again, even if it were for just a short while.

"What do you say, Lance?" Dr. Alexander asked.

"I don't know. The Geo-telescope project is at a critical phase right now. We might not make the schedule if I leave."

"We'll find someone to finish the project," Alexander assured him. "You've worked out most of the theoretical parameters already, now it's just a question of engineering. I can get someone else to finish up."

Alexander wasn't making this any easier. Lance knew a few of the engineers held reserve commissions, and he assumed the company just put up with their absences. But this was different. It was almost as if Alexander expected him to go help Kirk.

"I just don't know," Lance said, sensing he was lying to himself. "I need a little while to decide."

"We don't have a little while, Lance," Kirk said. "I need you in Albuquerque tomorrow. I'm going to have the plane checked out in Dayton and sent back to the hangar as soon as possible. I need you to start getting the beam pointer assembly ready."

"Then I'll let you know tomorrow, first thing in the morning. If I decide to help out, I can be on a plane before noon." Lance knew he was stalling.

"That's all I can ask. Walter, thanks for your time.

I've got to get going now. And Lance, we really need your help."

The line went dead. Dr. Alexander pulled a small black key out of the side of the phone and locked it in one of his desk drawers.

"It's your call, son," Dr. Alexander said quietly, folding his hands in front of him on the desk. "It goes without saying that if you decide to go, your job will be here when you get back. I don't normally pressure the people who work here to participate in the reserves or ask them to work on military projects. I figure they'll do it on their own if they want to. It's got to be for their own reasons, not because the company wants them to. But I think you should give this some serious thought, though. Kirk has never asked for anything from me, even though I owe him a lot. He's just not that kind of man. This must be important, possibly more than we'll ever know."

"Yeah. It must be important for him to look me up after all these years, but I still need to think it over."

"Go ahead. Take the afternoon."

"Okay, I think I will. I'll come tell you what I decide first thing in the morning."

"I'll be here," Dr. Alexander said as Lance got up to leave. After Lance closed the door, Alexander smiled to himself. He already knew what the answer would be. He hadn't served in the military himself, the enlistment physical had uncovered his diabetes, but his son had joined the Marines, and through him Alexander had come to appreciate the strength of the complex emotion called patriotism. He looked down at the picture on his desk, a blurred image of a young lieutenant in dress blues. Lance looked a lot like his son. Alexander had noticed the similarity years ago, when Lance first arrived for his job interview. Both men had perpetually deep tans and dark hair, though Lance kept his on the long side now. Like Lance, his son had been of average size, maybe a little on the thin side, and like Lance they both had a presence about them, an aura of competence, of energy, of enthusiasm. As usual a lump formed in Alexander's throat when he visualized the black marble wall where his son's name was permanently engraved, along with some fifty thousand other patriotic men and women.

Lance stopped his RX-7 in the driveway and got out. Santa Barbara Electro-Optics was more or less a "think tank," a company where the employees generally picked their own office hours. Even so Lance was home unusually early this afternoon. Mandy's car was in the driveway, she'd probably be surprised. The twins, Rachel and Sarah, wouldn't be home from school for another three hours.

Lance could hear Mandy in the bedroom when he went inside. He walked back to their room without her hearing him. Mandy was standing with her back to him, laying some things she had just bought on the bed. Lance stopped at the door, admiring her long, tanned legs. She was dressed for shopping, a white cotton sweater and walking shorts. Typical California.

He walked up behind her. "Guess who's home?" he asked as he put his arms around her.

Mandy jumped, surprised to hear a voice. She spun around in his arms.

"You scared me to death. What are you doing home this early?" she asked, returning his kiss.

"I decided to take the afternoon off," he replied, feeling the warmth of her body, the softness of her skin. He strained his neck, trying to see what was on the bed. At five feet eleven inches Mandy was almost as tall as Lance, and she kept moving her head to block his view. In spite of her efforts Lance caught a glimpse of a bag on the bed, he recognized it as one of the fancy ones from Victoria's Secrets, a lingerie store in town where Mandy liked to shop. "What did you buy?"

"None of your business." She turned him around and pushed him toward the door. "Go in the kitchen and find us something to eat. I'll be right out."

Lance did as he was told, turning his head to steal a glance at what she was trying to hide from him before she closed the door. She was too quick, he didn't see anything.

In the kitchen, Lance got bread and sandwich meat from the refrigerator. He laid it out on the counter while he gazed out the large kitchen window, looking past the pool and down the sloping hillside to the ocean below. Even the three offshore oil wells in the distance couldn't spoil the view. Lance watched a large sailboat, probably one of the yachts from the marina, sail off into the south. He had really come to love this place. That made it all the more difficult to consider leaving, for even a short period of time. He knew that was selfish, though, knew the freedom he had here was not something everyone enjoyed. Visions of a destroyed Israel invaded his thoughts, of people thrown from their homes, persecuted once more.

Lance had never been to Israel, had little experience with the Jewish people at all. Yet he sensed a tie to the people there. Perhaps it was his own heritage that spawned those feelings, his great-grandfather's hasty departure from pre-communist Russia.

"So, tell me why you're home so early," Mandy asked as she walked into the room, taking the knife from him.

"I got a strange phone call this morning, and I needed to talk to you before I made a decision." Lance backed away from the counter to take a seat at the kitchen table. He looked at Mandy while she finished preparing the sandwiches, admiring the long sun-bleached hair that cascaded over her shoulders.

"So what was it about?" she asked.

Lance thought for a moment before replying. What could he tell her about the call without revealing any secrets? Not very much. He wasn't comfortable with that, didn't like to keep things from her.

"You remember John Kirk, the major I worked for in Albuquerque?"

"Of course, he was at your going-away luncheon."

"He's the commander of the lab now, a colonel. Anyhow, he's got a special project he needs help on, wants me to help him out."

"So go do it. You always enjoyed the lab."

"It's not quite that simple. He wants me back in uniform."

Mandy stopped and turned to look at him. "Back in the Air Force? For how long?"

"Probably not long. I doubt if it would take more than a couple of months." That was certain. If Syria intended to attack in six weeks, they would have to be done before then. "But that's two months I'll have to be away from you and the kids."

"Well, what kind of project is it?"

"I can't really say, Mandy. It's secret." Lance saw Mandy's face take on a look of concern, one she hadn't displayed until now. Lance recognized the look. It was the same expression she wore when she found out what the Laser Lab tests involved back in 1983, and how dangerous the tests actually were.

Mandy wiped her hands on a cloth and sat down beside him at the table. She reached out and took his hand in hers. "Is this project going to be dangerous, Lance?"

"No, not really," he lied, knowing his eyes betrayed him.

"Is it an important project?"

"Yes. It could affect a lot of people."

"Are you going to do it?"

"I don't know yet. I owe Kirk an answer by tomorrow morning. He wants me to fly to Albuquerque."

They sat silently for a few minutes, Lance still trying to rationalize the decision he'd already made, Mandy trying to quell the fear that initially surged from within her, trying to appear supportive.

The love of his life looked him straight in the eye. "Sometimes you have to take time away from family for other things, the things that help you sleep well at night."

Lance squeezed her hand. "You're a philosopher beyond your years," he said, reaching to put his hand behind her neck, to pull her lips to his. He kissed her deeply.

Mandy broke the embrace to stand up. "Sounds like it's time for a run," she said, moving back to the counter. Mandy knew Lance always thought better when he was out by himself, running down the paved streets or up into the mountain trails.

"You're right. I'll wait to eat when I get back." He stood up and kissed the back of her neck.

"Okay, I'll have it waiting for you."

Lance went into the bedroom to change. Whatever was on the bed earlier was gone now, hidden away. Lance decided not to snoop. Things from Victoria's Secrets were best discovered when Mandy was wearing them. He changed into shorts and pulled a pair of his running shoes from the closet. No need for a shirt today, the weather was typical California—perfect. He pulled his hair back into a short ponytail and headed out the door. In just a few minutes he was on the road, running up the hill.

It was almost two hours later when Lance got back to his house. As he'd intuitively known all along, he'd decided to help Kirk out. Most of the run was spent sorting his thoughts, figuring out what he needed to do before he left. After a shower he'd write them all down. Alexander was right about the shuttle project. Someone else could handle the final design, so his work wasn't a problem. It was money that concerned him the most. The salary he'd get from the Air Force wouldn't even come close to making the house payment. There was enough money set aside for them to get by for a while, but if something unexpected happened and he ended up being gone for a long time, it could become a financial nightmare.

Lance stepped into the kitchen, before heading to the shower.

"Mandy, I've got to do it," he said, concerned she would be disappointed.

"I know." She was smiling.

Lance was relieved. He started toward her, wanting to hold her closely.

"No you don't," she said, burying her hands in his sweat-soaked chest hair and shoving him away. "Not until you're cleaned up."

"All right. But don't tell the twins just yet. I'll talk to them later."

"They won't be home until about six; they're going to a birthday party after school. By the way, a young man from Los Angeles Air Force Base stopped by while you were out. He was a lieutenant, I think. Anyway he left a package for you. I put it on the desk."

"I'll look at it when I get out of the shower."

Lance sat at the desk wearing only a pair of shorts, using one hand to massage his sore calf. The run had helped work out the stiffness, but the muscle was still tender. He'd just finished making a list of things he needed to do, the things he'd thought about when he was out running. He picked up the brown envelope with his name on it, obviously the one Mandy told him about. Inside were tickets for the noon flight to L.A., with a connection to Albuquerque. There was also a note from Kirk, apparently faxed to the lieutenant's office. Lance read it, smiling at Kirk's confidence. His old boss had assumed Lance would join the team. That was just like him.

"What's in the package?" Mandy asked from the doorway.

"A plane ticket," Lance answered. "Kirk figured I'd accept."

Lance turned around. Mandy was standing in the doorway wearing a white robe that barely came to the top of her long, tanned legs.

Mandy smiled and dropped the robe from her shoulders, revealing a white lace, French-cut teddy. The lace was sheer, leaving nothing to Lance's imagination.

"If you're leaving tomorrow, I have a going-away present for you to unwrap," she said, turning toward the bedroom.

5

D-Day minus Thirty-nine
Air Force Museum, Wright Patterson AFB, Ohio

Colonel Abraham "Ironman" Jones gazed down on the vast array of vintage aircraft immortalized on the museum floor below him. The aircraft spanned the days of the Wright brothers, represented by a replica of the Wright Flyer, to the early fighters of WWII. This half of the huge building was packed with the history of early aviation. He knew every airplane, every word on every plaque in the museum. Not only in this half of the building but in the other half as well, where the airplanes and spacecraft that represented the next phase of aerial flight, from WWII to early space exploration, were housed. This place had brought him solace in the last year, had beat back the depression that haunted him following Jenny's death. He still grieved, but the pain was finally easing up a little. He even planned to compete in his first triathlon since cancer took his wife. It would be his first race in the over-forty age-group.

Strange that the phone call that brought him here also reminded him of his loss. Kirk hadn't meant to hurt him, to bring back painful memories when he asked about Jenny. He hadn't known she was dead now, but it did hurt when he asked. It always hurt.

It was almost time for the museum to close, and there were very few people looking at the exhibits below. A young couple, Jones guessed some newly arrived airman and his wife or girlfriend, were wandering through the displays. And an old fellow, seemingly mesmerized by the Korean War vintage F-86. What memories he must be reliving, thought Jones.

The door to the VIP lounge opened, interrupting his train of thought. Jones turned as Colonel Talbot, the new museum curator, came into the room.

"Colonel Jones, I'm glad to see you again." Talbot came over to greet him.

Jones pulled the unlit cigar out of his mouth to reply. "It's good to see you, too, Colonel Talbot. How's retirement suiting you?"

"Pretty well. A round of golf once or twice a week, and I'm still surrounded by airplanes. Nice clean, quiet airplanes for a change."

"It is peaceful here." Jones turned to look out the plate glass window at the museum below him. "I've spent a lot of time here lately. In fact, I'd bet I know this place even better than your predecessor did."

"Yes, he told me you were one of the best supporters he had on base. Said I should give you a call if I ever needed a favor."

"Please do. But first, I need a favor from you."

"Shoot."

"I need my airplane back."

D-Day minus Thirty-eight

Jones sat with Talbot in the blue Air Force pickup. It was dark now, the hazy Dayton air almost completely obscured the full moon. They watched as a man in coveralls moved the big gate back, allowing them access to the apron outside the museum. Jones looked down at his watch. The standard blue Air Force pickup didn't have an air conditioner, much less a clock. He hit the orange button on the side of his Timex Triathlon, illuminating the liquid crystal display. He sighed. It was two o'clock in the morning. O-dark thirty in the vernacular of the unit he commanded, the 4950th Test Wing.

When the gate was fully open, Jones put the pickup in motion, slowly pulling onto the overgrown taxiway. Behind them a tow cart followed, and behind it a crew bus carrying a dozen men.

The dim illumination of the pickup's parking lights gave the procession an eerie quality. They drove through history, past an old C-133 CargoMaster on the right and a StratoFreighter on the left, the cargo version of the B-29. Next on the left was an EC-121 Constellation, its radar modification used as an early

Airborne Warning and Control System, an AWACS, over Vietnam. Then the KB-50J SuperFortress on the left just before they reached their objective back on the other side. The light fog swirled around, conjuring up the ghosts of these ancient chariots. Jones could almost feel the watchful eyes of their ancestral airmen, guarding their old birds, wary of their nighttime visitors.

The museum was full now. Even with the recent addition of an auxiliary hangar these big birds had to be parked outside, there was no room. Jones applied the brakes. One bird wouldn't have to wait for a spot in the hangar. She was being recalled to active duty.

The men in the crew bus clambered out. Mostly sergeants, they were specially picked men from the Test Wing. None of them knew why they were doing this, why they were moving the Airborne Laser Lab out of the museum and into one of the hangars on the other side of the fence. A few probably wondered why they were doing it in the middle of the night, but they didn't care. They would do it for Jones. Besides, they were retrieving one of their own.

Portable compressors came to life, pumping new air into old, sagging tires. Someone, a master sergeant, opened the hatch and climbed into the cockpit. He gave the thumbs-up when it looked like the front wheel would be free to move. With the tow bar engaged, men with orange-covered lights surrounded the plane, "wingwalkers," their job was to make sure there was no collision with the adjacent aircraft.

Jones had ordered the men to be particularly careful with this part of the movement. A damaged wing would ground this project for months, effectively killing it. Jones was betting the plane was nearly flight worthy. It had only been in the museum for a few years, and even though the Dayton weather wasn't the most hospitable for airplanes on static display, records showed this particular plane had very few flying hours on it. In fact, just before it was inducted into the museum, it was the oldest flying KC-135, yet it had the fewest flying hours of any 135 in the inventory.

Jones and Talbot watched as the plane was pulled slowly forward, abandoning its resting place.

"It's going to leave a hole," Talbot noted.

He was right. Jones looked up and down the line. There were six more planes toward the museum and two more in the other direction. The missing airplane would be quite conspicuous by its absence.

"I guess we better move these others up to fill the gap," he said to Talbot. "If that's okay with you, Colonel."

"That's fine, but you realize anyone who keeps a close tab on the planes out here will realize it's missing."

"I don't think many people will notice. If anyone gets nosy and asks about it, you can tell them it's being refurbished for another display."

"Sure, I'll send a memo to my staff in the morning."

Jones put the pickup in reverse as the plane was towed toward them. He backed into a small space between two other planes on display. They watched the procession in silence. First came the crew bus leading the way toward the gate, its parking lights creating a halo of light in the fog. The faded yellow tow truck passed next, pulling the plane. The wing-walkers, their orange lights aglow, surrounded the gray behemoth and moved with it. When they were past, Jones pulled in behind.

"Wait a minute," Talbot said.

Jones stopped the pickup, and Talbot jumped out. He walked over to the metal placard and picked it up, stand and all, then carried the sign back to the pickup and put it in the back.

"I'll put it in my office until you let me have the ALL back," he said when he climbed back into the cab.

"Good idea." Jones hadn't told Talbot he'd bring it back, hadn't even thought beyond the end of the mission, but he supposed that would be the reasonable thing to do.

Even though they moved slowly, barely faster than a normal walk, it would only take about fifteen minutes to get to the hangar on the other side of the old taxiway. Jones stopped and waited while the men opened the gates wider, allowing the big plane to pass through to the restricted side of the base. Beyond them the taxiway, now used as a service road, was blocked at both ends. With the lateness of the hour, it was doubtful anyone would come this way, but the odd car would be stopped by the security police and turned back.

As they started moving forward again, Jones grabbed the handheld radio off the dash and keyed the mike:

"Chief, this is Colonel Jones."

"What's up, sir?" Chief Master Sergeant Warren replied on his own radio. He was currently standing near the rear of the plane, keeping an experienced, watchful eye on the operation.

"We're going to leave a big hole back where we pulled the plane out. I've got Colonel Talbot's approval to move the other planes up one slot to fill it. It'll screw up our time line for the inspection, but it's important."

"I understand, sir. We'll get on it as soon as we have the ALL in the hangar."

Once through the gate they turned right, heading for the last hangar in the row of six on the other side of the taxiway. Earlier that day Colonel Jones had "requisitioned" the hangar. It was mostly empty anyway, having been used for storage over the last few years. The base civil engineers had come out on an emergency work order to hook up power to the building, not only the standard one-hundred-twenty-volt lighting circuits, but also the four-hundred-cycle and twenty-eight-volt circuits that would be needed for the aircraft maintenance work. They also covered all the windows with black plastic, keeping anyone on the outside from seeing what was going on in the hangar. Plumbing was going to be a problem, though. The engineers didn't have enough time to make the needed repairs to the water system, so they would have to use the latrines in the next building. Very few people, including the civil engineers, would be allowed in the building once the plane was inside. Limited access would be strictly enforced.

Once past the lone building near the access road, the airplane veered slightly left, cutting across the ramp toward the hangar. Jones looked past the airplane and tried to make out the accelerated runway he knew was there. In the foggy darkness all he could see were a couple of overhead lights.

He had always wondered what it would be like to take off on the specially designed runway in a plane as big as the 135. He would probably get to try it. The long runway on this side of the base, usually used to land aircraft that were going into the museum, was torn up. Like many other areas of the base, an old dump site had been discovered beneath the asphalt here. Lead from the dump had been discovered leeching into the ground water, and the site was being cleaned up. He would go through all the calculations, of course, but his gut feeling told him what was left of the long runway was too short. And his intuition was usually right. He would have to make sure the maintenance crew took a particularly close look at the landing gear, the huge upward ramp at the end of the accelerated runway would be very hard on the wheels and their support structures. In fact, that was why the concept was abandoned for such large airplanes, the gear couldn't take the stress.

They rode in silence as the plane was pulled across the tarmac to the hangar. When they got close, Jones pulled around the plane and parked near the side of the building. He and Talbot got out and watched the men pull the plane into the hangar. Once inside, the huge hangar doors were closed and the lights switched on, bathing the inside of the building and its new occupant with brilliant fluorescence. Half of Chief Warren's men got into the crew bus and headed back to the museum, the rest went to work on the ALL. Their orders were to check everything on the plane for flight worthiness. Chief Warren came over to Colonel Jones when he was sure all his men were gainfully employed.

"The rest of the men should be back before daylight. We should be able to give you an initial assessment before lunch, sir," he reported.

"That's great, Chief. She looks to be in pretty good shape to me."

"At least on the outside," the chief agreed. "Once you look past all the bird crap, anyway. It's what's going on inside that worries me, though. Especially the engines and flight controls."

"I've got a rule, Chief: Don't bother worrying about anything until you've got something to worry about."

"Sounds like a good rule, Colonel. By the way, do

you want us to pull the dummy turret when we get done with the inspection?"

"You know how?"

"Sure, I was assigned to Detachment 2 for a while, from '75 to '79."

"That's right, I remember now. You were just a tech sergeant then. Didn't the contractors always take care of the turret?"

Yeah, and you were just a major, the chief thought. "They were supposed to, but you remember how it was back in Albuquerque. Everybody pitched in when something had to get done. That's what made it so much fun. Anyhow, I can get the dummy off."

"We'll have to hold off for now. The plan is to fly the plane back to Albuquerque and integrate the systems there. You current?"

"Yes, sir, I just got my flight physical two weeks ago."

"Good. Plan to go with us. In the mean time, just get her ready to fly."

"Will do, sir."

The chief turned back to his crew, eager to get on with the job. It wasn't often he got involved with something that had this kind of priority, the "Wing King's" personal attention assured him he would have the resources he needed to get the job done quickly. The people he had working for him were just one example, half of them were in town on temporary duty, TDY, called in just for this project. It was going to be fun again, just like the old days.

Jones watched the chief walk away, trying unsuccessfully to stifle a yawn. He looked at his watch again. O-five hundred. O-dark thirty and a half. So far everything looked good. He walked back to the pickup, intent on getting a couple of hours of sleep before going into his headquarters.

"At least two of them, sir. Numbers one and four," Chief Warren reported over the phone. "Whoever readied it for display drained all the oil out of 'em. They're frozen solid. I don't think I'd trust the other two engines, either. Better to replace them all."

"How much time," Jones asked, biting down hard on the unlit cigar.

"If we had the engines, we could probably get them replaced in about four days. That's working two shifts."

"You've got the engines. We'll strip the new CF-100s off one of our other birds. And you've got three days."

There was a moment of silence on the other end of the phone. Finally Warren spoke up.

"All due respect, sir, but if we wait on the civilians to pull the engines off one of the other birds we'll be here at least a week. It'd be better if you let me use my men to pull the engines. The only drawback is that it'll take no less than four days to do the total job."

"Good point. Go ahead, Chief. You've got your

four days. You may have to work around some other folks while you replace the engines."

"Understood, sir. Should be no problem."

Jones hung up, assured the chief master sergeant would do everything in his power to get the engines replaced in the allotted time. Fortunately, all the other systems looked to be okay.

Jones picked up the phone again, punching the key that automatically connected him with the DO, the deputy commander for operations. The phone was answered in less than a full ring.

"Ops."

"This is Colonel Jones. Let me speak to the DO."

"One moment, sir."

"Good Morning, boss. What's up?"

"I need some engines. Free up 622, she's got the freshest."

"Sir, 622 is just about ready to fly that mission for NASA."

"I know, but this is important. In fact, get up here and I'll fill you in." He was going to have to tell him what was going on sooner or later. The DO would have to fill in as wing commander while he was gone, and no one was going to be able to talk him out of this mission. He had already decided he was going to fly it himself. After all, he flew the ALL back when it was just an experimental airplane. There was no one more qualified.

Jones killed the connection then released the switch,

hitting the intercom button this time. His secretary picked up.

"Track down Colonel Kirk and get him on the line for me." Jones put the receiver down. Kirk was going to be pissed, but there was nothing anyone could do about the engine problem now. Certainly not any more than was being done already. There was one chance for them to use the time to their advantage, they could bring the laser pointer from Albuquerque and mount it while the engines were being replaced. In fact, it might even save them a day or two off the original schedule Kirk had worked out, and even one day saved would help relieve the tight burden they were going to have to work under. He just had to convince Kirk. Meanwhile, after he briefed the DO he would have him find a C-5 and send it to Albuquerque. It would take a big plane to move the laser pointer up here.

Santa Barbara, California

"To be honest, I'm glad you decided to help Kirk. He's a good man," Alexander told Lance. "You don't have much time if your plane leaves at noon, and I'm sure you have a lot to do, so I'll be brief. Here's a packet of information on the program we've set up for the reserve officers who work here, consider yourself covered under it. One of the major points in the program is that our employees do not take a cut in pay when they do their reserve work, the company makes up the difference between what the government pays and what you would have normally made. You can read about it when you have time."

Lance was pleasantly surprised. He didn't know there was a program like that in the company. "You have no idea what a load that takes off my mind, Dr. Alexander."

"You have a uniform?"

"Yes, I dug it out of the closet last night. Still fits, too."

"Good, just a minute." Alexander punched the intercom. "Mary, call my barber and tell him we're on the way over."

Alexander released the intercom and got up, reaching for his cane. "Let's go, Lance."

"Your barber?"

"Yeah, I'm going to watch him cut off that damn ponytail," Alexander smiled. He hobbled over to where Lance stood and smacked him on the back.

6

D-Day minus Thirty-eight
Santa Barbara, California

Lance glanced nervously at his watch. The longer he waited, the more he regretted letting Mandy bring him to the airport. The small terminal was almost vacant. That left him, Mandy, and the kids with little to do but sit and wait until time to board the small, twin turbo-prop sitting out on the ramp. Mandy had been quiet all morning, content to sit beside him and hold his hand. The children were even subdued, staring curiously at his blue uniform. They were born after he had left the Air Force, after a qualified doctor had diagnosed and treated Mandy's illness, and had never seen him wear the clothes that had hung unused in the closet for almost ten years now.

Sarah, sharing the seat next to him with her sister, had seemed the most curious, asking him what each of the insignia represented. That was typical of her, older than her sister Rachel by almost five minutes,

Sarah had shown an insatiable curiosity since she could first communicate. Lance smiled as he thought back to the first words she had mouthed after mastering "mama," they were hard to discern but generally meant "what's that?" After the initial sadness that she hadn't murmured "dada" until later, Lance came to enjoy answering her endless questions. Rachel, not to be outdone, had gone with the other universal childhood question: "why?"

Now, older, the twins were in the third grade, but studying mathematics that some children didn't get to until the sixth grade. Lance was proud of them both, but constantly reminded himself they were just children, with games and dolls to enjoy before tackling the more complex problems of this grown-up world. He reached over and straightened Rachel's long black ponytail, and out of habit adjusted Sarah's as well. They both stared at him, somehow aware, he was sure, of the tension Mandy was silently communicating. He hated that, didn't want them to remember this as a sad event. He had been on business trips before, but never for this long, and he didn't want the girls to worry.

"Boarding all passengers for Trans World Express Flight 2301 to Los Angeles!" came the announcement over the speakers. Mandy's hand squeezed slightly tighter. Lance squeezed back, reassuringly. He stood and crouched down in front of the two girls, wrapping his arms around them both.

"I want you two to be good while I'm gone," Lance encouraged them, his heart breaking as he saw the tears well up in Rachel's eyes, just like they had when he told them how long he'd be gone.

"Now, stop that," he managed to whisper, his voice cracking. He wiped Rachel's cheek with his thumb. "Remember what we talked about last night; I'll be back before you know it, and I'll try to call as often as I can. Okay?"

Sarah nodded her head, then Rachel agreed. Lance squeezed them again and stood to say good-bye to Mandy. But the words wouldn't come. Instead he opted to hold her close.

After a minute or so she pulled away. "It's time for you to go."

Lance looked around, the other passengers, what few there were, had already gone through the door and were outside, climbing into the small plane.

He picked up his case and gave her one more kiss. "I love you," he told her as he began to walk toward the gate.

"I love, you, too," Mandy replied, her words barely audible. "Be careful."

Those near silent words rang in his ears as he walked out into the brisk breeze and over to the plane. He turned back and waved just before he ducked inside the door. His girls, standing just inside the terminal window, waved back and blew him kisses.

Albuquerque, New Mexico

Lance pulled his tie snug as the tires of the airplane squealed on the hot concrete. He looked out his window as the pilot applied the brakes and deployed the thrust reversers. They sped past the old chemical laser facility, its earthen-covered buildings several hundred meters from the runway that was shared by the Air Force base and the commercial airport. Eventually the plane slowed to taxi speed and turned left at the end of the pavement. Lance saw the old hangar pass momentarily into view. It hadn't changed, not on the outside at least. Hangar 760 still looked out of place, a huge building sitting alone at the end of the runway.

Lance sat back in his seat, absentmindedly running his hand through what was left of his hair. He hadn't worn his hair this short since he quit the Air Force. The uniform felt comfortable, though, like an old pair of socks.

The taxi back to the commercial terminal took a while, that hadn't changed, either. They passed the 150th Tactical Fighter Group, the Tacos. Lance remembered the initial flight tests of the Airborne Laser Lab, flown south of Albuquerque at White Sands Missile Range. The Tacos flew as chase airplanes for those tests, the venerable old A-7s as dependable as any of the airplanes they had used during the program. He didn't see any A-7s here now, though. It looked like they had been replaced with F-16s.

The airliner finally arrived at the terminal and parked at the gate. Lance stood up as soon as the pilot turned off the seat belt sign. He urgently needed to stretch his legs. It had been a long flight. He pulled his laptop computer from the overhead compartment and fell into line as the passengers slowly disembarked.

The information in the folder had said someone would meet him at the airport, but he didn't know who. He spotted a blue Air Force uniform near the back of the crowd. A first lieutenant. She saw him as well and approached, tentatively at first. When she got close enough to read his name tag, she smiled and held out her hand.

"Captain Brandon, I'm Dixie Carter, your reception party," she said slowly, her voice coated with Southern hospitality.

Lance was pleasantly surprised. She was pretty, very pretty. She wore her brown hair cropped short, probably to make it easier to comply with regulations, yet it didn't detract from her good looks. It was her smile that caught his attention, though, it was captivating. The only thing that seemed out of place was her accent. But like her short hair, her accent didn't detract from her persona, in fact, it added a bit of sensuality.

"Hi. Call me Lance. I've sort of outgrown the military title."

"The formality isn't really an option for me, sir," she said, smiling. "In fact, that's the first thing I was supposed to do when you got here, check to see if you were wearing the uniform properly. Colonel Kirk said you hadn't been in one for a while."

"Well, how's it look?"

114

She inspected him. Absentmindedly, Lance was inspecting her as well. He didn't recall Air Force uniforms fitting quite that well back in the old days. Lance realized what he was doing and stopped, not wanting to embarrass himself. Or her.

"There's only one problem, but one that can be easily fixed. Let's step over here," she said, leading him away from the crowd to a seating area. Dixie opened her black pocketbook and pulled out a small yellow envelope. She gave it to him.

Lance put his satchel down and opened it.

"What's this?" he asked, turning the epaulets over in his hand, fingering the gold oak leaves of a major.

"Captain didn't really suit you anyhow," Dixie responded. "The orders promoting you came this morning, straight from the Pentagon."

"Well, that's terrific," Lance said, with less enthusiasm than was probably appropriate. He was wondering how Kirk had managed it. Promotions usually required Senate confirmation.

"Let's go down to get your luggage. I'll help you put the rank on while we're waiting. Then we'll have to hurry out to the base. Your plane was a little late, and we're going to be pushing it to get to individual equipment before they close."

Near the luggage carousel, Dixie removed the old captain's rank from his epaulets and replaced them with his new major's gold oak leaves.

"Why do we need to go to individual equipment?"

he asked, bending his knees so she could reach his shoulder.

"There," she said, finished. Lance stood up straight. "We've got to get your flight gear issued before we leave. I got mine yesterday."

"Leave?"

"Yes. This evening. We're going to Dayton." She lowered her voice: "We're going to be working on the airplane there instead of here. It isn't flight worthy yet, so we're going to do our work in parallel with the maintenance."

"You're in on the project, too?" Lance asked. He thought she was just an escort, someone from public affairs or the protocol office sent to pick him up at the airport.

She looked at him intently. "Yes, but let's not talk about it here."

She was right, he'd been told not to discuss it with anyone, had probably put her in an uncomfortable position even asking the question. He changed the subject.

"So what do you do when you aren't busy picking up strangers from the airport?"

"I work at the lab. Mostly optical systems development. My pet project is an atmospheric compensation technique for low-energy laser beams."

Lance was more than a little surprised. In this day and age, there were more and more women involved in engineering, but optical engineering had been slow to recruit them. Apparently that was changing. Then he had another thought. "Dixie Carter, I thought that name sounded familiar. Didn't you have an article in the *Journal of Applied Optics* last year?"

"Yes, back in August. We were using the pointer from the Airborne Laser Lab to track some high-speed objects, drones flying over the old Sandia Optical Range. We incorporated a laser and deformable mirror to correct for turbulence and ended up with a pretty decent system. I wrote it up with a few of my colleagues."

A decent system indeed, a laser radar. No wonder she had been called in to help with the project, she had real experience. She had already put together just what the Syrians had supposedly built. If she knew how to build it, she would also have a pretty good idea of how to defeat it.

"I thought the pointer was on the airplane in the museum?"

"No. Fortunately, that was one system they took off the airplane before they sent it to Dayton. The laser and everything else is still aboard I guess, but we've been using the pointer/tracker for experiments here. We made quite a few improvements in it since then, too."

Dixie smiled at him. A bit of professional competition was possibly in the offing.

Though his uniform still fit, it was a little tight. That made the flight suit a welcome change. The flight suit was designed to be loose.

Lance stepped back, letting Dixie by.

"This is the MicroVax we use for data acquisition." She pointed at the computer behind the partition. "We can run a whole series of Bode' plots in fifteen minutes."

She had already impressed Lance with what she had been able to accomplish with the old laser beam director, and she continued to surprise him. He remembered taking a whole week to run a full series of Bode' plots on the beam director, usually in sixteen-hour shifts from four p.m. to eight the next morning. It was a real pain. Now she could do the same thing in half an hour. Wow!

Lance followed her through the tangle of cables and support equipment as she completed giving him the tour of her lab. There was little else for them to do right now. Technicians, mostly sergeants, were rapidly disconnecting the tracker from the test fixtures. Every now and then they would stop Dixie to ask her a question. About a dozen of the sergeants were wearing flight suits, the others wore standard camouflage uniforms.

"The plane's here," one of the sergeants came in to tell Dixie.

"There's not much more to see here, Major. Why don't we go out and watch the plane come in?"

"Sure," Lance replied. He followed her out of the air-conditioned test facility and into the empty hangar bay. The big hangar doors were open, letting the desert heat roll in.

They walked past several pallets that held equipment and supplies. The pallets were to be loaded onto the giant cargo transport and delivered to Wright Patterson Air Force Base. Lance had dropped his own suitcase off near one of the pallets earlier. he hadn't even opened his suitcase yet except to put his uniform inside.

"It sure is big, isn't it?" Dixie yelled to be heard above the high-pitched whine of the monstrous plane's engines.

Lance nodded, leaning into the stiff breeze, impressed with the size of the airplane. He had never seen a C-5 Galaxy before. It was the largest cargo plane in the Air Force inventory. They would probably need its size for the pointer/tracker and its test stand, and mounted in the test stand was the only way the tracker could be safely shipped.

The semipermanent fence around the hangar was being pulled back, and several airmen were guiding the plane toward the hangar. They would get it as close as possible and then close the fence again. It was obvious, though, that the plane wouldn't fit inside. They would have to move all the equipment outside and load it onto the plane from there.

Departing the Albuquerque airport in a heavy airplane was never something he looked forward to. Lance remembered several aborted Laser Lab tests, missions canceled because it was just too hot outside to launch the experimental aircraft. The heat thinned the air, leaving little for the plane's wings to bite into. Since the Laser Lab was already at maximum gross takeoff weight it needed all the help it could get to lift off from the mile-high Albuquerque airport. Lance's throat tightened as he felt the C-5 turn, beginning to taxi to the west end of the airport. That meant an easterly launch. A launch that would require a rapid climb out to avoid the Sandia Mountains guarding the east side of the city.

Lance looked back down the throat of the cavernous airplane. It seemed a waste to make the trip with so many empty seats, but that was necessary for security reasons. The fewer people who knew what was going on, the better. The pointer/tracker assembly, mounted in its test stand, was secured in the cargo area just below them. Chains and tie-down straps held it in place. Lance had watched the loadmaster check the connections just before they began to taxi. Lance pulled his seat belt tight as the engines started to spin up.

The plane strained against the brakes as the pilot applied the throttle. When the brakes were released, the plane worked to overcome inertia, slowly accelerating down the runway. Lance absentmindedly gripped the armrests as the plane slowly, grudgingly, picked up speed. To Lance, wishing he had a window to look out, it didn't seem they were moving very fast at all when he felt the nose of the plane lift off the ground. His own flying had taught him the effects of a stall, when wings lose lift because they didn't cut the air fast enough. In a stall the plane fell from the air. Like a rock. He shivered at the thought and closed his eyes, leaving the flying to the aircrew.

"What are you running?" Dixie asked, almost shouting to be heard above the noise inside the airplane.

Lance had been so engrossed with the computer display run he hadn't even noticed her take the seat next to his. "It's a fairly simplistic atmospheric propagation model, first-order approximations. I'm trying to get a handle on how much power we'll need to knock out the other laser." Lance had decided she probably knew all about the mission, although Kirk hadn't told him who else had been indoctrinated. Even so, he was careful not to say anything that she might use to figure out what was going on if she hadn't been told.

"A first-order model won't cut it. I mean sure, it'll give you a rough idea of how much power we'll need, but that's not going to be enough information to tell us how close we'll have to get."

"You're right, it's a trade-off." She had been read in all right, even knew where their big problem was going to be. They would have to use the big gold vapor laser at Wright-Patterson Air Force Base's Wright Laboratory, and its power was limited. If they needed to put more power on the target, they would have to get closer to it, but how close could they get before the target used its own laser to lock into them, guiding a Syrian missile to the Airborne Laser Lab? Could they get close enough to kill it without getting shot down first?

"I've got a high-fidelity model on a Convex computer back in Santa Barbara. I'm going to have to set up a data link between there and the computer center at Wright Patt. Then we'll be able to make some accurate runs."

"How does it look so far?"

"Not good. I'm using power levels I've seen published in the open press. I hope the unclassified numbers don't reflect the actual power they can get out of the laser. If that's all the power they can get, we'll never get close enough to damage the target. If they can get more, then maybe we've got a chance."

"At least we can blind it. We'll shift the wavelength a little and go after their sensors."

Lance knew that was an option, but blinding the sensor was a risky proposition. They wouldn't know if they had failed until it was too late, until after they were shot down. He continued making computer runs, varying the parameters while Dixie looked over his shoulder.

"So how'd you get interested in optics?" Lance asked while they waited on the computer to plot the output from the last run.

"My dad was an astronomer. I grew up spending my summers on top of a mountain in Arizona while Dad collected data. I kind of fell in love with the big telescopes."

"That doesn't explain the accent."

"Born and raised in Arkansas, but I eventually went to college in Arizona."

"The Optical Sciences Center?"

"Yeah. Dad taught there some, and it seemed like a good school."

Just one of the best. Lance admired her courage; it was probably a challenge to break into such a male-dominated field. "And the Air Force?"

"It paid for school. I got married right out of high school, and we didn't have a lot of money. I signed up with a recruiter when they offered me a scholarship. Plus, I like airplanes."

"You're married?"

"Was. We divorced about halfway through college. He wanted me to stay home and have kids, but I wasn't ready for that yet. He finally told me to take a flying leap. Some of the best advice he ever gave me. I started skydiving, one of my favorite hobbies."

"Let me get this straight, you pay people just so you can jump out of perfectly good airplanes?"

She nodded. "Let's take a look at this." Dixie pointed at the computer screen.

Quite a young lady, Lance thought as she pointed out an anomaly in the computer output.

7

D-Day minus Thirty-eight
Wright Patterson Air Force Base, Area A

Lance was studying the graphic display on the laptop computer, deep in thought, when the tires of the C-5 Galaxy grabbed the pavement. The landing startled him. He had lost track of time while he ran through scenario after scenario, trying to refine the parameters of the experiment. Experiment. Lance shuddered. He would have to quit treating this like an experiment—it was anything but. The lives of the ALL crew, not to mention the fate of the Israeli people, would be at stake. If this "experiment" didn't work, they would all be in grave danger.

He grabbed the small computer as the airplane braked hard. When they slowed to taxi speed, Lance saw the loadmaster get up and begin making preparations for their arrival. He looked around for Dixie. She had disappeared after their conversation, and he wondered if he had gotten too personal. He spotted her coming down the steps from the crew compartment, probably went up to get a bird's-eye view of the landing.

She came over to where he sat and started to say something when the engines changed pitch, drowning out all possible conversation for a few seconds. The plane jerked to a stop, almost throwing Dixie to the floor. Quick reflexes saved her as she grabbed a nearby seat and regained her balance.

The engines wound down, and she was finally able to ask her question.

"What did you find out?"

"Not much really." Lance felt a cool breeze, an indication the loadmaster had begun to open the clamshell doors in the back of the plane. "It's just about what I suspected," he continued, getting up from the chair and putting the computer into its carrying case. "Everything depends on how much power we can get out of the laser. Unless they've made some significant improvements in efficiency, we're going to come up short, not nearly enough energy to do damage. Of course, that begs another question: Is there enough energy to blind the other laser's tracking system? That may be what we'll have to do. I'll need to make some runs on the higher resolution model to answer that question."

"It's late already," Dixie said after thinking about what Lance had told her, "but I used the radio up front to call a friend of mine who teaches at the Air Force Institute of Technology over in Area B. As soon as you're ready, he'll come out to the school and let you into the computer center. He's also up to speed on the latest in high-power gold vapor laser technology research here at Wright Lab. If you're not too tired, you can go over tonight. I've got to make sure they get the tracker unloaded, and then I'll try to drop by the institute to see how it's going."

"I'm not too tired. I'm still running on California time, three hours earlier. Besides, I want to know what the answer is going to look like. If I know Kirk, he'll want to know as soon as he gets here. If he isn't already here, that is."

"No, I don't think he's here yet. He'd have come out to meet us if he was. Let's grab a ride down to Operations and check in. They'll be able to get us into the 'Q,' the Visiting Officers' Quarters, and fix you up with a ride over to the institute."

Dixie and Lance stepped onto the stairs that had been brought up to the giant airplane. The spring air was unexpectedly cool. They saw the crew bus, an old panel truck, parked up by the front of the plane. The aircrew was already getting aboard, leaving the loadmaster and two civilians from the 4950th Test Wing, the only active unit at the base, to secure the plane. Dixie yelled as the crew bus started to pull away. Someone in the back of the truck heard her above the scream of the ground power cart and told the driver to stop. Dixie and Lance trotted up to the open rear doors and plopped down inside, their legs dangling off the back. The crew bus lurched forward into the darkness.

Five minutes later they pulled up to the operations building. Inside, Lance looked out the window while he waited for Dixie to place a phone call to her friend in Area B. A staff car jerked to a stop outside just as she hung up. A major in a flight suit stepped out of the passenger's door and ran up to the building. He stuck his head in, his red hair closely cropped and barely visible beneath his flight cap.

"Is there a Lieutenant Carter here?" he asked above the din of noise from the aircrew.

"Here, sir," Dixie answered, walking toward the door.

"Hi. I'm Billy Tipton, everyone calls me 'Red.' Colonel Jones asked me to come over and pick you up. He's waiting for you at his house."

"Pleased to meet you. This is Lance Brandon, the project officer for the test we're here to run."

"Hi."

"Welcome to beautiful Dayton, Ohio," Red said. "I suggest we get going, the colonel doesn't like to be kept waiting."

Lance and Dixie followed Red out to the staff car. Red got in on the passenger's side, and the two newcomers got in the back.

"Don't worry about your gear," Red said as their driver, an airman, pulled away from the curb. "We went down to the plane looking for you first, and I told the loadmaster to make sure your bags got over to the 'Q.' I've already made reservations for both of you there. Have either one of you ever been here before?"

"I was here once about a year ago, giving a presentation over at AFIT. I didn't get to see much of the area, though."

"No," Lance answered.

"Well, AFIT is over in Area B, about ten miles away. This is Area A. They're practically two separate bases. Area B has AFIT, of course, and the museum, and several of the labs. Here in Area A we have the Test Wing on that side of the runway. We're just crossing the end of the approach now, and on this side there's the senior officers' housing, the Air Force Material Command headquarters, and most of the base civil functions. The 'Q' is over here, too, as well as the officers' club. That's it there," Red said, pointing to a large brick building.

The housing area they were in now was impressive. Lance had never seen this kind of architecture at Kirtland or any of the other Air Force bases he'd ever been to.

"These are nice houses," Lance said.

"Yeah. This is the senior officers' housing. It was built back in the thirties, in one of those job programs after the depression. Colonel Jones lives here. I'm kind of surprised they haven't asked him to move out, though. His wife passed away a little over a year ago. Cancer. They usually only let married officers stay here. Guess they felt kind of sorry for him."

"That's too bad," Dixie said.

"Yeah, she was a great lady. Everybody in the Test Wing felt it when she died, but no one more than the colonel. It very nearly trashed him, but from all appearances he's over it now."

The car pulled to a stop in front of one of the smaller brick homes. Red led them to the door. He knocked once, but there was no answer. He got out a key and unlocked it himself.

"Come on in. The colonel's probably out running."

Lance and Dixie followed Red inside.

Lance studied the house. It was quite nice, the furnishings were modern but didn't detract from the antique trim. Yet the rooms lacked something. It took him a while to figure out what it was.

"How long did you say it's been since his wife died?" Lance asked.

"Thirteen months and two days," came a voice from the door.

Colonel Jones walked in, dressed in only a pair of running shorts, carrying his shoes, his dark black skin coated with a shimmering layer of sweat. He reminded Lance more of a weight lifter than a runner.

"Sir, I'm sorry," Lance stumbled for the words. "I was just wondering . . ."

"Don't sweat it, son." The colonel stopped him short. "I take it you're Brandon, the kid Kirk keeps taking about?"

"Yes, sir. Lance Brandon, Colonel." What an idiot,

he thought to himself. Lance couldn't believe he had said something so stupid.

"And this is Dixie Carter." Red finished the introductions.

The colonel shook each of their hands, then took a new cigar from a box on the polished mantle. He unwrapped it and shoved it in his mouth.

"Red, get the roast out of the 'fridge and shove it in the microwave. I'm sure these folks are hungry. There's beer in there, too. If you'll excuse me, I'm going up to shower and then I'll be right down."

The colonel tossed his shoes into a room off to the side and bounded up the steps, taking them two at a time.

Lance followed Dixie and Red into the kitchen. He hadn't realized how hungry he was until the colonel mentioned the roast. It sounded good.

"Beer?" Red asked.

"No, thanks," Lance replied. He still had a lot of work to do tonight.

"Sure," Dixie answered. Red tossed her a Bud, and she popped the top. "Where are the plates?"

"Look in the dishwasher."

Lance finally understood what it was about the house that had bothered him. While it had a woman's touch in the way it was decorated, the house was now occupied by a lonely bachelor. The small signs were everywhere: dirty dishes stacked in the sink, several days worth of newspapers lying in the corner of the living room, stacks of *Time* and *News-week* on the coffee table.

They were all sitting around the kitchen table, enjoying the roast, when Colonel Jones came back in. He was still chewing on the end of the unlit cigar, wearing a flight suit now.

"How is it?" he asked, sitting down at the table to pull on his boots.

"Great!" Lance said, honestly.

"I used to cook for Jenny when she was with me," Jones said. He sat up when he had his boots laced and got right down to business. "We've got the plane in a hangar on the other side of the base, over in Area B near the museum. The engines are shot, that's why we didn't fly it down to Albuquerque for the installation. It'll take a couple of days to get them replaced. There are some other things that have to be worked on as well."

"That's okay, Colonel," Lance said. "We've got a lot of work to do ourselves. The laser, the computers, not to mention installing the beam director."

"How long?"

"Don't really know yet," Dixie said, finishing her beer.

"That's right," Lance agreed. "I've got to make some computer runs before we do much of anything. The results will determine which tracking algorithm we use."

"We don't have an open calendar on this one,"

Jones said. "I haven't been told exactly when we'll have to be ready, but I'd guess we have less than four weeks. And I'm sure you've been listening to the news—the Syrians walked away from the table in Madrid about two hours ago."

"It's going to be tough to meet that schedule. It took a dozen years to get the ALL flying the first time," Lance said. He was surprised at the news about the Syrians, but then again he realized he shouldn't have been.

"We've got no choice. Besides, you've got experience now."

Lance took a napkin and wiped his mouth, stalling, trying to figure out what to say. He could feel Jones's eyes bearing down on him.

"I guess I better get over to AFIT, then," Lance finally said.

"Good, Red will drive you over. What about you, Dixie, what do you need to get started?"

"I want to see the plane first. Then I'll need to get the equipment moved over there."

"I'll take Lance over to the Engineering School, then drop Dixie off at the hangar," Red said.

"Okay. I'll go over to the Wing and check on the equipment." Jones stood up. "We'll have it over to the hangar before morning. By the way, do you remember a sergeant named Wallace, Lance?"

"Sure, he was with us for the last part of the test program. If it weren't for him, we'd still be trying to figure out what went where."

"Well, he's here, working at the Wing. I've got him heading up the effort to get the plane ready. He says he even knows how to install this beam director of yours."

"He probably does, I'd be surprised if he didn't know how to program the computer as well." Maybe they stood a chance of making this project work after all.

Jones moved over and opened a drawer near the phone. He dug around inside and finally pulled out a notepad. From the small pocket on his sleeve, he pulled a government issue pen and began to write.

"What's your home phone, Red?"

"Two three six, two four nine four."

Jones finished writing, then tore the sheet off, folded it, and tore it in half. He gave one piece to Lance and one to Dixie. "Here are all the numbers you two will need while you're here. There's my home phone and my office phone, plus the number of the Ops shop at the Wing. If you can't get me on either of the two lines or Red on his phone, call Ops. They'll get me in less than an hour or I'll have their ass. And they know it. Need anything else?"

Neither engineer spoke up.

"Let's move out, then."

The staff car was gone when they walked outside, and the night air was cooler than before.

"We'll have to take my car," Red said. "It's over here. It might be a tight fit."

Red led them to a bright orange BMW, a two door, parked in the drive next to the house. Parked just in front of it was a dark gray Jaguar. Dixie held the passenger door while Lance climbed into the back. It was cramped. Lance had barely dug his safety belt out of the crack between the seats when Red slipped the little car into reverse and rocketed out of the drive. Lance grabbed the armrest to stabilize himself as Red shifted gears and the car lurched forward, the sound of squealing tires coming through the partially open window.

The ride to Area B and the Air Force Institute of Technology was fast and frightening. Lance suffered in silence, used to the relaxed style of southern California. He wondered if Red wasn't a frustrated fighter pilot, stuck flying the Test Wing's big, slow birds. Dixie seemed to be enjoying herself, though.

Once through the gate into the other side of the base, Red slowed down.

"The security police on this side of the base are strict," he said. "They've been very aggressive lately, and I've already got six points against me. Four more, and I lose driving privileges on base."

"Pull up to the main entrance," Dixie said. "Ron said he'd meet us there."

There were no cars parked in the drive leading to the front entrance, not surprising this late at night. A man in a blue windbreaker walked toward the car when they stopped.

"That's him," Dixie said. She jumped out and gave

the man a hug while Lance struggled out of the backseat.

"Lance Brandon, this is Ron Justin." She made the introductions while holding Ron around the waist. He had to pull his own arm from around her to shake Brandon's hand.

"A pleasure," Justin said, his own voice mimicking Dixie's Southern accent.

"Ron, if you'll be a sweetheart and give Lance a hand getting started, I'll go check on some other things. I'll be back around in a while to see you."

"Sure, I'll be glad to."

"Good, I knew you'd help." Dixie kissed him on the cheek and got back into the car with Red. The tires on the car squealed again as he pulled away.

"You guys must be good friends," Lance said as he followed Ron through the glass doors into the building's foyer.

"Pretty good. She was my sister-in-law for about three years. Fortunately, when the marriage broke up we stayed close. Kind of had to, our parents live next door to each other in Little Rock. Dix said you needed to make some computer runs?"

"Yeah. All I really need is a terminal with communications software. I'll connect it to the mainframe back at my office in California and make the actual runs there."

"We can do that if you want. We have several dumb terminals but they can't run classified information. If the runs you want to make will involve classified data, we'll have to do it another way."

"I don't know if it will be classified or not. I'll be running a laser propagation model, unclassified, but I need to use the gold vapor laser data Dixie said you had."

"That data is classified. Secret. The dumb terminals are out. How about importing the propagation program into one of our computers, then we can make the runs here?"

"What kind of machine do you have?"

"There are half a dozen VAX machines, and a couple of CONVEX super computers if you need that kind of power."

"The VAX will work fine," Lance said as they stepped from the dimly lit hallway into the artificial brightness of the computer center. Even though it was late on a Saturday night, the center was buzzing with activity. Over two dozen terminals were in use.

"It's a bit like a zoo in here," Ron said. "Several of the engineering classes have computer projects due on Monday. Bugs are being trapped and exterminated as we speak. Don't you miss school?"

"Not at all." Lance remembered with disdain the many computer projects he'd had to prepare at MIT. Most of which made no sense at all to him at the time. Now, he admitted, he had learned something from each one, mostly programming tricks. "Which terminal can I use?"

Ron crossed his arms and looked around, trying to

decide. "You know," he said finally, "we won't be able to connect to your machine from here. It's against regulations to hook the classified systems up to an unclassified one—it's a security risk. We might accidentally port some information out, or worse yet, we might import a virus. Besides, it's too noisy down here. Let's go up to my office." Ron led him back out the door as he continued to explain his plan.

"We can use the personal computer in my office to hook up to your machine. We're not supposed to go outside the Local Area Network, but I do every now and then. I've got a modem I bought myself, and I can disconnect from the network while we're tied into your computer. I've got a virus checker as well. We'll download the program onto my tape drive, check it for viruses, and then hook back up into the network and load it into the VAX. How big is the program?"

"The tape drive will hold it easily. Since I already know what laser we'll be playing with, I can select the particular part of the database relating to the gold vapor atmospheric transmission information. It'll be a snap."

Ron opened the door to his small cubicle. It was a typical professor's office, textbooks filled the bookshelves, papers stacked high in boxes, and a whiteboard on the wall with numerous equations scratched across its surface. In the corner behind the desk, was the computer. The console was already on, mapping out multidimensional surfaces on the screen as if the computer was practicing while its master was away.

Lance pulled up a second chair and watched over Ron's shoulder while he logged on. The two men began the process. Time stopped.

D-Day minus Thirty-seven

The next time Lance looked at his watch, it was four a.m., California time. They had been working at the computer for over eight hours, but they finally had the program loaded on the VAX mainframe computer. Now they were ready to make some preliminary runs.

"Let's break for some breakfast," Ron said.

"Great idea. I'm starved."

"There's a Bob Evan's Restaurant near here. They make terrific sausage gravy."

"Sounds great. Why don't I call Dixie and see if she wants to join us."

Ron agreed, and Lance got out the numbers Colonel Jones had left him with. He tried the one labeled "hangar 4C" first. A sergeant answered the phone on the first ring, and Dixie was on the line a few minutes later.

"Tell Ron to go on to breakfast, but have him drop you off here first. Colonel Kirk just got here, and he wants to talk to the both of us."

"You look tired." Kirk welcomed Lance into the makeshift reception area just inside the hangar door.

The guard, carrying an M-16, handed Lance a special green badge with his name and photo on it.

Lance hooked the clip onto one of the zippers of his flight suit, then reached over to shake Kirk's hand. Kirk hadn't changed much, his hair was a little grayer now, but he still embodied a sense of urgency about everything he was doing, even greeting old friends.

"A little, Colonel. I probably should have knocked off last night to get some sleep," Lance said.

"Yeah, right. I know how it is when you guys get your heads buried into those computers; you hardly ever come up for air. You were the same way when you were a lieutenant."

True, Lance admitted to himself. He'd been known to spend twenty-four hours at a time working on a problem. It was one of those things that had taken Mandy a little time to adjust to.

"I want you to go get some breakfast, and then I want you both"—Kirk pointed to Dixie as well—"to go over to the 'Q' and get some sleep. Even though we're going to have to push this project fast, there's no room for screwups or accidents. I'm going to be here now, at least for the next few days, and I'll help make sure things get done as needed. Understood?"

Dixie nodded. Lance did, too. It was just as well, he knew that during the day the computer would be bogged down with the computer projects the AFIT students were running. He could make better use of his own time running the problem at night.

"I'd like to take a look at her first, Colonel," Lance said.

"Certainly." Kirk pulled back a black tarp shielding the inside of the hangar from the reception area.

Lance followed the colonel through. "How's Nancy?" Lance asked, finally remembering Kirk's wife's name. He had met her at a party when he first arrived at the Lab as a lieutenant. He remembered her as being somewhat aloof.

"Beat's the hell out of me," Kirk replied, letting the tarp fall back down as Dixie came through. "I haven't seen her in over two years."

Once again, Lance had stuck his foot in his mouth. Kirk's voice dripped with venom as he spoke of his wife. Lance didn't know what to say except "I'm sorry to hear that, sir."

"Don't worry about it," Kirk replied. "It was probably as much my fault as it was anyone's; I was on the road a lot. Subject closed." At least I've still got my work, Kirk thought to himself, again reliving that painful moment when Nancy told him she was leaving.

Lance got the message. He wouldn't bring up Kirk's ex-wife again. He turned his attention to the old airplane sitting inside the hangar.

The unmistakable fairing on top of the fuselage marked this plane as unique. The gray and white paint was faded, and there were men working on one of the wings, removing an engine. The other wing had already been stripped. In spite of that, he recognized her easily. Bathed in the glow of countless work lights sat the Airborne Laser Lab, waiting for one final mission.

Lance climbed the portable stairs and stepped aboard, entering through the aft access door. It was like stepping into history, stepping into his own past. The smell caught his attention first. He had never really figured out where the smell came from, guessing it was the insulation or the wiring. It was different than the smell of commercial planes, their molded plastic and luxurious cloth and leather seats filled the airliners with a distinct, not unpleasant aroma. No, this smell was different, primitive.

There on the left was the muster, painted on the back of the test director's console, the side facing the rear of the plane. He ran his fingers down the list of names, stenciled in that uniquely government style. Old friends, mostly long forgotten, the crews of the two ALL test missions lettered in a tribute to their efforts.

One quick glance around was all he would allow himself. It was time for a rest.

8

D-Day minus Thirty-seven
Damascus, Syria

Ha'im pushed the cart slowly down the hall, and headed for the closet where he stored the cleaning equipment. He was glad to finally be out of the conference room. The guard had watched him carefully, almost caught him making the switch. His shirt was still soaked with sweat. Security was tighter than he'd ever seen it.

Ha'im bowed his head low as several men passed him, apparently headed for the conference room he had just left. Ha'im recognized one of them. The man wore the rank of *fariq* (lieutenant general). He was the commander of all Syrian air forces. The general was smiling broadly as he walked past. He looked as if he had just received some great bit of news and was happily passing it along to the aide walking at his side. Ha'im listened for some tidbit of information, but the general stopped talking when he noticed the old custodian. All Ha'im heard was the general bragging to his aide that he had been right all along. Ha'im pushed the cart a little faster.

Ha'im was worried. The wax seal was broken. Someone had been inside the storage closet. He checked to make sure there was no one in the hall before gingerly opening the door, listening intently. He breathed a sigh of relief when he found it empty, hoping whoever had been in there had simply been looking for supplies, maybe just some more toilet paper.

Once safely inside the storage closet, Ha'im wasted no time in retrieving the ashtray from its hiding place. He wiped the tray clean and quickly removed the miniature tape. He put it in a small playback machine, similar to the one he kept in his apartment. He listened quietly, fast-forwarding the microcassette until he heard voices.

Ha'im raised his eyebrows in concern. The first voice he recognized on the tape was the same one he had just heard in the hallway, that of the general. Even in the taped recording Ha'im could tell he was yelling at someone in the room, demanding to know why the timetable couldn't be moved up. The Syrian air force commander was confident everything could be ready two weeks early. Someone else argued against the change, said the two backup laser radar planes weren't ready, hadn't been properly checked out.

The Israeli spy listened as the argument went back and forth, often highlighted by the general's angry outbursts. Ha'im pushed the fast-forward button, then backed the tape up slightly when he got to the end of the meeting.

"By this time tomorrow you will give me an answer, and it had better be the one I want or I will make sure your families share your fate!" he heard the general warn. There was a pause. Then: "The time is right. We must move as quickly as possible before word of this reaches the Israelis and they have an opportunity to counter our attack. The timetable I have just proposed is appropriate, and we can meet the schedule if our industrial team can validate the performance of the reserve planes. Until tomorrow."

Ha'im heard notebooks closing and chairs scraping as the meeting broke up. He shut off the tape player.

The general was smiling in the hallway, was happy. He had apparently gotten the word already. The timetable must have been moved up. Ha'im had to get this word out fast. Out of habit he reached down to the bottom of the cabinet where he stored the fresh cassettes, intent on replacing the one he had just removed. He pulled the box of tapes from beneath some old cleaning rags.

Ha'im stopped, stared at the open box. There were only five tapes, three were missing. Only one tape should have been gone, he was certain. Someone had been snooping around. And the guard had searched his cart before allowing him to leave the briefing room. That had never occurred before, either. Ha'im didn't believe in coincidence. He was considering his options when he heard the doorknob turn.

Ha'im snapped his head to the side, watched the knob turn all the way around. Then there was a soft push as the door pressed against the bar he had placed across it for security. He heard muffled voices from outside.

"I know I saw him go in there." Ha'im heard someone say.

"Get the *naqib* (captain)," someone replied. "And something to break down the door."

The sweat returned. It wouldn't take long to break down the wood-panel door, it wasn't made to resist attack. Ha'im dropped the microcassette into a small leather pouch and placed the chain over his head, letting the pouch fall down into his shirt. He wasn't sure how, but he was certain his cover was blown. He had to get away, had to get this information back to Israel as quickly as he could!

Ha'im had several escape plans laid out ahead of time, part of his training. He checked his watch. It was almost time for the workers to go home. Good. His best escape plan was timed to coincide with the evening hours. Ha'im stood on the cart and removed a ventilation grate from the ceiling, letting it hang from one side as he pulled himself up into the darkness.

The duct was small, tight, he could barely fit through. He stuck his head in and climbed forward until his feet were inside, then used his hands to back up. When he got to the opening, he reached down and pulled the grate back up, hooking it in place with a bent paper clip.

He continued to back away, trying to be as quiet as possible. In spite of his efforts the duct rumbled and boomed, the thin metal shell buckling as his weight passed over it, slammed loudly back into shape as he passed. The noise reminded him of a drum, announcing his presence wherever he went.

Ha'im heard banging, then the cracking sound of splintering wood. The Syrians would break into the storage closet shortly. He had to hurry.

He continued to back down the duct, faster now. He clearly heard the door crash in, the Syrians burst into the room. They made a great deal of noise themselves as they searched the utility room, covering the drumbeats of Ha'im's frantic attempt to escape. He continued to crawl backward, blindly, until his feet touched something solid. He heard one of the Syrians, apparently an officer, order someone to look up in the ventilation system. Turning on his side, he continued to back up, feet first, around the corner of the T-shaped connection.

Ha'im grabbed at the large, flat mirror he had earlier placed in the other branch of the T, pulled it to him and stood it up, reflective side facing away from him. He angled it at forty-five degrees and held it steady as he heard the grate come down. He continued to hold it, certain one of the Syrians was inspecting the shaft.

The mirror did its job, making the T-shaped connection look instead like a long, straight, empty shaft.

"Nothing here." Ha'im heard a voice echo throughout the duct as the Syrian reported to his captain, fooled by the reflection of the empty shaft in the mirror.

"Impossible, let me look." Ha'im heard a muffled voice order, followed by scraping sounds as the first Syrian climbed down.

Quickly, Ha'im wired the mirror in place with more paper clips and started to back farther down the duct.

He passed over another grate, peered down through it as he went by. It was an office, unoccupied, but not where he wanted to exit.

The captain used a flashlight to look up into the conduit, knowing the spy could only have escaped that way. In each direction the tunnel appeared to go on for quiet some distance. The captain knew, however, that the building couldn't extend so far to the east, they were already near the outside wall. He stared in that direction, wondering how the duct could possibly reach so far. A cool blast of air poured over him as the building's huge air-conditioning system came on. The mirror, fastened only at the top, tilted up in the breeze. The Syrian looked in surprise as the duct appeared to climb into the air.

"He's down there," the Syrian yelled at his men, jumping down the ladder. "Get him. KILL HIM!"

Ha'im couldn't tell exactly what was going on now, the wind of the air-conditioner blew past his ears, and he was by now far from the supply closet. Only the words "KILL HIM" were loud enough to be heard.

Ha'im dropped out of the duct into a warehouse area, the little noise he made was covered by the rumbling of a huge shredding machine. The machine was destroying the classified material generated by the headquarters, turning entire sacks of the paper into a fine powder. Large carts of the powder surrounded him, and two other carts were being filled by output pipes in the wall. Ha'im went through a door to the outside, to the loading dock.

Two old dump trucks stood nearby, nearly full of the fine gray powder. At the end of the day, the trucks would carry the waste to the country, to a smelly, overflowing landfill. Ha'im had followed them once, hoping to sift through the powder to recover remnants of the documents. It had turned out to be a waste of time, the machines had not passed even a scrap of paper intact. Near the landfill he had hidden a small motorcycle for just such an emergency.

Ha'im jumped into the back of one of the trucks, the full one. He heard the shredder shut down, finished with its day's work. He buried himself in the powder near a corner of the truck, leaving only a small part of his face uncovered. Once under way it would be impossible for the driver to see into the bed of the truck, and he would be able to climb out of the dust.

The workers came to the dock and dumped the final load into the adjacent truck. Ha'im didn't have to wait more than fifteen minutes before the trucks started and began to pull away. Once they were moving down the road, he climbed up and peered over the edge of the bed. What luck. The truck he was in brought up the back of the column. He should be able to escape undetected.

It wasn't a pleasant ride. The gray powder stirred in the wind and billowed up in the back of the truck, making it extremely difficult to breathe. Ha'im waited, counting the stops and the turns. By his estimation they were getting close to where he had hidden the motorcycle. He climbed out of the powder and fought his way to the back of the truck, the dirty gray soot trying to suck him under with every step.

At the back of the truck he waited again, covering his mouth with a rag torn from his shirt, trying to breathe through the blizzard of powder. The truck slowed, and he quickly jumped over the tailgate. He hung there with his hands while his feet flailed, blindly searching for a grip.

He was still trying to find a good footing when the truck started to accelerate again. Ha'im dropped to the ground, knowing the truck was pulling out of the turn. He stumbled, then fell and rolled on the packed dirt. Billowing clouds of sand churned up by the truck hid him from the driver's view. Before he even stopped rolling, Ha'im stood and dashed for the side of the road, diving into an empty ditch.

Ha'im checked the chain around his neck, patted his chest until he was reassured the pouch with the microcassette was still in its place. He crawled to another, better hidden area of the ditch and waited, using the time before nightfall to brush away some of the powder from his clothes and to rest. It was too dangerous to go back to Damascus, and that left him with no way to pass the cassette to his old contacts. His only choice was to head southwest, toward the border. It might well take all night, and he might not survive the trip, or the border guards, but he had to try. He had to get the word out.

Ha'im topped the small rise and stopped, killing the motorcycle while he rested. It was difficult to see much of the land stretching out before him, the sun was still below the horizon at his back and his eyes burned from the prolonged exposure to sixty-kilometer-per-hour wind. His throat was parched. He should be almost there, almost back to Israel, almost home.

Now came the hard part. What lay before him was

a no-man's-land, the deadly region that separated the Syrians and the Israeli army. The question became one of how to cover the last few kilometers. Should he move slowly, and risk being stopped by a Syrian patrol? Or should he move quickly, push the old motorcycle to its limits, risk being mistaken as a Syrian by the Israeli soldiers and shot for his trouble? Neither option was attractive. In the end it was the sense of urgency that helped him decide. He took the lid off the dented blue fuel tank and tried to see inside. Darkness. He rocked the bike back and forth between his legs, listening to the minuscule amount of liquid as it splashed against the sides of the tank. Enough?

Ha'im kicked the engine to life, eased out the clutch, and accelerated. He moved up through the gears, throwing a cloud of sand into the air behind him. The road turned back to the north, but he kept going straight. It wasn't going to be easy, he realized almost immediately. The motorcycle, designed for paved roads, strained as the thin front tire plowed a groove into the loose sand. He fought the bike, urging it onward, riding toward solid dirt whenever it appeared in the gloom before him.

The strain was beginning to tell. His brow dripped sweat, the salty liquid stinging his already burning eyes. He moved forward blindly, watching the ground immediately in front of his machine, not daring to look away from his path for fear of losing control. He never saw the hair-thin wire stretched across the desert floor.

Time seemed to drag by. Ha'im was sure it had been over thirty minutes since he left the road. Surely he should be in south Lebanon by now. There must be a village somewhere nearby. He stopped again to look and rest. Wiping the sweat from his forehead with a dirty sleeve, he searched the horizon. There was nothing, not even the lights of a town. Checking the stars, now barely visible due to the light from the rising sun, he reoriented his heading, pointing the bike more to the south.

Kicking the machine to life once again, he started forward, intent on achieving his goal. After less than five minutes, the engine coughed then died, starved for fuel. Ha'im dropped the motorcycle, stood on shaky legs, and started walking. Rapidly marching at first, it took little time until he was barely moving, slowed by exhaustion and dehydration. His mind wandered. Five more minutes and he stopped, dropped to one knee. He knew he had to keep moving, but didn't really remember why.

Ha'im stared at the shadow looming on the ground in the distance. It grew rapidly, then separated, half rising above the other. There was a breeze. It turned into a gale. Then a sandstorm. Ha'im squeezed his eyes shut, the only response his exhausted body would allow him. Something grabbed his arms and pulled him away.

Lawrence Livermore National Lab

Steve Sympson watched as the missile, the infamous Pegasus, was unloaded from the truck. In the crate at the other end of the closely guarded building was one of only three working models of the Brilliant Pebble. His job was to integrate the two, as fast as he could. It wasn't going to be easy. He had gotten his orders from the top, though, and had been told to do whatever was necessary to get the job done, had been given authority to commandeer whatever resources and people he needed.

He was sure it could be done; it was the kind of job he was good at. In fact, it would even be fun if he weren't under such a time crunch. The schedule was going to be nearly impossible to meet. He looked at the memo again, wondered how much work the sensor guys were going to have to do, wondered why they had to modify the tracker so it would work *inside* the atmosphere. His main concern was how much the sensor guys were going to be in his way, slowing him down.

Sympson scratched his head. What kind of Defense Department experiment was this, anyhow?

D-Day minus Fourteen
CENTCOM HQ, MacDill AFB, Florida

Kirk was going over some of the schedule data with "Ironman" Jones when General Wainwright finally arrived with another Army officer.

Both men came to attention. "Good morning, General," Kirk said.

"Good to see you again, Kirk. This must be Jones?"

"Yes, sir. Good to meet you. I go by 'Ironman.'"

"Okay, Jones. I want you guys to meet Lieutenant Colonel Delaney."

They shook.

"I believe he goes by Lieutenant Colonel Delaney." Wainwright glared at Jones.

Kirk realized he hadn't prepared Jones for Wainwright. This was one general who was no-nonsense about everything. Must have been his West Point training.

"Now," General Wainwright began the meeting, "how in the hell are we going to make this happen?"

"Why don't I give you an update on the Brilliant Pebble progress thus far, General?" Lieutenant Colonel Delaney said.

"Yeah, but make it quick. Give me the top-level view, leave all the technical mumbo jumbo out of it."

"Yes, sir. There are three Brilliant Pebbles being prepared for flight. One of them will be ready in about ten days. They had already prototyped that one to fly with the Pegasus and the required mechanical interface parts were already available. The other two will take another thirteen or fourteen days. Parts fabrication is causing most of that delay."

"This is no kidding? The scientists aren't blowing smoke up your pants, are they?"

"No, sir. I've been watching the effort firsthand.

There's a good man down at Livermore, a guy named Sympson. He's been very honest with me so far on what's going well and what's taking extra time.

"My biggest concern is testing. We really need to use the prototype as a test asset, find out if it's really going to work or not."

General Wainwright held up his hands to stop the discussion. "I don't think that's going to happen. I've just been told the Syrians have moved up the invasion schedule. The Israelis now say we have only fourteen days before the Syrians make their move. I'm afraid some kind of field test is out of the question."

"I have a suggestion, General," Kirk said.

"Let's hear it."

"Okay." Kirk didn't know the schedule had been moved up, didn't know for sure if they would have time to get the ALL ready. That was secondary, though. The main objective was to defeat the Syrians before they could effectively attack. He thought his plan through out loud, scientifically looking at the problem.

"First, I think the Brilliant Pebble is the safest approach. It's biggest advantage is that it will limit casualties on both sides. If the Pebble concept works, the Syrians won't know what hit them. They'll simply have to fall back and try and figure out what went wrong. With some luck they might come to the conclusion they have a faulty system that blew itself up and abandon the whole idea. I don't know. It's biggest disadvantage, as I mentioned previously, is that it probably won't work. I'm guessing your Mr. Sympson has quite a few doubts.''

Delaney nodded.

"Our other option is the Airborne Laser Lab. Using this system has disadvantages as well. First, we'll be flying directly into Syrian airspace. They'll know we're coming and will have time to prepare their backup plane. I believe you had pointed this out in our first meeting. Our problem will be to take out the Syrian laser plane, clearing the way for the Israelis to come in and knock out the missiles, particularly the ones with the chemical warheads. The Israelis will have to come in fast, and accurate. If they don't get there in time, or if they miss their targets, the Syrians will be able to launch their backup plane and this will all be for nothing. The big advantage of the ALL is I'm sure it will work.''

"So what's your suggestion." Wainwright was listening intently.

"Try the first Brilliant Pebble out, but test it against the Syrian plane. If it works, great. They'll be stopped, at least for a while, and maybe they'll abandon the whole project. We have nothing to lose.''

"And if it doesn't work?''

"We'll continue to prepare the ALL. If the Pebble fails, we'll launch and go take out the laser plane. The rest will be up to the Israelis.''

Wainwright thought for a few moments while Kirk waited to hear what they thought of his plan.

"What do you think, Delaney?" Wainwright asked.

"I think it's a good plan, but I don't think we should wait until the Syrians are ready to launch. We should preempt their strike."

Wainwright nodded. "Ten days enough for you to get the Brilliant Pebble ready?"

"I think so. One other thing."

"What is it?"

"Putting my infantry hat back on, I'm thinking about Colonel Kirk's system and how the Israelis are going to support the strike. The colonel makes an excellent point, the Israeli Air Force is going to have to come in fast and accurate. There is something they should do to improve their chances of accuracy, but they may not be able. I think they should use a Special Ops FIST team."

"A what?" Kirk asked.

"Fire Support Team." General Wainwright liked to explain the intricacies of the ground war to Air Force types. "Laser Target Designators, the works. We sneak these guys in all the time. How do you think the Air Force bombing accuracy scores stay so high?"

"I've trained some very good Israeli Special Forces Teams," Delaney said. "They liked to be called Special Night Squads, they do their best work in the dark. Infiltration may be a problem, though."

"You're right. The Syrians are getting ready for

war, and the border is going to be tight. We may have to help them out," General Wainwright said.

The general leaned back in his chair. It didn't take him long to decide. "I'm going with your plan, Kirk. We'll use the Pebble. If it fails, you go in with your plane and the Israelis will mop up. Delaney, I want you at SPACECOM J3 when the Pebble goes up. I want you to report directly back to me. I'll also have a plane over the Med to monitor the situation there. If the Pebble doesn't work and we have to use the ALL, I'll coordinate with the Israelis from here."

Wainwright leaned back in his chair again. He didn't like leaving so much of the fight to the Israelis, would rather have his own boys there to finish off the Syrians. But their orders were to help the Israelis, not to fight the war for them. "All right, I'm going to head for Israel in the morning to talk to the Israeli Defense Forces General Staff. They'll have to agree to the proposal, although I don't think they're in any position to argue. You boys go get your operations ready."

Conner took the call over the intercom. It was good news for a change. He made his way back through the Rangers, waiting along either side of the web seats to pass the news to the Army captain as the C-130 pulled into an easy bank to the left. Conner steadied himself, using the cable that held the warriors' static lines as he spoke to the company commander. The first sergeant listened closely.

"The mission has been canceled." He had to speak loudly to be heard above the drone of the engines. "We're going to fly back over to the Omaha drop zone and let you out there. No sense getting all suited up for a fight, then not letting these guys have at least a little bit of practice."

They passed the word quickly back up and down the line. Smiles broke out on many of the faces. Frowns on a few. The diplomats had scored a victory. There was no need for these men to go into harm's way, at least not tonight. A simple practice jump was a pleasant alternative to what they could have faced.

Conner walked back toward the front of the airplane. He felt a bond with these men. They were ready to go to war, battle dress uniforms, camouflaged faces, M-16s. Conner had once worn that same uniform as an air liaison officer to the Rangers. The Ranger tab he wore on the sleeve of his flight suit garnered more respect than these warriors afforded the other special operations loadmasters. It had been a few years since he had worked directly with the Rangers, and Conner would be the first to admit he missed the excitement.

Conner walked past the last Ranger, glanced down at his face. He was asleep, helmet-covered head leaned back against the sheet-metal skin of the airplane, an M-16 cradled in his lap like a childhood toy. Conner didn't see how anyone could sleep under these conditions, but he had seen Rangers sleep in much worse. He took a second look at the private.

There was something hauntingly familiar about his face. It was the same face he had seen in many dreams, many nightmares. Conner made a decision, one he had been putting off for several years. He called the navigator on the intercom and confirmed they were going to return to Fort Bliss to await further orders, probably to stand by in case the diplomats screwed up the remaining negotiations. Conner asked him to make a radio call.

The morning sun was fully exposed when Conner finally finished securing the airplane, cleaning up the trash the Rangers had left behind before they jumped into the cold night air over the training range. The copilot had stuck around to give him a hand, and they called for a crew bus to take them back up to field operations.

Conner grabbed his small suitcase and helmet bag, carrying them into the reception area of field operations. The copilot asked Conner if he needed a ride out to billeting. Conner looked into the reception area and spotted the petite blonde he had hoped would meet him there.

"No, thanks," Conner said.

"Woah, I haven't seen her before," the pilot said. "Woman in every port, eh, Conner?"

"She's my sister-in-law."

"Oh, I didn't know you have a brother. Give him my compliments. She's quite a catch."

"Had."

"What's that?"

"Had a brother. I'll check back in after crew rest." He left the pilot and went to meet his brother's wife. He was exhausted after the long mission. Perhaps that's why he felt himself shaking so. He dropped his bags when he reached her, and they wrapped their arms around each other in a silent welcome. A reunion of sorts. After a moment they separated. Conner felt his voice crack. "I think it's time I went to see him."

She nodded.

The cemetery was quiet. The cool, crisp spring morning air at Fort Bliss hadn't yet been polluted by the many fireplaces burning in the adjacent town of El Paso, farther down in the valley. Conner stood at the gate, tired and dirty. He wondered if he shouldn't have cleaned up before coming, perhaps waited until another time when he could have worn his service dress. No, the flight suit was more appropriate. He asked her to wait behind, to give him a few minutes to himself, then walked through the gate.

The short white markers were in precise alignment all the way across the field. Conner counted down six rows, then turned and walked between them. He was supposed to count to seventy-three, but lost count at about thirty-five. He read the engraving on the stones, searching for a particular name. There were many friends among the names, no one he knew personally, but friends none the less. They were mostly soldiers, a few airmen, sailors, and marines. Some graves had been decorated with small flags, a black banner with the word RANGER formed in gold letters. He almost passed the marker he had been seeking. This grave had one of the Ranger flags.

Conner stood at the marker for a long time, reading the inscription over and over again. He hadn't known how he would react when he came here, one of the reasons he had avoided this place for the last eight years. Conner had been the one to convince his brother to join the Army, to fight to earn the Ranger tab. His brother had done it, and the process had turned a wild, unfocused young boy into a keenly disciplined young man. Then he went to war and died. Conner felt sorrow, but more than that he felt pride.

The noise he had been hearing came closer. A strange noise. Conner turned to look. A horse-drawn caisson bearing the remains of another comrade was passing along the narrow road nearby. A short procession of people followed the honor guard. Parents, a brother, a wife. Was his brother's funeral like this? Conner had been flying over Iraq at the time, and the Special Operations tempo was such that he couldn't be spared to attend. Conner watched the procession in a stupor, imagining a similar one many years ago.

Conner's right hand flew to his eye when he heard the squad commander bark "Present Arms." A quick succession of shots was carried out in precise unison as the twenty-one gun salute was presented to the fallen warrior.

The playing of taps is what finally did Conner in. The bugle's sorrowful hymn brought the tears to his eyes. Conner's knees began to shake as he fought to maintain the salute. He thought he might fall, but she came then. She held his arm and gave him strength. The strength of his brother.

Conner's beeper pierced the calm air as the solemn procession retreated. He wiped his eyes and checked the message. They used a code. This one told him to return to base. Fast.

9

D-Day minus Thirteen
Wright Patterson AFB

Lance stepped out of the shower, exhausted from the long day he had put in. How many hours had it been? He looked over at the clock next to the bed. It was only three in the afternoon, but he had gone to the hangar at about this same time yesterday. Twenty-four hours straight. He sat down on the bed, planning to get a few hours sleep and then head back over. Getting the beam control system ready had been more of a job than anyone had expected.

If it hadn't been for Dixie's help, they would have given up long ago. She had been phenomenal, working more hours than even Colonel Kirk or himself. The young female lieutenant had performed more than one apparent miracle, not only with the beam control system but with the installation of the new laser modules as well.

Laying back on the bed, Lance started to shut his

eyes but opened them after a few moments. He reached over and picked up the phone, dialed his home number.

"Hello," he heard on the other end after only two rings.

"Hi, sweetheart," Lance said, "it's good to hear your voice."

"Lance!" Mandy yelled, "it's good to hear you, too. Just a second."

Lance heard Mandy call for the twins. In a moment they were both on the phone.

"Hi, Daddy!" they squealed in unison. "We miss you."

Obviously something they had been practicing. Lance didn't care, happy to be able to hear their voices. They talked for quite a while, caught up on the latest news from the school and the girls' friends. After a while Lance could tell he was rambling, tired. He hoped the girls didn't notice.

"Are you both being good?" he asked.

"Well, pretty good," they both admitted, honestly.

"That's good. I love you both."

"We love you too, Daddy."

"Let me talk to Mommy now."

"Okay. Bye, Daddy."

Mandy came back on the line, Lance realized it was only noon there, wondered why the girls were home so early.

"Lance," Mandy said, "it's Saturday. You know

the girls don't go to school on Saturday. Are you all right?"

"Saturday? Oh. Yeah." Lance knew he was tired now, had lost rack of what day it was. "Just working some long hours."

"Well, try to take it easy. Do you know when you'll get to come home yet?"

"No, but I'll be here for at least another month. That much is for certain. How are you doing? Keeping busy?" he asked, hoping to change the subject.

"Terribly. The shelter has started a new fundraiser. They want me to head it up, but I told them I couldn't."

"Why not?" Lance asked, hoping that his being away wasn't keeping Mandy from doing what she loved, hoped the kids weren't keeping her so busy she couldn't help out downtown.

"I don't think I'm going to have time," she answered. "The city council called me yesterday, they heard about what we've been doing for the shelter and want to start up a program for the homeless. They've asked me to help manage the effort."

"Mandy, that's terrific," Lance said. He couldn't be more proud of his wife. They had talked about the increasing number of people who seemed to be wandering aimlessly along the beach, wondered how they could help.

Mandy began filling him in on all the details about what she planned to do. Lance, though interested, found it difficult to concentrate. Finally she changed the subject.

"Do you really think Syria started it?" she asked.

"What? What are you talking about?"

"I guess you haven't heard the latest news. They interrupted all programming about an hour ago, there was a fight along the Syrian/Israeli border. Israel is blaming Syria for starting it, and Syria is blaming Israel. It wasn't a big fight, but I keep hearing more and more bad news from over there. Thank God we don't have to live where there is so much violence."

"Yeah. Thank God." Lance promised himself he would take time to read a newspaper tomorrow.

D-Day minus Ten

"What the hell do you mean, Major?" Jones asked, close to losing his temper.

"Sir"—Lance wondered why the colonel was being such a pain—"we won't have another plane flying nearby to tell us which system is giving us trouble. If we expect to be able to do any in-flight troubleshooting, we'll need to leave the recorders on board."

Lance watched as Jones bit down hard on the unlit cigar, could tell his anger was almost to the boiling point. The colonel looked down at his list again. Brandon wondered what else he wanted to take off the airplane.

"How about the safety console?"

Here we go again. "Without that system we won't be able to monitor the pressurization levels in the laser compartment."

Lance jumped as the colonel threw his paperwork against the nearest console. Jones put his hands on his hips, fists clenched, staring at him.

He could feel the colonel's breath, his face only a foot away. Lance knew not to back down.

After thirty seconds Jones backed away. "You obviously don't understand the problem."

Lance said nothing, waiting for the colonel to speak his mind. He wasn't sure what they expected of him anymore; first they cut another two weeks from the schedule, now they wanted to take off every piece of gear they could.

Jones looked around, then had a thought. "You're a runner, aren't you?"

"Yes, sir," Lance replied, still standing at attention.

"Got your gear here?"

"Yes, sir."

"Let's go."

Lance followed Jones out of the gym, actually a converted hangar near the one where the ALL was hidden. Jones took off without warming up. Lance stayed with him, habitually reaching down to start the stopwatch function on his wristwatch, glad he had decided to wear a shirt since it was so cool. Jones was wearing only his shorts, the bulging muscles in his back and shoulders made an impressive sight.

They headed south, along the row of hangars. They ran in silence.

Lance was breathing hard when they turned the corner at the end of the taxiway. They hadn't run even a mile yet, but Jones was pushing hard, a much faster pace than Lance was used to. Lance looked up, a sinking feeling hit him when he saw the hill they faced, at least a quarter of a mile long, with an even sharper rise at the top. Jones sped up, sweat glistening on his bare black skin.

Lance saw Jones turn at the top of the hill, already over fifty yards ahead of him. He dug in, forcing himself to hurry to the summit. Jones made a circle, then jogged in place while he waited for Lance to catch up.

"See that," Jones said, pointing back down the hill.

He looked back without speaking, stopping with his hands on his hips, his breath came in heavy gasps. He could see the vast expanse of concrete that hadn't been obvious from the hangar. Beyond the bottom of the hill, the concrete extended for another four hundred yards or so. Probably so the planes could get a running start.

"That's what they call the 'accelerated runway,' " Jones explained, still jogging in place. "Unfortunately, it's our only way out of here. The cross runway is too short due to the construction. If we don't lighten the ALL, we'll never make it off the hill. That's why we must take off every piece of equipment we don't absolutely, and I mean *absolutely*, need."

Lance didn't think the runway looked long enough for a small plane to take off on, much less the big ALL. Now he knew what Jones had been getting at. A picture is worth a thousand words. He looked back at Jones: "I'll do what I can, Colonel," he gasped between gulps of air.

Jones smiled. "Good. Are you warmed up yet?"

Lance watched in amazement as Jones pulled away, heading up a trail cut in the trees at the end of the runway. "What the hell," he said quietly as he bowed his head and set out in pursuit of the old colonel.

"I don't know." Gurion opened the door and let Reitman enter the hospital first. "He just said to come here and wear civilian clothes. When you get orders from that high up, it's best to follow them explicitly, no matter how strange they sound."

Gurion hated the thought of being in a hospital, even a special military hospital such as this. They reminded him too much of pain, of death, of friends.

They found the room they were to report to on the second floor and went inside.

There was only one man there. He was sitting at a small table, the hospital bed was empty.

"Lock the door behind you," the man instructed.

Gurion turned the bolt and tugged at the door to ensure it was locked.

The occupant of the room waved at the two empty seats next to the table.

Gurion studied him. There was something strangely familiar about this patient.

"We have met before," the patient said, apparently anticipating Gurion's question. "Though under much different circumstances."

When the stranger held out his hand, Gurion noticed the index finger was missing. Scarred skin covered the years-old wound.

"I remember." Gurion wondered if Reitman recognized the man.

"You were ordered to come here?" he asked.

"Yes. I was told you had information that might be useful to us on our mission."

"Perhaps. I presume your mission is to destroy the missiles?"

Gurion said nothing. They were here to receive information. Not provide it.

The patient nodded, then began. "I was just rescued from an undercover operation in Syria. They put me here because I was badly dehydrated. While I was there, I found out our friends to the north are returning to their evil ways. They plan to attack Israel in less than ten days."

"Are you sure of this?" Reitman asked.

"I heard it from the Syrian defense minister himself."

"Surely they recognize the futility of such a move." Gurion believed the man, remembered the night in

Lebanon when he sliced the throat of the terrorist who had cut off his finger. "We've shown them before how they will suffer."

"Their plans this time are quite different. They have developed an aerial weapon that will incapacitate our attack aircraft. A laser system. They intend to use it as an umbrella for their ground forces and the precursor for a missile attack. Chemicals. We won't stand a chance."

Gurion recalled the fear of his fellow Israelis during the Americans' Persian Gulf War, the terror inflicted by Iraq's ineffective missiles. What if those missiles now came from Syria, laced with poison chemicals . . .

"I believe it is your mission to destroy the missiles before they can be launched. I don't know exactly how you intend to accomplish such a feat, but let me tell you all I know about their current situation."

Gurion listened as the spy corroborated much of the information he had already been given by the intelligence unit. There were a few details that might come in handy, particularly the command and control equipment and deployment sequences they intended to use.

10

D-Day minus Five
Wright Patterson AFB, Ohio

There were only a few people left working on the plane, most of the modifications were already complete. Kirk sat down in one of the metal chairs near the entrance to the hangar and waited for the photographer to finish up.

The photographer was setting up for his last shot, something for the history books. With any luck this project would help secure the needed funding for the follow-on program called the Air Based Laser, already in its developmental phase. It was being touted as the ultimate defense against ballistic missiles, the kind that had bloodied the coalition forces in Iraq. The photos would help with the public relations campaign that would be needed on Capitol Hill to garner the needed funding for the program. It was going to be expensive.

Colonel Jones stepped through the canvas partition, holding a piece of paper. "We've got our orders," he said.

Kirk held up his hand, stopping Jones from saying anything else.

"I'm all finished, Colonel," the photographer said. "Anything else you need?"

"No, thanks. How quick can you have the prints ready?"

The photographer looked at his watch. It was only noon. "Probably first thing in the morning. I was told this had priority."

"Good. Can you bring them by here tomorrow, first thing?"

"Make it about 1500," Jones said.

"No problem." The photographer left carrying his camera and tripod.

"Why so late?" Kirk asked.

"We'll be launching tomorrow night, about 2200."

"The PEBBLE hasn't even flown yet."

"I know. It isn't supposed to fly until the day after tomorrow. Problem is that we have to be close to the theater in case it fails, so we get to leave before we know if the PEBBLE works or not. Best case is we get a free trip to Crete. Worst case is we keep going to Syria. How are the kids doing?"

"They're just about finished. I'm really impressed with how they got this thing together so quickly. All we have left to do is ring out the system in flight, make sure nothing airborne will affect its performance."

"Good. I want them to go get some rest, but there's

something we have to do first. Tell you want, I'll buy the first round over at the Fly-Wright. Can you bring them over in about half an hour?"

"Sure."

"Tell them to bring the paperwork I asked them to get from home."

"Okay. We'll see you in a little bit."

The Fly-Wright, the officers' club annex in Area B, mostly catered to the AFIT crowd, students from the graduate school found it a good place to hang out and unwind after the grueling academic pace they were under. The lunchtime crowd was thinning, but there were still a few officers having lunch on the patio and a small, rowdy group playing crud at the billiards table. The side room was mostly empty, so Jones took a table there with the captain he'd brought with him. The captain looked out of place, long sleeves and a tie, while most of the AFIT students preferred the short-sleeve shirt, no tie. The rest of Jones' crew showed up in just a few minutes. Lance and Dixie came with Kirk. Red and Chief Warren arrived just behind them. They were wearing flight suits.

They all ordered from the menu, and Jones asked for two pitchers of beer, then he introduced the captain.

"We've got orders to fly out of here tomorrow evening. I'm not going to go over the details of our mission—we'll have plenty of time for that later. I do want to point out that this can get very dangerous. I imagine you all realize that. Our guest is from the legal office, he's going to look over your wills and update them with any changes you might want to make."

The captain opened a laptop and pulled a small printer out of his case.

Dixie was first. She didn't have a will, but asked that her assets revert to her parents.

Lance had called his lawyer in California the previous day and updated his will over the phone. His lawyer had then transmitted the electronic file to Lance's computer, and Lance handed the floppy to the Wright Patt lawyer. He printed it out and witnessed Lance's signature.

Jones would be last. He stared at his old will for a long time, ran his fingers across Jenny's name. Who would he leave his assets to now? There was quite a bit in his stock portfolio, plus his life insurance if something went wrong. Chief Warren was telling the lawyer something about his youngest son, only five. That gave Jones an idea. He allocated half to Chief Warren's family, the other half to the Air Force Aid Society.

Chief Warren joined them for one beer, then excused himself. "If we're leaving tomorrow, I'd like to spend a little time with the family."

Jones and Kirk entertained them for the next hour, trying to one up each other with their past exploits. Two more pitchers of beer, and the stories got much more interesting. Eventually the stories began to focus on family life, what there had been of it. Red challenged Lance and Dixie to a game of crud. They admitted they didn't know how to play, so he offered to teach them. They left Jones and Kirk solemnly discussing their wives, one now dead, the other too much alive.

D-Day minus Four

Lance checked his watch, 2200 hours. He smiled when he noticed he automatically thought in terms of military time now. Lance sat in the same seat he had occupied back during the ALL's test series, directly in front of the beam control console. The console was different now, though. Upgraded. Instead of the multitude of switches he'd had to deal with before, the panel now used a touch screen monitor. The symbolic switches were displayed on TV screens, their function dependent upon which menu he selected from the master program. There were only a few mechanical switches left, most importantly the shutter switch on the joystick. At least that was still the same.

"Stand by to switch power!"

Lance touched the screen to bring the computer back to its top-level mode, then punched the master power switch, turning the whole system off. He stepped on the foot switch that activated the boom mike connected to his headset.

"Beam control ready," he said.

Looking back over his left shoulder, he saw Colonel Kirk glance in his direction. Kirk reached up to his own console, still filled with the mechanical switches it held in the early years, and disabled the master ready switch.

"Systems powered down." Kirk's own screen went blank.

Dixie walked up from the very back of the plane, trailing a cable from her own headset. "Everything is ready back here," she informed Colonel Kirk, the mission commander for the flight. She took the seat next to Lance's, at the laser device operator's console, and strapped in.

"ECS coming off!" Chief Warren said from the front of the plane, shutting down the Environmental Conditioning System, the air conditioner, in preparation to disconnect the airplane from external power.

The plane was bathed in silence. Lance could hear his own breathing as the high-pitched whine of the blowers wound down. The lights went off next, plunging the back of the plane into almost total darkness. Only a tiny amount of light from a bulb in the hangar filtered through the single window next to the test director's console. For a moment it was peaceful. Then Lance felt a small tug as the tow cart jerked the plane, initiating its move out of the hangar.

"Put your helmets on," Kirk ordered them, his voice loud in the confines of the quiet airplane.

Lance knew why the helmets were necessary. It wasn't due to risk of depressurization; that wouldn't be a factor until they were ten or twelve thousand feet up. No, the runaway itself presented the greatest risk on this first flight. The runaway was short, never designed for an airplane this large. The ramp at the end, resembling the upswing used by ski jumpers before they rifled into the air, probably presented more of a problem than a solution. Even with every piece of excess equipment removed from the airplane, it was going to be tough to get airborne. Lance put his helmet on and strapped the oxygen mask on tight. He leaned back into the seat and tried not to think about what was about to happen.

The interior of the plane went completely black as the big bird was pulled out of the brightly lit hangar. There must not be a moon out, Lance decided. That didn't really surprise him, he hadn't seen the moon in the three weeks he'd been here, and only saw the sun once. The clouds and haze seemed to be an ever present entity in Dayton. He missed sunny southern California.

Before the plane came to a stop, Lance heard a high-pitched machine start up outside. He remembered hearing the same sound years before, the machine that was used to start the KC-135's four engines. He flipped his intercom to the aircrew net to listen to what was happening.

"Ready on number one," someone outside the

plane called, hooked to the interphone system through an auxiliary umbilical connector.

"Starting number one," Jones answered.

Lance felt the plane vibrate slightly as the turbine spun up to speed, and the fuel ignited in the burner. The engine ran quieter than he remembered, much quieter. These new engines were different, bigger than the ones the ground technicians removed. He hoped they had more thrust as well. That would help them get up the ramp and airborne easier. Safer.

"Ready number two."

"Starting number two."

The noise was constant inside the plane now, loud, but Lance still heard the second engine light off. Chief Warren had told him this was the first time the engines would be started, warned him it would take a little time to check them out. Obviously he was confident in his men, waiting until the day of the launch to test the newly installed equipment. Or else he just hadn't had enough time with all the other maintenance he had ended up doing.

"Ready number three."

"Starting three."

Lance felt a puff of cool air from the vent overhead.

"ECS on."

That would be Chief Warren up in the front of the plane, sitting at the navigator's console. It would be his job as flight engineer to maintain all the aircraft systems during the flight and, if Lance guessed correctly, during the mission itself. Good. Warren had proven himself more than capable during the last few weeks, repairing more discrepancies than even Jones had guessed could be wrong with the plane after its long period on display. The internal lights came on next. In the old days he would have gotten busy firing up his own system, but now he just waited. There would be plenty of time to run the system through its paces once they were airborne. It was going to be a long trip.

"Ready number four."

"Starting four."

When the vibrations abated, all four of the engines were operating.

Lance listened as Chief Warren began conferring with the ground crew, going through a detailed checklist on each of the engines. When it appeared the chatter would go on indefinitely, Lance pushed the "aircrew" button on his ICS box in, turning off that channel.

After a few minutes of relative quiet, the plane started to shake rather violently, the engines bellowing louder and louder. Lance gripped the armrest without thinking, wondering how long they would sit there with the engines running at what sounded like full power. Part of the checkout, he presumed.

Eventually the engines were cut to idle, the vibration ceased, and the noise level dropped markedly.

"Mission Commander, this is the pilot," Lance heard over the test crew net.

"Mission Commander," Kirk replied.

"All systems check out, we're ready to taxi."

"Roger. Ready here."

Lance pulled all the knobs out on his ICS box, hoping the communications net to the makeshift air traffic control van was patched in. If anything went wrong on the takeoff he wanted to know as soon as he could, and he figured the ATC net would broadcast the news first.

". . . Three Three. You are cleared to taxi onto the active."

The pitch of the engines increased slightly, and the plane lurched forward. Slowly at first, but picking up speed when they were well away from the hangar. Lance and Dixie strained to look through the window just behind Kirk, barely saw red and blue lights flashing in the distance. The plane turned, and they saw the hangar doors closing, green fire trucks pulling in behind them and racing for the runway.

"INS?" Jones followed the checklist on the thigh pad strapped to his leg.

"Set," Chief Warren replied, verifying the Inertial Navigation System was ready to log their position and monitor their flight plan.

"Flaps?"

"Twenty degrees," Red answered from the copilot's position.

"All right." Jones closed the checklist. "We're going to have to pull the gear up right away. As it is, we're barely going to clear the hill, not to mention the trees on top of it."

"The trees aren't there, Colonel," Chief Warren said.

"Aren't there? What happened to 'em?"

"I had the civil engineers cut them down, figured that was one obstacle we could do without."

"Good job, Chief," Red muttered into his own microphone.

"Yeah, why didn't you think of that, Red?" Jones asked, his smile hidden by his own oxygen mask.

"Turning," the copilot said, ignoring the question as he followed the flashing lights of the police car just ahead of them.

The taxiway lights were long broken, neglected from lack of use. Same for the runway lights. Chief Warren had taken care of that as well, bringing large floodlights from the Test Wing over and positioning them on either side of the runway to guide them up the asphalt, all the way to the top of the hill. Two red lights marked the point of no return, the point beyond which they would not be able to get the ALL stopped before she crashed at the end of the runway.

Instead of turning onto the runway, Colonel Jones stopped short. He went into a quick rehash of emergency procedures, then called the ATC van.

"Tower, this is Eagle Three Three, ready for take-off." Jones used the new call sign the project had been issued.

Inside the "tower," two men coordinated with the

real tower on the other side of the base, verifying via telephone there were no launches taking place there.

"Eagle Three Three, you are cleared for takeoff."

Jones and the other two men pulled their safety harnesses tight. Jones called Kirk: "Mission, we've been cleared for takeoff."

"Roger. Prepare for takeoff," Kirk instructed the two engineers in the back. They each pulled a handle on the bottom of their seats and rotated to face aft, the safest direction in case they crashed. "Test crew is ready."

Jones pushed the throttles up to thirty percent, accelerating around the corner as he brought the nose wheel onto the faded runway centerline. Without slowing, he pushed the throttles full forward, intent on using every bit of available real estate to get them up and off the hill.

The floodlights passed by, slowly at first. The plane lumbered grudgingly forward, the end of the runway rapidly approaching. It didn't seem like the heavy plane had picked up any reasonable speed when the halfway marker flashed by.

Just as Jones was considering aborting the takeoff, the efficient new engines proved their worth. The airspeed indicator practically jumped from sixty knots to over ninety-five.

"We're going for it!" Jones called into the interphone as they passed the red light, the point of no return.

The spurt of acceleration tapered off dramatically

as the plane started up the hill. The G forces pushed each member of the crew deep into his seat. Red began calling off the airspeed as they plunged forward.

"One hundred knots."

Jones watched another floodlight pass out of sight. They were still well below the necessary one hundred seventy knots required for a safe takeoff.

"One twenty."

They pulled out of the main part of the curve at the bottom of the hill, and the G forces leveled off.

"One thirty."

Jones' concern returned. The plane wasn't picking speed up as rapidly as he'd hoped. There were only three more floodlights in front of them, less than four hundred fifty feet.

"One forty."

Two more floodlights.

"One forty-five."

Jones could feel the tension in Red's normally emotionless voice.

"One fifty."

This was it. They were less than one hundred feet to the end of the runway, still twenty knots below the calculated safe rotation speed.

"One fifty-five."

Jones held the yoke forward, squeezing out every available inch of asphalt.

"One sixty."

The final floodlight passed, and the runway fell

away, the big aircraft lofted into space by its own momentum, still well short of its normal takeoff speed. Jones jerked the yoke back, using his strong arms to lift the plane into the darkness.

"Gear up!" he ordered, concentrating intently on flying the plane.

Red pulled the handle, and the landing gear hydraulic system pulled the wheels up into the belly of the plane.

It was a risk, Jones knew. There would be no time to get the gear back down if they augured in, but the gear was causing too much drag, keeping them from building airspeed. Fortunately, the ground effect, air forced between the wings and the ground, added extra lift, helping to keep them airborne. Between that and the upward direction of the takeoff, Jones had enough leeway in his airspeed to push the airplane to one hundred feet above the ground.

"Gear up," Red called when the indicator showed the wheels were stowed.

Jones breathed a sigh of relief. It looked like they might make it. Then the ground effect went away, and they were still ten knots below stall speed. A warning horn blared loudly.

"Stall warning!" Red stated the obvious.

Jones twisted the yoke slightly to the right, pushing it forward, forcing the nose down. The slow speed caused the plane to buffet, the left wing extremely close to losing lift. Jones noticed the sign and eased off slightly on the turn. By the time he pulled out of the twenty-degree bank, the plane had lost all but twenty-five feet of altitude, but the trade-off gained them five knots of airspeed. While the warning horn continued to blare, he kept the nose pointed down.

He could sense the tension rise in the cockpit as the plane plunged forward into the darkness. The radar altimeter clicked off the range to the unforgiving earth below. Every eye was on the display.

Red was tense. His hand was on the throttles, holding them full forward. An accidental loss of power would be fatal.

Chief Warren sat back and held tight to the arms of his chair. He wasn't in a position to provide any assistance, and he felt helpless. He could only hope the new engines would maintain their thrust. He didn't even want to think about what the stress of the takeoff had done to the already weak landing gear.

Jones was tense, too. This had been a lot closer than he had planned. He kept the nose of the plane down as the stall warning horn blared in his ear. The altimeter continued to read between twenty and twenty-five feet. All the while the plane was descending, picking up airspeed. At one hundred seventy knots, the stall warning horn wavered and finally went silent. Jones leveled off, the altimeter showed the ground falling away until it steadied at fifty feet. They were only ten knots above the stall speed when the altimeter showed the ground approaching again. Jones pulled the nose of the plane up slightly, keeping it at fifty feet. Now that they were above stall speed, the plane continued to pick up velocity. At one hundred eighty knots, Jones pulled the nose sharply back, pushing it into a normal rate of climb.

"I don't know what the hell you did," Red said, "but it worked."

"There was a little valley just off the runway centerline. I saw it yesterday when I flew over here in one of the Aero Club's Pipers. We just flew down into it until we stabilized. There's just one problem. I figure we flew over the base commander's house at about twenty feet. He is really going to be pissed."

"Oh, well."

"Yeah. Chief, let's get out of here. Give me a heading."

11

D-Day minus Three
An airfield in Western Kuwait

It had been a long flight. After receiving their warning orders, the entire Special Ops crew had rested
up for a few short hours, then began the trek across
the Atlantic to the Kuwaiti desert. They had been
there before, most of them, back when there was a
war to fight. Thankfully that was over. The airman
Conner was talking to hadn't seen that war, hadn't
been in the Air Force at the time. He was a rookie,
but had already been baptized by fire, barely escap-
ing the terrorist bomb that killed so many in Saudi.
Still, he hadn't fought the enemy and was full of
questions about what it was like back then. Conner
had answered most of them, others were too painful.
Changing the subject, Conner pointed across the
runway.

"Are you sure?" Conner asked.

"That's what I heard," the airman replied. "They

189

got here yesterday, on a Navy transport that landed about three hours ahead of you. Word is you're supposed to take 'em somewhere."

"Yeah, that's probably bullshit. You know how rumors float around this little base. There's always talk of something weird going on. It's the boredom. The guys assigned here for short tours spend their free time making up shit like that to give them something to do. That kind of rumor is dangerous, though. Can you imagine what would happen if the Kuwaitis heard there was an Israeli Special Operations platoon on their precious Arab soil?"

"There's one way to find out if they're Israelis," the airman said, ignoring Conner's question.

"Yeah," Conner agreed. "But are you going to be the one to go ask them to drop their pants?"

Both men laughed, then became silent. They looked out across the tarmac, watching the small unit of men mill about on the other side of the taxiway, their brown tents billowing in the gentle breeze.

Segen Gurion stared blankly at the Kuwaiti sunset. Another night approached, another night with nothing to do. Gurion felt naked here, and he was sure most of his men felt the same way. They'd had to leave all their personal identification behind when the U.S. Navy aircraft picked them up in Tel Aviv. The Mossad had tried to convince them to use false passports, papers that would identify them as Kuwaitis. He had refused. The Mossad had no qualms about impersonating Arabs, but it would disgust the men he led. They would prefer to remain anonymous rather than be confused with the forces they were sworn to defeat.

Gurion patted the shirt pocket where he normally kept the picture of his wife, it, too, left behind with his other personal effects. He wandered around the little camp, aimlessly checking on his men. They were all doing what they could to keep busy, sharpening knives, cleaning weapons. Rav Samal Reitman, his top noncommissioned officer, stopped him as he walked by.

"Any word on when we move out, Naqib Gurion?" Reitman asked, using a Syrian rank designator for his commander. The men had been told not to use their Israeli titles, in case anyone was eavesdropping. Reitman had gone one better, using Syrian titles, and promoting Gurion to the equivalent of a captain in the process.

"None. I doubt we'll be moving out tonight, but it's possible."

"Then I think I'll run the men through some physical training. They're getting bored. I've never seen their weapons so clean."

"Go ahead, but stay close. And do the Egyptian routine in case someone is watching."

"Yes, sir."

Gurion considered whether he should join them. The Egyptian routine was the easiest standard exercise they did, and one that would not tax the men.

They wouldn't be overly tired if they got orders to move out on short notice. On the other hand, since it was so easy, the workout would do little to alleviate the boredom. Gurion decided to join his men, deciding it was better to do little than nothing at all. When Reitman had all the men gathered in the center of their little compound, Gurion joined the formation, standing at the rear while the sergeant went through the commands for the calisthenics.

As Conner came out of the side door of the hangar, he saw the men doing some sort of exercises on the far side of the taxiway. He laughed to himself. If they were Israelis, they certainly weren't what he expected. He'd always heard the Israelis were top-notch, heard they were prepared to endure physical and mental hardships that would incapacitate the soldiers in most of the world's armies. From what he watched them doing, a few jumping jacks and some stretching exercises, he doubted they were in very good physical condition. Conner took a long drink from the clear plastic bottle of spring water, regretting again he hadn't thought to bring along some Kool-Aid to give it a little flavor. In this environment it was necessary to drink a lot and do it often, dehydration could wipe you out quickly and without warning. His last assignment here had proven that often enough.

"Sergeant Conner," he heard someone yell from behind him.

Conner turned to see one of the pilots yelling at him from the door. Conner turned and trotted back to the hanger.

"What's up, sir?" he asked as he stepped inside, following the captain, already walking across the hangar floor.

"We've got a mission. We launch in three hours, I just got the brief. You won't believe where they're sending us."

Edwards AFB, California

The dark gray B-52 sat silently, waiting for its next mission. It didn't fly often, this old bird, but this morning it would fly again, another job for NASA. Until then it waited on the tarmac near the shuttle recovery facility, shrouded by an eerie, early morning fog.

Just before dawn a convoy pulled up to the old A-10 hangar at Edwards AFB, three cars and two large semi-trucks. The vehicles were white, even the trailers were painted a sterile shade, and they all bore government license plates. Someone had been waiting for them, and he opened the door to the hangar, letting the trucks pull inside. After the doors were closed, the lights inside the hangar came on.

A dozen men climbed out of the cars and joined the trucks inside the hangar. All the men wore white jumpsuits, Lawrence Livermore National Laboratory emblazoned across the back. The men split up and went to the trucks. They unlocked the trailers and began removing their equipment. Some of the boxes were quite large, heavy enough to require a forklift.

Eventually everything was out of the trucks except for a particularly large box, over thirty feet long and six feet square. Several men gathered around the back of the truck while others began unpacking the computers and setting up the prelaunch test equipment.

"We'll be ready to unload the missile as soon as the contractors arrive," Dr. Byron Sympson, standing with the group near the back of the trailer, told the DARPA director.

"Well, where are they?" Kashwa'ar asked impatiently.

"They should be here any minute," Sympson replied.

"We can go ahead and pull the box out of the truck if you want, Byron," one of the Livermore engineers said, knowing Kashwa'ar was a difficult man to deal with if he were made to wait.

"Yeah, that's a good idea, let's get it out. How about a cup of coffee, Dr. Kashwa'ar?" Sympson hated having to baby-sit the man from DARPA, but that was one of his primary jobs here. The further the DARPA director was kept from the equipment and the engineers, the better chance they would have of a successful and timely launch.

Everyone could tell Kashwa'ar was having reservations about going with Sympson, worried he would miss something important if he wasn't right in the middle of everything. He only agreed to go with Sympson after he was assured they were only going to take the box out of the truck.

The contractor personnel, men from Launch Services, Inc., started to arrive just as the sun was coming up. Unlike the engineers from Livermore, these men trickled in one at a time. Generally their first stop was the coffeepot set up in one corner of the hangar. A few of the Livermore engineers went over to talk with the new arrivals. Some of the contractors were the same men who delivered the Pegasus to the lab just over two weeks earlier. They were having coffee and discussing the launch procedures when Kashwa'ar came out of the bathroom at the side of the hangar. He rushed to where they stood. Sympson saw him and tried to intervene, but couldn't head him off in time.

"Why aren't you men unpacking the missile?" Kashwa'ar asked, fidgeting, wringing his hands.

"And just who the hell are you?" one of the men from Launch Systems asked. He was a big man, wearing a western hat, blue jeans, and old boots. The others quit talking when he spoke.

"John," Sympson interrupted, addressing the man in the hat, "this is Dr. Kashwa'ar. He's the director of DARPA, the man who's funding this project. Dr. Kashwa'ar, this is John Campbell, he's president of Launch Systems."

"Well, get him busy unpacking the missile," Kashwa'ar ordered Sympson, his voice cracking. "We don't want to risk missing the launch window."

"Dr. Kashwa'ar," Campbell said slowly, knowing he had to take care of the problem Sympson had warned him about. "Let's go take a look at the crate."

Campbell put his big arm around Kashwa'ar's shoulders and turned him around, leading him away from the group. The other men just smiled and sipped their coffee.

"Now, listen, Mr. Kashwa'ar," Campbell said, lowering his voice and purposefully omitting Kashwa'ar's title. "You gave Sympson a fair amount of money to hire me to send this little payload of yours into space, and I'm going to do it because that's what I do for a living. But I'm going to tell you something right now, I don't like bureaucrats looking over my shoulder while I work. I've launched over two dozen of these little babies, and I haven't missed a launch window yet. If you have doubts about my ability to get this thing into space, then you can just go find someone else to launch it for you. Otherwise, just stay out of our way, and everything will be fine. Any problems with that?"

"I didn't mean to imply you couldn't do your job," Kashwa'ar protested, "but this is a very crucial launch."

"Every launch I make is crucial, Kashwa'ar. My name goes on every one of these birds. Now, why don't you go help the Livermore boys get ready to check out their payload and stay away from my men." Campbell slapped Kashwa'ar on the back and walked away before the DARPA bureaucrat could say anything else. "Let's get this box unpacked boys," he yelled across the hangar to his men.

Kashwa'ar watched from a distance as Campbell and his men removed the protective fiberglass from the missile and positioned the PEGASUS on a wheeled cart. From outward appearances it was impossible to tell what the payload was. Only the Livermore personnel had any idea what was going on. The contractors thought they were launching a missile defense experiment. Kashwa'ar smiled at that, pleased he knew something the overgrown Campbell didn't.

The Livermore engineers hovered over the missile once the protective cover was removed. Several computers were hooked up to diagnostic cables protruding from the missile's upper side. Automatic computer programs queried the payload subsystems, checking the operational status of the first Brilliant Pebble to be launched into space. It took over thirty minutes to complete the tests. Fortunately, all systems checked out properly.

"All set," Sympson told Campbell. "You can mount it up as soon as you're ready."

"We're ready now, the BUFF's hooked up to ground power already."

Campbell ordered one of his men to bring in the

tow truck, then supervised them as the missile cart was attached. The hangar doors slowly opened, and the entire group followed the missile out. The procession was reverent.

It was only a quarter of a mile to the plane, so most of the men walked, following the slow-moving cart, its cargo glistening white under the glow of the bright sodium lights lining their path.

The B-52 was still waiting in the dissipating fog of the early morning, its internal systems powered up. The mighty bomber was ready to accept its newest cargo.

"It's a lot quieter out here than I expected," Sympson told Campbell as they walked to the plane.

"Yeah, it's nice when we get to use Pad Fifteen to load the missile. It's one of the few pads where ground power is already available. Otherwise we'd have to start up a ground power cart, and those things make a hell of a racket. This is the same pad they used to get the X-15 ready for flight. That's why the ground power is already out here, they didn't want to have any auxiliary engines running with such volatile fuel around."

"Is that what all this plumbing is for?"

"No, that was put in when the Airborne Laser Lab was flying its missions over China Lake about eight years ago. Those pipes were used to load the fuel for the onboard laser. Is there anything else your guys have to do before we can load the missile?" Campbell asked, getting back to the business at hand.

"No, we're ready to load it now. We'll need to fill the liquid nitrogen tank, but we can't do that until the missile's mounted. We'd like to wait as long as possible before topping off the dewar so we don't have too much nitrogen boil off."

"We can wait until about ten minutes before launch if you want to load the nitrogen while the BUFF's engines are running, otherwise you'll have to fill the dewar about twenty minutes earlier."

"We'll go for T minus thirty, that should give us plenty of coolant reserve for the sensor."

Several of Campbell's men were manhandling the missile cart under the wing of the B-52, lining it up. They jacked the missile up and attached it to the wing pylon, carrying out several tests to verify the electrical systems were connected. At thirty minutes before launch, the Livermore engineers filled the Brilliant Pebble with liquid nitrogen, coolant for the seeker's highly sensitive infrared sensor.

Aboard the B-52, somewhere over the Pacific Ocean

John Campbell watched the video screen, the status of all the missile subsystems was displayed on the computer console he faced. Everything looked okay. So far. The missile was ready to go, if only the Livermore boys could figure out what was wrong with the payload. He looked back over his left shoulder to watch the flurry of activity at the payload console. He pulled the master switch on his intercom station to listen to what they were saying. The first thing he heard was Kashwa'ar's panicky squeal.

"Why won't it cool down?" he asked.

"We don't know yet, Dr. Kashwa'ar." Sympson tried to calm him down. "As soon as we finish this test sequence, we should be able to give you an answer. Now, how about letting these men finish their work without interruption?"

Campbell shook his head. He felt sorry for Sympson. Sympson had told him how Kashwa'ar volunteered the payload for this test, well before it was ready to go and without asking for input from the developers. Then Campbell had an idea, there was one thing he could do to help get Kashwa'ar out of the way. He twisted his intercom knob to the AIR CREW position and hit the foot switch to activate the boom microphone attached to his helmet.

"Pilot, this is Test," he called.

"Test, Pilot. Go" came the reply from up front.

Campbell was glad NASA had contracted out to a civilian company to fly the old BUFF. It was easier to get the civilians to "bend" the rules than the straight-laced Air Force guys who used to fly the missions.

"Let's begin the climb to altitude," Campbell requested.

"I don't have a 'payload ready' indication up here," the pilot replied.

Campbell knew the flight rules specified the payload as well as the missile had to be ready for launch before the pilot was supposed to begin his climb. "I know," Campbell replied, "but we're pushing the launch window. I've got this feeling that if we climb out now, the payload will be ready by the time we get to altitude."

"Roger that." The pilot trusted Campbell, knew his hunches were usually right. He pulled back on the yoke.

Sympson and Kashwa'ar were still standing over the payload console, Kashwa'ar still interfering with the engineers, asking irrelevant questions. Sympson obviously hadn't been able to talk him into leaving them alone.

The klaxon in the back of the airplane went off as the nose of the plane pitched up. Campbell was watching Kashwa'ar when the klaxon sounded, laughed as the little bureaucrat almost jumped out of his skin. He had intentionally omitted mentioning the klaxon alarm in the safety brief to the man from DARPA. Campbell hit the master override on his intercom, allowing him to talk on all the circuits at once.

"All right, gentlemen. We're beginning to climb to launch altitude. I want everyone to get strapped in and get their masks on. I don't want anyone getting hypoxic."

Now Kashwa'ar had no choice but to leave the engineers alone. Sympson pointed toward Kashwa'ar's seat and ushered him aft. Sympson turned back to look at Campbell, already wearing his flight helmet. While Kashwa'ar's back was turned to him, Sympson gave the thumbs-up sign to Campbell. Campbell waved back, then resumed listening to the engineers, hoping they would be able to sort their problem out in time.

USSPACECOM, *Colorado*

"Sir, the launch platform is climbing to altitude," the chief petty officer manning the communication center informed him.

"Roger that. Check on Argus. See if they're in position. Then pass the word to CENTCOM." Lieutenant Colonel Chris Delaney, United States Army, had taken command of this mission and the supporting Space Operations staff. Some of the assigned personnel had complained, but one phone call from CENT-COM had shut them up. Besides, he'd served a tour here before, was fully qualified for what needed to be done. He and the chief petty officer were the only ones who had been cleared on what it was they were doing. The rest of the staff thought it was merely a routine Pegasus launch.

"Argus is on orbit. She reports four point four hours of fuel available and all systems operational."

Good. They'd need the old range control aircraft to get a clear picture of what the reentry looked like. It had been Delaney's idea to send Argus to Saudi

Arabia to monitor target and reentry activity. There was nothing else that could provide that information. "What about the target?"

"Argus reports he's still flying the same orbit he's held the last two days."

"Good. Make sure they keep an eye on him. What about other traffic in the area?"

"Not a lot. A few airliners have flown near the target after departing the civil airport in Damascus, but they've stayed at least a hundred miles away."

They shouldn't be a problem. The Livermore engineers had told Delaney their seeker had a narrow field of view, wouldn't even see a target that stayed at least fifty miles away.

"Fighters?"

"A whole shit load. But again they're staying to the east."

"Do they get closer than fifty miles to the target?"

"Yes."

Again, that shouldn't be a problem, their infrared signatures were quite different than the target's. The seeker should reject them on that basis; at least that's what the design predicted.

Delaney looked up at the huge video screen that covered the front wall. He was always amazed at the vast array of space "junk" that floated through the vacuum above the earth. Every new launch had to take into account the limited amount of clear flight path available to it. Launch windows became narrower and narrower as more and more satellites fought for the best positions above the earth.

The computer calculated the projected route and plotted it on the front display. So far the Pegasus flight path looked clear. None of the "junk" in space would come close to the track. Unless something really bad happened, this particular payload would reenter after only one orbit. They wouldn't have to add it to the computer catalog, listing it as a piece of orbital debris to avoid on future flights.

The only other asset that concerned SPACECOM was in position as well. A small, elongated circle on the display showed the track of Argus, a modified KC-135 orbiting over the Mediterranean. They had used Argus before; its optical and radar subsystems were extremely useful for mapping the first pass of Pegasus launches. The satellites were low enough for the optical systems to pick them up on the initial orbit. That helped SPACECOM refine the data in its space catalog, but Argus had a different mission this time.

"Okay, it looks like we're a go. Pass the word to launch, and let me know if you see anything that might be trouble."

USCENTCOM

"General, SPACECOM reports the Pegasus is preparing to launch," the major interrupted General Wainwright's staff meeting.

"Thanks. I'll be right down. Gentlemen, I'm afraid I'll have to ask your indulgence on the rest of these issues. We'll continue tomorrow." Wainwright stood to leave. The general's staff came to attention as he departed.

It was a short walk to the Operations cell. Wainwright found the room a flurry of activity as he walked in. Many of the personnel in the Ops cell were leaving, not cleared for Operation Eagle Fire.

"How's it going?" the general asked the Ops officer as he took his seat in what he liked to call his "war room."

"All systems look good, General. Anticipate launch of Pegasus in thirty minutes. All the players are in position. We just need to bring the Israeli fighters up."

"Not yet. I don't want them airborne until we have a launch. They're supposed to be on fifteen-minute alert anyhow. What about the Special Ops bird?"

"On the ramp, General."

"Good. We'll have to launch him in thirty, as soon as we know Pegasus is airborne. I'd rather not launch them this early, but it's going to be tough to get them in place in time if Pegasus fails. He is not, however, to cross into Syrian airspace yet. I'll tell him when. Get SPACECOM on the horn. Is Delaney on the net?"

"Yes, sir."

B-52

"All right!" Campbell heard one of the Livermore engineers yell over the intercom. He looked over at that console. All the engineers were strapped into their seats, but the two nearest the primary payload operator were leaning over to stare at the readout.

"Test, this is Payload," the lead engineer called.

"Go."

"Test, the payload is ready to launch."

"It's about time. We've been at launch altitude for over fifteen minutes. What was the problem?" Campbell had seen too many payload problems that seemed to "magically" correct themselves, only to crop up again just before launch.

"It was a temperature transducer in the coolant line. Looks like it frosted over when we loaded the liquid nitrogen. We're good to go now."

Campbell's display finally showed a green light for the payload. All the other systems showed green as well.

"All right, crew, this is Test. We're ready to go. Pilot, bring us to a heading of three zero zero."

"Wilco."

The crew felt the plane move into a hard right bank that lasted over ten seconds.

"Three zero zero." The pilot pulled the plane out of its turn.

"Roger," replied Campbell, habitually checking his own heading indicator. He hit a switch on the console and waited for the computer to run through the prelaunch check. It didn't take long.

"Crew, this is Test. We're ready for launch. Stand by on my count." Campbell hit the switch that began the countdown, reading the numbers as they were displayed on the digital console. "Five."

The consent light on his console went green, the pilot had keyed the switch on his yoke, providing his manual approval.

"Four . . . three . . ."

Two other lights, one from the data link and the other from the payload separation package, also went green, the computer determining the systems were GO in its final checks.

"Two . . . one . . . Fire!"

The computer sent a final command to the electrical solenoids on the pylon, releasing the pins holding the missile on the plane's right wing. Campbell watched through his small window as the polished white missile dropped silently away, slowly falling down and back as atmospheric friction slowed its speed. Less than two seconds later the missile's rocket motor fired, sending flames spewing aft of the high-tech bullet. The missile passed beneath the wing as it accelerated, angling upward and northward as it climbed away.

"We have successful separation and ignition," Campbell said over the intercom and the radio, knowing USSPACECOM was monitoring the frequency. He watched the computer display and read out the data as it rolled up on the screen.

"Altitude: 55,000 feet, Speed: 500 knots, heading: three zero six.

"Altitude: 72,000 feet, Speed: 850 knots, heading: three zero seven.

"Altitude: 92,000 feet, Speed: Mach 1.6, heading: three zero seven. Missile is now downrange seven miles. Heading is stabilized. Estimate T minus twelve minutes until payload separation. Pilot is clear to start descent."

Campbell continued to call out the data until they approached the next critical phase: payload separation.

USSPACECOM

"Sir, we're getting telemetry from the ground station. Data looks good," the Chief Petty Officer reported.

"Good. How long until separation?"

"About ten minutes."

"Argus still up?"

"Affirmative."

"Bring the data up on the display."

A new track appeared on the video map covering the front wall. Lieutenant Colonel Delaney watched as the track extended northward from its current position over the Eastern Pacific. The numeric readout next to the point of the track incremented, showing the satellite approach fifty miles in altitude.

"Clear the BUFF to return to base," Delaney ordered the sailor.

Delaney picked up the STU III telephone handset,

checking the display to make sure they were still secure. It read TOP SECRET, USCENTCOM/J3.

"Major, we've established the data link. All systems are nominal and separation is now expected in," he looked up to check the display board, "nine minutes."

USCENTCOM

"General, launch was successful, separation expected in nine minutes. Everything looks good."

"Keep that line open, Major. Let me know the instant anything, I mean anything, goes wrong. And check the Special Ops bird, see if it's up yet."

Wainwright also picked up a secure phone, one connected to his Israeli counterpart's own "war room." "General, launch your birds. Then wait for my go ahead to initiate the strike."

Israel

He held the binoculars up to his eyes. From his vantage point in the hills, he could see the airfield clearly. He began counting as the F-16s launched below him. After ten minutes there was a lull in the launch activity. He had already counted over twenty-four aircraft in the air, had watched them streak north, away from the airfield, the fire from their engines bright against the late night darkness. He jumped in his car and drove rapidly down the small mountain, hurrying to get to the phone.

B-52

"Like hell we're going home," Campbell told the pilot. "Just keep this bird airborne for fifteen more minutes, at least until I can make sure the payload separates properly. NASA can afford the gas."

"Okay, Campbell, we'll stick around. By the way, we're down to thirty thousand feet. You can release your guys to move around."

"Thanks." Campbell wasn't about to tell Kashwa'ar he could get out of his seat. The only information that made any difference now was being displayed on Campbell's monitor, and he sure as hell didn't want Kashwa'ar hanging over his own shoulder.

"We've got a good launch," Campbell reported over the test crew net. It wasn't fair to let them all wait without word. "Stay put for about twenty more minutes, then you'll be free to move around."

Campbell checked the display, watched the clock tick down to the time for payload separation. When the payload left the booster, his job would be complete. It would be another successful launch, another fat paycheck from Uncle Sam.

Brilliant Pebble

At an altitude of ninety-six miles above the earth, the Pegasus booster ignited a small rocket motor to give its payload a final push into outer space. Electrically actuated bolts ejected from the mating collar between the rocket and the payload. The rocket motor burned out just as small panels in the booster airframe extended, using the thinning air at that altitude to slow the spent missile casing.

The Brilliant Pebble continued onward, and internal, battery-powered systems came up on-line. A small patch antenna on the outside of the Pebble's case started searching for the Global Positioning Satellite it knew should be directly overhead. Once the satellite was located, the onboard navigation system used the GPS data to compute corrections to its preplanned course.

Simultaneously, the infrared scanner began to search the earth below, hunting for the target it was programmed to destroy.

USSPACECOM

Signals from the payload indicated the booster had successfully separated. The booster itself continued on a ballistic course, heading for the atmosphere under the force of the earth's gravity.

"Sir, we've got separation. Payload is now transmitting. Course is displayed on the screen."

B-52

Campbell was watching the data coming from the payload navigation system. He had talked them into letting him have direct access to the data in case something went wrong with the launch. Nothing had, of course, but it gave him something to do while they flew back to Edwards.

The data had looked normal for the first twenty minutes, but now it was looking a little strange. The payload's orbit seemed to be decaying. Watching the screen, Campbell hammered a command into his computer, calling up an orbital prediction program. When the code prompted him, he typed the trajectory data into the machine. It took less than thirty seconds for the machine to spit out an answer.

"What the F . . . ?"

The payload was going to reenter the atmosphere somewhere over Syria.

12

D-Day minus Three
Brilliant Pebble

The Brilliant Pebble turned back toward the earth. Even though it was night in the target area, the earth was still emitting the heat it had absorbed during the day, threatening to overwhelm the seeker's infrared detector. The sensor turned its automatic gain control down as far as possible to avoid saturation. That helped for a while, but eventually the shroud covering the front of the Brilliant Pebble, made from the same material used to protect the space shuttle from the rigors of reentry, began to heat up. The sensor couldn't compensate for the infrared emissions of the hot shield, and the onboard computer sent a message to the sensor, shutting it down and deploying a shield over the sensor to protect it.

A small piece of the heat deflecting material on the shroud peeled back slightly, the glue holding it weakened from the heat. The material didn't break away as designed, instead acting as a small air brake, deflecting the air rushing past it.

USSPACECOM

"Sir, we may have a problem," the Navy lieutenant responsible for watching the reentry trajectory called out.

"What is it?" Delaney asked.

"The Internal Navigation System shows an ambiguity. It looks like the payload is starting to spin."

"What would cause that?" Delaney asked the Livermore rep, sitting at a desk near him.

"I don't know. The internal gyros are supposed to keep it from spinning. There must be some external force competing with the gyro stabilization system. It'll take time to look at the data to find out what's causing it."

"Well, what will happen to it?"

"That's hard to say. If it keeps spinning, it could tumble out of control. It'll burn up if that happens. If it stops spinning it may correct its course, if it isn't already too far off to compensate."

"Shit!" Delaney grabbed the phone to CENTCOM.

Brilliant Pebble

Heat continued to build up where the small strand of material remained attached to the falling body. Eventually the heat melted the strand away, releasing the aerodynamic forces causing the Pebble to spin. The internal gyroscopes slowed the spin until the Pebble returned to a stable descent. The Pebble slowed and cooled, eventually releasing the shutter that covered the infrared sensor. The sensor resumed its hunt for the target, trying to match the infrared signature of the objects it saw below to data stored in its memory. It acquired a close match and fired thrusters to correct its course. The computer armed the onboard warhead.

USSPACECOM

"Sir, we definitely have a problem," the lieutenant said.

"I thought it quit spinning," Delaney said.

"It did, sir. This is another problem. Somewhere in the reentry, probably because of the spin, the payload has acquired a tilt in its trajectory. It's going to miss the target, the payload's coming down in the wrong area."

"What do you mean? Where?"

"Near the border, over Iraq, sir."

Thank God, Delaney thought to himself. It'll probably impact somewhere in the middle of the desert. Then he had another thought.

"Are there any airplanes in the new reentry area?" Delaney shouted over at the Air Force liaison officer.

"Can't say for sure," the Air Force captain replied. "We're not set up to monitor aerial activity that close to Syria. There could be some commercial airliners, maybe even a few military transports, but air traffic in the region has been pretty scarce lately. At this time of night, I doubt if there's much of anything."

Only Delaney knew the full picture. He remembered another plane that was somewhere in that particular area. Delaney picked up the phone to CENTCOM again.

Aboard the Special Operations C-130, somewhere over Northern Saudi Arabia

Conner walked up and down the middle of the plane as the C-130 droned through the air. He was keeping a close check on his cargo. There were twenty-three men, all silently waiting as they sat on the netting that served as troop seats for the Special Operations airplane. They were intent men, silent. He had heard only two of them speak since they came aboard, and they only talked when they needed to issue orders to the others. With no other information, Conner had to rely on what he saw to guess who they were.

Their uniforms provided no clues. The only consistent thing about the uniforms was their inconsistency. They seemed to be a mixture of garb from several different armies. Some wore sandy-colored uniforms like the desert-pattern battle-dress uniforms the American soldiers had worn during the Gulf War. Others obviously weren't of American origin, possibly Saudi, or even Syrian. It almost looked like they had equipped themselves at some army surplus store.

The cord to Conner's headset snagged on a tiedown in the floor, and he reached back to jerk it free. As he did the pilot called a diving turn and pushed the nose of the airplane down and to the left. Conner, off balance, stumbled and almost fell into the laps of two of his passengers.

Some of the men burst out in laughter. Conner's face turned red as he made his way back to the jump door. He keyed his interphone to contact the pilot.

"What the hell was that all about," he asked.

"Sorry, Conner. We only have a little time to be in place, and we got the call to move in just as we were at the top of the orbit. Keep the men strapped in until we pass the word to get ready."

It only took ten minutes for the C-130 to get in position. By now Conner had pretty much figured out what was going on. They had crossed into Iraqi airspace from their orbit in Saudi Arabia and then turned back to the west. They were heading for Syria.

"Tell our passengers to stand up," the pilot called.

"Roger," Conner replied, hooking a long safety line from an overhead cable to a special belt he wore around his waist. He punched the switch to open the cargo door in the very back of the plane. The wind blew in his face as the ramp leveled off, exposing the darkness, giving the men aboard a sense of what awaited them.

SPACECOM

"What have you got?" Delaney was standing over the petty officer's shoulder, staring at the data that was being piped in from Argus.

"Still have that infrared source on the far side of the country, high up. It's too bright, saturating the sensor. With it in the field, I can't make out anything else."

"Keep looking," Delaney ordered. He was concerned. If that infrared source was indeed the Pebble, its trajectory was all screwed up.

"What about radar on the target?"

"He's still there." The petty officer tapped a small green light on the larger display. "Still just flying holes in the sky."

"Keep an eye on him. Contact Argus. Have them make a sweep of the border region, between Syria and Iraq. The Pebble is coming down in that area, and I want to know if anything is there."

C-130

"The seeker indicates it's locked on, it could very well be coming after you," Delaney warned the C-130 pilot over the satellite radio link after explaining to him the similarity between the infrared signature of the target and that of the C-130.

"No shit," the pilot answered, craning his neck to

see up into the dark sky. Too late, he never saw the Pebble streaking toward his plane.

The missile impacted the fuselage near the right wing, clipping the major hydraulic line that provided rudder control.

Conner was knocked down again, this time all the way to the floor. The wind from the hole in the plane gushed in, almost blowing him back out the open jump door. The safety strap saved him, giving him something to hold on to while he climbed back to his feet. When the smoke cleared, he could tell at least six of the men sitting in the jump seats near the missile impact point were gone.

Up front the pilot grabbed the yoke, fighting to hold the plane level. The elevator felt mushy. The rudder was dead.

"What the hell happened back there," the pilot yelled into the intercom.

"We've been hit," Conner answered. "There's a big hole in the right side, just aft of the wing spar. At least half a dozen guys are gone. She's bleeding hydraulic fluid all over the place!"

"Get the rest of the men out. This bird isn't going to make it home. Tell them we're barely inside Syrian territory. I'm going to point this thing back toward Iraq. All kinds of shit will break loose if anyone finds out we're in Syrian airspace."

Conner grabbed the guy he guessed was in charge, the one who had given all the orders when they were loading up.

"You've got to get out! Now!" he yelled to be heard over the wind rushing through the airplane, streaming in from the hole in their side.

Gurion nodded, signaling his men to stand up. They quickly checked their equipment and began jumping out the back, the static lines pulling the chutes out of their packs.

The C-130 started into a climb, shallow at first but becoming much steeper.

The pilot fought to maintain level flight long enough for the men to get out of the back. It was futile at first, the nose ignored his commands due to the elevator problem and climbed higher and higher into the air. He shoved all throttles full forward to stave off a stall as long as possible. The engines strained under the load.

Finally, the auxiliary hydraulic system brought the runaway elevator back under control. The pilot eased the yoke forward, forcing the nose down. He looked at the airspeed indicator, it warned him he was just five knots above a stall. At the rate they were losing airspeed, the big plane would have dropped from the sky in only a few more seconds. It would have fallen like a rock.

"Fire light on number three engine!" the copilot warned.

The pilot reached over and retarded the throttle, then engaged the fire suppression system. Some of the missile debris must have torn into the rear of the big turbojet. The plane started to yaw to the right as the two engines on the left side pushed harder than the single functioning engine on the right. He retarded the thrust on the left outboard engine to fifty percent. They were still much too close to a stall to kill the engine completely. The big bird still pushed to the left, the nose started to fall in that direction as it came down. The pilot shoved hard on the right rudder pedal to try to overcome the side slip. That proved to be a fatal mistake.

Conner heard one of the engines shut down. Almost all of the other men were out when he heard the sound of metal tearing. His stomach tightened.

The strain on the already weakened fuselage was too great. When the rudder was forced out into the airstream, two of the main wing spar supports ripped loose.

The yoke went soft. Sweat poured down the pilot's back, and the ailerons failed to respond to his commands. The plane slipped into a tight left diving turn and entered a spin.

Gurion shoved Reitman out the door and turned to make sure all of his men were out. The only one left aboard was the American sergeant. Gurion grabbed him bodily and moved toward the open cargo door.

Conner fought back. His plane was in trouble, and he needed to help. Both men watched through the gaping hole as the entire right wing fell away. Conner knew then that the plane was doomed. He released the safety strap from his waist and, facing the Israeli, hooked his arms around the man's neck. He threw off his headset, and the two men launched themselves off the edge of the jump door.

USCENTCOM

"General, call off the strike," Wainwright spoke over the secure line to his counterpart in Israel. "The system didn't work." He listened quietly. "Yes, sir, I understand, but we have another plan, a backup. I think we should meet to discuss how to implement it. I'll fly over tomorrow."

Wainwright hung up the phone, then turned to his aide: "Major, get me a plane to Tel Aviv."

Somewhere over Syria

Conner counted to three then held tight, anticipating the opening of Gurion's chute. The jerk of the opening chute was almost too much, Conner's hands started to pull free. Fortunately, Gurion had a secure grip on Conner's safety belt, saving him from a fatal plunge. In seconds the rush of wind in his ears was replaced by the floating sensation Conner was so familiar with. Even with over two hundred assault jumps to his credit, this was the first time he had gone out without his own parachute. Conner swore to himself it would be the last. From now on he was going to wear a chute whenever he flew in a C-130, he didn't care who laughed at him.

He felt Gurion let go of him with one hand, watched as he reached up with his free arm to pull the toggle on the chute, guiding them in a circular motion. As they turned, Conner could see the C-130 in the distance, diving for the ground, flames bright against the dark sky. It was in a tight, spiraling turn, one wing missing and the other ablaze. There was a bright explosion when the plane hit the ground. Loud. Then peaceful silence.

"Don't look down," Gurion warned. "Look at the horizon and keep your knees slightly bent."

"No problem," Conner answered, surprised at how loud his voice seemed. "I've done this before."

"So you have," Gurion said, noticing the small patch near the shoulder of Conner's left sleeve. "When we get down, you'll have to tell me how an Air Force sergeant gets to wear a Ranger tab."

The landing was actually quite routine, the only problem occurring when Gurion fell on top of him, pulled that way by the drag of the chute. A small, sharp rock gouged Conner's head, just behind his right ear.

"Are you all right?" Gurion pulled the parachute toward them so he could release the couplings.

"Yeah, peachy." Conner sat up.

"Good. I was afraid you might be hurt from the

sound you made when we landed, like a soccer ball being squashed."

"That's about how I felt. How much do you weigh, anyhow?"

"Only a hundred kilograms. I've been on a diet."

Conner made a quick calculation in his head. The answer was just about what he suspected. "Two twenty. No wonder you knocked the breath out of me."

"Sorry."

Gurion got up and started to pick up his parachute. Conner stood to help.

"This may be a bad time to ask," Conner said, "but I didn't get briefed on much of anything before we left. Mind telling me who you are and what you're up to?"

Gurion didn't know how to respond. The American had put him in a difficult position. He couldn't just leave him there, not in the desert. His only option was to take him along, all the way to the missile site. In order to do that, he had to divulge several State secrets, secrets known to virtually no one outside the Israeli Defense Forces establishment, and to only a few within the establishment itself.

Conner thought he was being ignored, and was about to repeat the question again, more forcefully this time, when Gurion spoke up.

"I am Segen Gurion. Segen is approximately equal to a first lieutenant in your country. My men and I are with the Israeli Special Forces, a Special Night

Unit. Our mission is to destroy a surface-to-surface missile site here in Syria."

"You're talking about starting a war," Conner noted, alarmed, wondering how the U.S. government had gotten involved in this.

"Not really," Gurion said. "As it turns out, and this must not be told to anyone, it is the Syrians who are about to start a war. We are simply trying to stop them."

It sounded like so much bullshit to Conner. He didn't know a lot about politics in this part of the world, but he did remember how the Israelis attacked the Iraqi nuclear reactor project back in 1982, using the same excuse. Not that he really cared about the Iraqis—if it weren't for them his brother would still be alive. Just the same the Israelis took a very liberal attitude when it came to preemptive strikes in the name of defense.

"Just you and your little squad of men?" Conner asked, deciding to question the feasibility of the idea rather than the political reasoning behind it.

"Yes. It is a little bit of overkill, I agree, but my superiors insisted I bring this many men along."

Conner could see Gurion flash a smile in the darkness. He smiled back himself, understanding the blustery overconfidence in the Israeli's comments.

"I guess it's a good thing I have extra men now. I'll need them to help you keep up with us."

"Don't worry about me," Conner countered. "I've been through this drill before. You asked about the

Ranger tab earlier, I had to go through the Army's Ranger school before I became an air liaison officer."

"I thought as much. I, too, have been through Ranger school. Normally I would be wearing the Ranger tab as well, but not on this mission. We have to be discrete, our identities unknown if we are captured. That's also why we wear such an assortment of uniforms."

Conner helped Gurion stuff his parachute in a small depression, then covered it with sand.

Several of the other men arrived just as they finished. The group waited in silence until the others joined them.

"That's all of us, Gurion," Reitman said.

"Technical Sergeant Conner, this is Rav Samal Reitman, my lead NCO."

The two men shook hands.

"As I see it, Conner, you have two choices," Gurion continued. "I can detail two of my men to lead you back to the Iraqi border, where you would be on your own to try and get back to one of the security zones near the Khurdish camps in the North. Or, you can come with us, join us on our mission."

Conner really had no choice. The land he would have to cross to get to the Khurdish camps would be filled with Iraqi infantry. He had to go with the Israelis.

"I'll take my chances with you."

"Good. Make sure you get rid of everything that could identify you or your nationality," Gurion ordered. "From here on we will use no rank, will travel only at night, and will rest only when absolutely necessary."

Conner felt sure Gurion's speech was directed at his own men as well as to the lone American.

"Reitman, make sure there are no traces of our landing, then we'll move out. I want to cover at least twelve kilometers before we establish communications with headquarters. We'll have to tell them what happened and ask for new orders. We must get away from this area first. Whoever shot down the transport will be scouring the area for survivors."

Reitman took several of the men and made a quick check of their surroundings.

When Reitman returned, the Special Night Unit, plus one American, took off at a quick pace. Conner knew he would have no trouble keeping up with them, he had no pack to carry like the others. As he walked, he began thinking. The more he thought about it the funnier it got. He started to snicker, then laugh quietly.

"What is it?" Gurion asked, frowning at the noise the American was making.

"I was just thinking," Conner answered quietly, but loud enough for those nearby to hear. "If we get captured or killed, my presence is going to confuse the hell out of the Syrians."

"Why is that?" Reitman asked.

"I'll be the only one who isn't circumcised."

It took several minutes for the laughter to die down. When it did, the men moved off quietly, without a noise. Even the American.

Edwards AFB

Campbell was helping the pilot inspect the pylon on the B-52's wing, the pylon where the Pegasus had been mounted, when the Livermore guys finally climbed down the ladder from the plane. Kashwa'ar was the first one down, and he waited to greet each of the engineers as they followed, shaking their hands and slapping them on the back. Kashwa'ar was ecstatic.

"What's with that jerk?"

"Nothing, that's just his way," Campbell said. "He's just a desk jockey, apparently doesn't get out in the field very much. He was about to drive these Livermore guys nuts before we made him go sit down."

"Oh."

"Looks like the pylon made it through the flight okay, no damage that I can see," Campbell said.

"Hey, Campbell!" called a full colonel walking up to the two men.

"What's up, Colonel?" Campbell asked. He recognized the man as the base commander, his staff car parked near the ramp.

"You guys got a character name of Kashwa'ar around here?" the colonel asked.

"Yeah." Campbell jerked his thumb over his shoulder. "The noisy one."

"What's he done, Colonel?" the pilot asked.

"Beats the hell out of me, but I got a call from a three star out of CENTCOM about fifteen minutes ago, said he wanted the jerk on the phone as soon as he hit the ground."

13

D-Day minus Three
Somewhere in Eastern Syria

Conner was sure they had covered at least fifteen kilometers. Fifteen fast kilometers. Even without a pack he was sweating profusely, the heat making its presence known with a merciless vengeance. The Israelis were also soaked in sweat, but they didn't appear to be nearly as tired as he was. He must have lost the edge since being reassigned to Special Operations Command. When Gurion called a break, Conner flopped down near a rock and tried to catch his breath. Reitman came over and offered a drink from his canteen.

"Thanks," Conner said. He put the canteen to his parched lips and tilted it skyward, gulping down the life-preserving liquid. He swallowed several times before noticing the water tasted funny.

"It's a potassium supplement," Reitman told him, seeing the expression on Conner's face. Almost everyone looked the same way when they got their first

230

drink of the special additive. "It helps replace the minerals that contribute to dehydration. Some say it gives the water a bad taste, like rotten bananas. I don't think so," he said, taking a long drink himself.

"What's he doing?" Conner pointed to another soldier near Gurion.

"Setting up the radio. Come over and watch, you might find this interesting."

They both moved over to the small rise where the soldier was working. First he spread a small reflector, made of metal ribs covered with aluminized plastic. It looked like the underside of an umbrella when fully open. Then, where the handle of the umbrella would have been, he inserted a small box with a wire attached. An audible tone from the equipment in his rucksack told him when the antenna was properly aligned.

Gurion took a small keyboard, like those found on the new, compact, electronic address books, and began to type in a message.

TASK FORCE LIGHTNING REPORTING. TRANSPORT ATTACKED, SHOT DOWN. SIX CASUALTIES. LOCATION, 325245N 364730E. STANDING BY FOR INSTRUCTIONS. END TRANSMISSION.

Gurion looked up at Conner, who had been watching over his shoulder, while he waited for a response.

"SATCOM?" asked Conner, referring to the standard military tactical communications in use by most modern armies.

"Yes," Gurion replied, not wanting to discuss much of the classified system.

"Aren't you afraid of being picked up?" Conner asked after it became obvious Gurion wasn't going to offer any further information.

Gurion studied the American closely, then made a decision. Even if the American sergeant got out of this alive, he probably wouldn't be able to report anything of much value about this system. Most of the technology had been procured from the Americans anyway. He had even heard the relay satellite was owned by an American company.

"That's not likely," Gurion answered. "Burst transmission. Plus, it's going out encrypted. The Syrians wouldn't be able to decode it even if they picked it up. At least not in time to . . ."

A sharp beep from the instrument interrupted Gurion's explanation, the reply was coming in. Conner watched as the words marched slowly across the liquid crystal display:

TASK FORCE LIGHTNING. CONTINUE MISSION IF POSSIBLE. DELAY OF FORTY-EIGHT HOURS EXPECTED FOR START OF EXERCISE. ADVISE IF UNABLE TO PROCEED. END TRANSMISSION.

Gurion nodded at his communications officer, who began taking down the antenna. Conner still stood there, not understanding what they were going to do. Gurion stood up and answered his unasked question.

"Well, my American friend. There is good news and there is bad news. Which do you prefer to hear first?"

"I always like good news," Conner answered as the Israeli officer put an arm on his shoulder and led him away from the small summit.

"The good news is we won't have to walk all the way back to Israel, but before the helicopters can pick us up we'll have to cover about one hundred thirty kilometers in the next two days."

"By foot?"

"Of course," Gurion smiled. "Now for the bad news . . ."

*Aboard the Airborne Laser Laboratory,
above Cypress*

Lance opened his eyes when he felt someone tugging on his shoulder. Too bad, he thought, he'd been dreaming of home, and Mandy. His ears popped as he looked around, his neck stiff from sleeping upright in the seat.

Dixie sat down in the chair on his right after she was sure he was awake. She plugged her headset in and punched up on the test crew net.

"We're about to land," she said. "Last stop before the desert."

"You ever been to Greece?" he asked sleepily.

"Never."

"Let's take a look," he said, reaching over to power up the beam control system. He'd already run a complete system test on the trip over. And then tested it again. There had been plenty of time. Without even counting the three-hour layover at Torrejon Air Base in Spain, they'd been flying for over fourteen hours. They had already busted the crew-duty day limitation as prescribed in the regulations, something they would never have done during the ALL tests. Obviously this was different. If it wasn't for Colonel Kirk's assistance up front, Jones and Red would have been wasted by now. Kirk wasn't an Air Force pilot, but he held a private twin-engine rating. Catching on to the techniques of flying this four-engine behemoth didn't take him long.

During the approach to landing in Spain, Lance had found the beam director's targeting video camera gave them a rather good view of what was going on outside the plane, and he could aim it to look any direction he wanted.

With the system powered up, he went through a quick readiness check and then touched the appropriate area on the monitor to release the controls to the manual system. Using the joystick he pointed the system forward, checking on their flight path. They were heading east, according to the direction readout at the bottom of the display. Panning to the right he could see the blue waters of the Mediterranean. The shoreline was beautiful. Clean. Except for one area farther to the east, where the beach looked black.

Probably a remnant of the huge oil spill from the previous year.

"Eagle three three, turn north to heading zero seven zero and descend to five thousand feet. Contact Tower and good day." Lance and Dixie were both monitoring the aircrew net on their interphones.

Lance punched up auto-track on the console and released the grip. He hadn't had a lot of chance to check this new feature during the straight and level flight of the past dozen hours, and this was as good an opportunity as he might get.

"The auto-track works pretty well," he said to Dixie as the plane banked to the left. The image in the monitor didn't move, the beam control subsystem imparting signals to the control motors in the turret to compensate for the turn of the aircraft.

"Yeah," Dixie replied. "Let's see what it does when the wing moves into the field."

Just as she released her microphone button, the airplane's right wing came up and into the screen, passing slowly from right to left. Once the wing was out of the picture, they studied the image closely.

"It's rotated slightly," Lance commented.

"Yes, but that's unavoidable. You can see the point in the center of the frame is unchanged. As we move, the field has to rotate if the target is to remain centered."

"Right." Lance knew he should have realized that. Too tired.

By now the target was nearly behind the plane,

and Lance keyed the grip again, sluing the turret to select another target. Just ahead and to the right of the plane was another aircraft, its signature clearly visible in the other display, an infrared scanner.

Lance took advantage of this excellent opportunity and switched back to auto-track. They could obviously track stationary targets, but what about something airborne, something moving. It would be just like their planned mission. He released the grip. The infrared image remained motionless in the center of the frame.

"Excellent!"

Dixie smiled.

"Eagle Three Three to Tower, we have you in sight."

"Roger, Three Three. Continue descent and be advised of a commercial jet at twenty miles, three o'clock. You are cleared to land, runway two-one."

"Roger, Tower, cleared to land. We have the jet in sight."

Lance recognized Kirk's voice, wondered if he was going to land the plane. He wouldn't be a bit surprised if Jones was going to let him. The commercial jet they were tracking looked like a 727 from the twin heat plumes near the tail, and was passing to the four o'clock position now. Lance reached forward to key the auto-focus mechanism when he noticed the image was getting fuzzy. Before he touched the focus control, the target plane disappeared from the screen. A slight jolt indicated the pointer had slammed into its mechanical stops.

"What the hell was that?" Dixie asked. She reached up to disable the auto-track mode.

"I don't know," Lance replied, sharing her concern. Whatever the problem was, it could be fatal if it weren't corrected before the mission. "It wasn't me. I didn't even touch the stick when the system broke lock."

"Try it again," Dixie instructed, punching up the tape drive to record the electrical signals from the FLIR. "It looked like the tracker lost signal and the servo control mechanism had no idea where to point the system, but it should have caged in the center instead of running away like that."

Lance swung the beam director aft, looking for the jet again. He spotted it, still close enough and bright enough to track. Dixie enabled the auto-track, and Lance keyed the grip, then released it.

"Looks good," Lance said.

Less than half a second later, the gimbals ran away again, the beam director stopping only after it rammed the mechanical stops a second time.

"Damn it!" Dixie practically screamed. "Try it again."

Lance took control of the system and searched for the target. He found it, but it was too far away, its signal too small to track.

"Try a stationary target," Dixie instructed.

Lance rotated the beam director forward, looking for a ground target. He could see the approaching runway, could tell they were close to landing. He hadn't even locked on anything when the system broke away again. Lance hit the reset button and caught the runaway system before it slammed into the stops.

"We better secure it," he told Dixie. "We're almost on the ground."

Dixie reached up to shut off the recorder, and Lance hit the switch to shut the eyelid, the movable plate that rolled up to cover the beam directing telescope. They powered down the system and rotated their seats into landing position just as the pitch of the engines decreased. Lance felt the nose of the plane come up slightly, and seconds later they were on the ground.

As if they didn't have enough problems, it felt like the plane was skewing to the side as the thrust reversers were applied. Then the brakes were engaged, much earlier than Lance thought they should be. The brake linings screamed in protest, then began to chatter as they got hot. Lance hoped the plane wasn't having problems now, too. If it was, Chief Warren would lose his rest time making repairs.

He wouldn't be alone. Lance knew he and Dixie would have to try and figure out why the system kept crashing before they could even consider taking on the Syrian plane.

Lance looked at the printout again, hoping to see something he'd missed, something that might explain the erratic action of the beam director.

"Anything?" Kirk asked, leaning against the side of the aft door frame.

Lance jumped, he was so lost in concentration, he didn't notice anyone had come in. "No, not a thing."

Kirk walked up behind Lance and looked over his shoulder. The printout, a lazy flat line broken by three vertical marks, was dimly illuminated by the glow of the beam control subsystem console lights. "Are these the break-locks?" he asked, tapping each of the vertical lines in sequence.

"Yes, this is the signal from the azimuth position transducer. It gives me the position of the beam director as a function of time. The elevation transducer signal looks the same. Then here"—Lance pulled over another sheet, laying it on top of the first and holding the pair over a makeshift lightbulb—"are the signals from the computer telling the servomotors where to position the gimbals. They show the same ambiguities."

Kirk nodded in agreement. He could see the shadows of the bottom trace through the upper paper with the added illumination from the light.

"Now," Lance continued, "here are the signals from the computer, after it has processed the tracker signals. Nothing."

The line was mostly flat, only slowly rising as the target apparently moved past, mostly in Azimuth.

"So what's the verdict?" Kirk asked, stepping forward to let another worker by.

Lance didn't know what to answer, slowly shaking

his head. "I don't know," he finally replied. "It almost looks like some kind of interference. But from what?"

"Isolated?"

"To what?" Lance didn't understand the question.

"Is the interference isolated to the immediate area? Did it happen anywhere else?"

"I can't really say for sure. We never had a chance to use the auto-track against a real target until we were in the landing pattern here, and that's when it broke lock. If it doesn't work . . ." Lance stopped himself when some more workers came into the back of the plane.

"If it doesn't work against our primary target," he continued, his voice lower, "we're going to be in bad shape. I might be able to track it manually, but only if it doesn't move around much. And even then it will be risky."

Kirk sat down in the chair next to Lance. "Is there anything else you can check?"

"I can't think of anything."

Kirk looked up at the console. "It's a lot different than the displays we used to use, isn't it?"

"A lot."

"Even back then we were taking a risk. No one really knew if the system would work."

"We had a pretty good idea it would."

"No, *I* had a pretty good idea it would work. As I recall, you were still a skeptic."

Lance smiled. "You're right. The eternal pessimist."

Kirk returned the smile, recalling the night before the last test mission in California when Lance had voiced his concerns. Kirk remembered calling him an eternal pessimist then. "Still the pessimist?"

Lance thought for a second. "I suppose."

"Well, you're going to have to ignore your pessimism one more time. We're going in. There was a chance we wouldn't have to, but I just found out we're the only option left. Less than fifteen hours before launch. The mission brief is in twelve hours. You better get some rest. Where's Dixie?"

"I sent her back to the hotel. She's more worried about this problem than I am. She worked on it for almost twenty-four hours straight." Lance stopped speaking as the last worker walked by and out the aft door. "Who are all those guys?"

"Some of our friends from Israel. They've been putting in some special equipment. Among other things an IFF transponder. Identify, friend or foe. It's loaded with the codes to help us get through Israeli airspace without getting shot down by their own defense network. Unfortunately, it's only good on the western border, the eastern border doesn't recognize any IFF signals. They're afraid the Syrians or Jordanians might discover the codes and use them to sneak through."

"Then, how do we get through to Syria?"

"That'll be part of the mission brief, but essentially

there'll be a no-shoot corridor set up at the time we expect to go through. It's a standard way of allowing your own aircraft to transit an air defense zone, by setting up a specific time when all weapons are on hold, and then closing the corridor after the period has elapsed.

"I don't know what else Jones has had them putting in. I know he made several long-distance phone calls directly to the Israeli defense minister's office before we left, and he had some of the engineers from the Avionic's Laboratory at Wright Patt putting some stuff on the plane while we were there. Did you see the flare and chaff dispensers mounted outside the plane?"

"No."

"Well, they're there. Let me show you what's in the cockpit."

Lance got up and followed Kirk forward. He had to stoop over to get through the aft bulkhead door, a small opening in the wall that separated the laser from the back of the plane. Once through they walked along the narrow passageway on the left side of the plane.

"How much gold did you say was in these?" Kirk asked, pointing at the spot where the nitrous oxide tank once resided. A large flat box was now installed, one of two dozen. Below each box was the power supply for an electrical heating system, used to vaporize the precious metal.

"Only about six pounds," Lance replied. "In each box."

Kirk shook his head as he continued toward bulkhead. Once through the small opening, they shut the door behind them.

"What *is* all this stuff?" Lance asked.

"To tell you the truth, I don't even know," Kirk replied, looking at several new video monitors between the pilot and copilot's seat. There was also a new panel back by the navigator's console. It held a variety of switches, mostly unlabeled, and a new radio set. "Jones must think he's a fighter pilot again. I wouldn't be surprised if he's got a Gatling gun mounted in the nose. If he doesn't, it's not because he didn't try, probably didn't have enough time."

"I hope he won't need any of this stuff."

"Me, too. Just make sure your beam control system is up, and we won't have to worry about it."

"We'll do our best."

"I know. Let's get back to the hotel and get some sleep before the brief."

Kirk led the way, climbing down the ladder just behind the pilot's seat. Once both men were down, he pushed the ladder back up into the hatch and swung the door shut, locking it.

"So much for seeing Cypress," Lance said, following the colonel out of the hangar into the crisp night air.

"Yeah, there isn't always a lot of time for sightseeing. Maybe on the way back . . ."

14

D-Day minus Three
USS Nimitz

> PERSONAL FOR: COMMANDER, AIR WING SEVEN
> FROM: COMNAVCENT
> SUBJECT: OPERATION SILENT EAGLE, CLASSI-
> FIED TOP SECRET/SPECIAL ACCESS REQUIRED
> REFERENCE: PERSONAL FOR MESSAGE DATE/
> TIME GROUP 164523Z.
> (TS/SAR) CENTCOM OPERATION SILENT EAGLE
> IS GO FOR IMMEDIATE IMPLEMENTATION. SI-
> LENT EAGLE REQUIRES SPECIALLY CONFIG-
> URED AIRCRAFT FOR OVERLAND MISSION.
> BEGIN IMMEDIATE MODIFICATIONS OF TWO
> AIRCRAFT IN ACCORDANCE WITH THE ENGI-
> NEERING CHANGE DOCUMENTS ATTACHED. A
> TOTAL OF FOUR AIRCRAFT, TWO MODIFIED AND
> TWO UNMODIFIED, WILL FORM AN EMBARKED
> DETACHMENT AND WILL BE OPERATIONALLY
> SUBORDINATED TO USAF LEAD ELEMENT,
> CALL SIGN EAGLE THREE THREE. PERSONNEL
> GIVEN ACCESS TO THIS PROGRAM WILL BE
> HELD TO THE ABSOLUTE MINIMUM AND WILL

BE INDOCTRINATED ACCORDING TO NAVAL
SECURITY DIRECTIVES.

Commander Adkins flipped through the attached
sheets, then looked up from the message. "What's
Silent Eagle, sir?"

The admiral pulled a small folder from the open
safe in his at-sea cabin. "It's all in here. From now
on *you* are Silent Eagle. It's a hell of an opportunity
for your band of electron shooters. May even put the
Prowlers on a par with the real attack pilots."

Adkins fought the urge to say something about the
A-6s, but held his mouth in check. Everyone knew
the admiral held little interest in the electronic warfare capabilities of his Air Wing, instead giving most
of his attention to the fighter wings, the F/A-18s,
and F-14s. The A-6s, the Intruders, were held slightly
below the fighters, being the "real" attack planes
as he called them. He held the Prowlers in even
lower esteem than the Intruders, feeling that "electrons" were only slightly useful at best. Adkins
read the message both for what it was, an important mission, and for what the admiral was going
to use it for, a way to get the Prowlers out of his
hair for a while.

Adkins finished the document and handed it back.

"Do what it says, Commander, limit the number
of people you read in. When your guys see the missiles going up on the planes, they're all going to want
in. Believe me, I know. But you don't need all the

ECMOs, certainly not on the planes with the Sidewinders."

He knew the admiral was right, on both counts. There would be no need for the electronic counter measures officers on the Prowlers with the air-to-air missiles, but everyone would want the chance to be aboard a "real shooter."

Cypress

Jones continued, biting on his cigar, using the expandable pointer to indicate the specific area on the map where the Israeli's would be making their strikes after they had taken out the Syrian laser plane.

The mission brief had been interesting, Lance had no idea the whole thing was going to be this complicated. They were even going to have to rely on the Navy for part of the mission, as evidenced by the naval officer, Commander Adkins, sitting near the door. Lance wondered if all the sailors wore the gold-colored scarves. The others involved—Kirk, Dixie, Chief Warren, and Red—all crowded around the front of the table in the small briefing room just inside the hangar.

After a while Lance stopped listening. He was wondering why he hadn't thought this through. The idea of killing everyone aboard the Syrian plane was something he'd had difficulty accepting before, back when it looked as if they would be destroying it with the high-power laser. The relief he experienced when finding out they would only be able to blind the laser radar's sensors had been welcome. Now, finding out their mission was to blind the plane long enough for someone else to destroy it with a missile, his anxiety returned.

The feelings didn't last long, Lance's neck tensed when Jones brought up an aerial photograph on the overhead projector.

"Finally," Jones continued, "with the laser radar plane destroyed and Israeli F-16s taking care of the surface-to-air missile batteries, we will have eliminated Syria's capability to achieve air superiority. Specially inserted Israeli teams will be using laser designators to mark these SCUD missiles for destruction by a squadron of KFIR fighters."

Lance couldn't believe the photograph, taken at apparently close range by a reconnaissance aircraft. There were at least two dozen of the cigar-shaped canisters, most mounted on trailers for rapid repositioning. He wondered about the other tanks at the maintenance facility, the large ones. Surely they weren't all needed for fuel. "Are those . . . ?" he started to ask, pointing at the largest of the tanks.

"We think so," Jones answered. "These SCUDs are armed with chemical warheads, capable of devastating entire cities. So you see our part of this little war is very important, but we aren't the only major players. Our job is to open the hole, the Israeli Special Ops team and the KFIR attack jets will finish the fight. Finish it for good."

"I didn't know the Syrians were planning to use their SCUDs," Dixie said.

"I didn't even know they had them," Lance said.

"The Israelis believe the Syrians plan to use the SCUDs as a negotiating tool, and it makes sense. Simply achieving air superiority wouldn't buy Syria anything. To gain what they want, they would have to launch a ground offensive. They already know they would have a tough time defeating the Israeli armor, even if they control the air. By threatening to use chemical warheads in the SCUDs, maybe even launching one or two to prove they mean business, the Syrians can blackmail the Israelis. For our mission to be truly successful, the SCUD batteries will have to be destroyed. That will buy Israel some time, time needed to complete testing and deployment of their Arrow antimissile system."

"There's going to be a lot of planes in the sky over there," Kirk said.

"A hell of a lot, but that shouldn't bother us. Most of them won't show until after we've finished our job. We're going to be a small but important player in this little air battle. Until we knock out the laser radar, no one else can play. It'll be an Air Force gig until then."

"Don't forget the Navy," Commander Adkins stood up in the back of the room.

"Right." Jones nodded at the sailor. "You guys ready?"

Adkins looked at his watch, a large silver timepiece. "Should be, I'm going to head back to the carrier as soon as the brief's over. The Prowlers should be armed by the time I get back. We'll wait until we get word you're airborne before we launch, that'll conserve fuel. We'll rendezvous near the coast."

"Okay. Unless there are any questions, I think we're done."

There were none. Adkins grabbed his helmet bag and rushed out the door. Lance waited for Dixie and walked out with her toward the plane. The hangar doors were partly open, and they stopped to watch Adkins as he walked toward the A-6 waiting on the ramp, pulling a parachute over his shoulder as he went. The Intruder was already running, a Marine captain sitting at the controls. Adkins pulled his chute on and climbed into the right seat. In less than three minutes, the round-nosed plane was taxiing toward the runway, the canopy coming down as it moved. They watched it take off.

"Hell of a way to get to work," Lance said as the noise from the Intruder's twin engines abated.

"Yeah," Dixie replied. "I thought the pilots sat on the left?"

"They do," Red answered, walking up behind

them. "He told me he had to catch a ride from the A-6 because his plane was getting checked out for the mission."

"A-6? I thought that was an EA-6B," Lance asked.

"They're almost the same thing, the EA-6B, the Prowler, is the electronic warfare version of the A-6 Intruder. The Prowler has four seats and a lot of electronic gear. Adkins will be flying lead off the carrier."

USS Nimitz

Adkins didn't like riding in the right seat, didn't like relying on someone else making the trap, let alone a Marine. He checked the ball and pushed his head back against the restraint. The gear slammed against the deck as the hook grabbed the number three wire, engines roaring as the pilot pushed them to full throttle, a safety precaution against a failed landing attempt. When he was sure he was safely on the deck, the marine pulled the throttles back, raising the canopy to let his passenger get out.

Commander Adkins pulled off his helmet and safed the ejection seat before climbing out. He tossed the helmet to the plane captain and climbed down. The Intruder was already being towed to the elevator when he got to the hatch.

The crotch straps of his parachute were choking him, so he popped the buckle loose as he made his way down the passageway to the ready room. He walked into the smoke-filled room and, with the assistance of a lieutenant, shed his chute and stood it upright in the corner. He counted heads—the nine men he needed to brief were all present, as well as the chief of maintenance.

"Get the door," he began as he pulled the charts out of his thigh pocket. "Senior Chief, are the planes ready?"

"Ready and armed, sir," the maintenance chief replied. "You got two Prowlers with AIM-9s and two with HARMs. Ordinance wanted me to let you know the Sidewinders were patched into the HARM launch switches. They wanted me to tell you good luck, too, this ain't never been done before."

"I know, hell of a deal isn't it, Senior Chief, Prowlers shooting air-to-air missiles. We're writing a page in history here," Adkins said, as much to pique the interest of the other men in the room as to reply to the maintenance officer. "Go check with the air boss, tell him we expect to launch at zero three hundred."

"Aye-aye, sir."

Adkins waited until the senior chief left, waited until the door was closed.

He tossed the chart to a lieutenant, the one who helped him with the parachute. "Put it on the board."

The lieutenant took the chart to the front of the room and started to hang it while Adkins began.

"I'm dead serious about making history today,

gentlemen, and not only in the way the senior chief thinks. Unfortunately, this is one of those bits of history you won't be able to tell anyone about until after you're dead.''

15

D-Day minus One
Cypress

The hangar doors opened, exposing the ALL to the darkness preceding dawn. Chief Warren supervised, coordinating the ground crew's efforts to pull the aircraft out of the hangar. The British ground crew was inexperienced with the big Boeing aircraft, but you couldn't really tell by the way they handled themselves. Meticulous. Every move checked and rechecked. The penalty paid was in the time it took them to get the job done. Warren cursed under his breath as yet another crewman checked the connection to the tow cart. He had already checked it himself, it was fine.

"What the hell's going on out there, Chief?" Jones asked over the interphone.

Chief Warren, connected to the airplane's communication system by a cable hooked to the plane just aft of the forward door, keyed his mike switch and shouted to be heard above the loud roar of the ground power cart sitting nearby.

"The hired help is kind of slow. We're almost ready to move now."

Another crewman, the foreman, held his flashlight above his head. The others, wingwalkers stationed around the airplane, held their lights aloft as well, signaling they were ready. The foreman waved his light. The man driving the tug acknowledged the signal with his own light, and Warren breathed a sigh of relief. They were finally ready to move the plane.

Warren looked back to make sure the chocks were pulled. The muscles in his neck tightened, and he filled with rage when he saw the plane move *backward*, then jerk to a stop.

"What the hell are they doing?" he could hear Jones scream in his ears.

Warren didn't answer immediately, waving his light and running toward the tug driver, screaming at him to stop. The idiot still had the tug in reverse. Warren reached in the tug and hit the kill switch. The foreman came running up behind him.

"Don't say a word," Warren screamed at the apologetic look on the foreman's face. "I'm going back to check the tail, then I'm going to look at the front gear. When I get back, you better have a new driver, one that knows what the hell he's doing."

Warren trotted back to the rear of the plane, flipping the interphone cord out of the way so it wouldn't get hung on the tires.

"The idiot forgot to put the tug in forward," he yelled into the microphone. "I'm going to check for damage to the rudder."

"Hurry your ass up," Jones yelled, barely capable of containing his own anger. "The window is close enough as it is, we don't need any delays."

Warren looked up when he got to the back of the plane. The rudder appeared to be in good shape, still a good twelve inches from the back wall. At the closest approach, Warren estimated, the tail was probably only two or three inches from the wall, two or three inches from screwing this mission for good. Before they launched, he'd have Jones go through the range of motions of the elevators and rudder just to make sure there were no problems.

Running back to the front of the plane, he bent down to check the nosewheel where the tow bar was hooked. Everything looked good on the wheel, but the upper strut had more hydraulic fluid on it than Warren felt comfortable with. Looking up into the wheel well, he could see no cause for the excess fluid, but the pressure from the takeoff on the accelerated runway and the erratic wheel control on landing here in Crete had him worried about the front landing gear. He knew Jones wasn't going to like what he had to say.

"We've got a lot of hydraulic fluid leaking from the forward strut. I recommend taking a hit, pulling the access panel to make sure we haven't broken anything."

Jones knew Warren wouldn't have said anything unless he was sure it was a flight safety issue. "How long?"

"Two hours if I do it myself, three if these guys help."

"You've got one hour; Red will give you a hand."

Red was out of his seat and on his way down the ladder before Jones could give him the order. "Mission Director, this is pilot."

"Go," Kirk answered, having already heard what had happened.

"We're down for an hour. Flight safety."

"Roger. Can you get back to the office and make the call to CENTCOM?"

"Can do. I'll go right now."

Lance, having monitored the net himself, asked permission to power up the computer.

"Negative," Kirk replied. "We won't be able to afford the time. I don't want these locals to fool with the power cart, and Warren's too busy to hook it up. And I don't want anyone leaving the plane, either. You can get up and walk around, but that's all."

"Understand," Lance replied, resigning himself to a long, restless hour in the back of the plane while he waited for the flight mechanic to check out the strut.

"See anything?" Red asked.

"Yeah, plenty, but I still can't tell where the hydraulic fluid is leaking from. It doesn't look like the main seal, though. That's good. It could be that it only leaks under high pressure."

"Like during landing?"

"Yeah."

Warren climbed back down out of the front wheel well. He was still concerned, but there was nothing he could really do. If it was leaking under high pressure, the whole assembly would probably have to be removed and checked out on a test stand. Certainly couldn't be done here, they didn't have the facilities.

Red took a cloth from the tool cart and tried to wipe the hydraulic fluid off his flight suit. There were several spots on it now, not the kind of presentation he liked to make.

"You'll never wipe that stuff off," Warren told him, smiling at the pilot's predicament. "You'll have to turn your flight suit in when you get back to the base and get a new one. Unless you want to keep it, sir, you almost look like you work for a living now."

"Not hardly," he replied, still wiping at the stain.

Warren checked his watch. Forty-five minutes. Add five minutes to get the panel back on and the tools pushed out of the way, and he was going to beat the colonel's deadline by ten minutes. Not much, but this was one of those times when every second counted.

"Give me a hand putting this panel back on."

Red dropped his rag and grabbed the sheet metal cover, hoisting it into place so Warren could install the fasteners.

*   *   *

The new driver was steady, pulling the plane from the tight confines as directed by the foreman. He never took his eyes off his guide, following the flashlights into the new, crisp morning.

"Clear," Warren called as the wings brushed past the hangar doors without touching.

Twenty more feet and the foreman crossed the lights over his head, signaling the tug driver to stop. Another man rushed forward and disconnected the tow bar from the nose gear. The tug cart moved away. Warren hooked the start cart up to the number one engine, and Jones started it.

"Switching power," Red called over the interphone as he reached up from the copilot's seat and flipped the switch.

Lance could hear the Environmental Control System come up first, the blowers working to reduce the temperature in the plane. It was warm back there. Lance was sweating, even without his flight jacket on. Thank goodness he didn't have to wear his helmet this time, the runway was more than long enough for them to get airborne. They didn't even have to limit their fuel this time. Four hours and fifteen minutes worth. More than enough. He hoped.

"Beginning preflight checklist," Lance called on the test net, using the more comfortable headset in place of his helmet, still sitting in the helmet bag at his feet.

"Negative," Kirk replied. "No time."

"But, sir, we don't know if the glitch is still there. We were relying on the preflight to tell us."

"Sorry. We have to hope it's not. Besides, we can test it on the way out. Pilot, this is Mission."

"Go."

"We're going to skip the system's preflight. That'll save us twenty minutes."

"Roger. We should be airborne in fifteen minutes, then."

Lance glanced at Dixie, sitting on his right, then over his shoulder at Kirk. Kirk had his helmet on, the sun visor pulled down. Lance couldn't see his face. He was sure Dixie held his same concern, could tell from the way she avoided his gaze. She turned her chair to the rear in preparation for takeoff. Lance turned his own chair around as well.

"Request permission to power up as soon as possible after we're airborne," Lance asked over the test crew net.

"As soon as we can," Kirk agreed.

Jones jammed the throttles home, letting the new engines push the airplane forward. Slowly at first, then faster as the efficient engines wound up to 100 percent of thrust.

"It still feels stiff," he said, centering the nosewheel on the centerline of the runway.

In the back, the plane felt like it was jerking from one side of the runway to the other. At first Lance thought it was the wind, but there had been only a slight wisp when they got into the plane earlier. Surely it wasn't that.

"It's locked up. I can't move it." Jones was struggling with the nose gear, trying to get it back on the centerline. It wouldn't budge, and they were heading for the grass at the edge of the asphalt.

Jones glanced at the airspeed. They weren't going quite fast enough to take off. "Pull it up!" he yelled anyway, hoping to use ground effect again.

Red yanked back on the yoke, jerking the plane into the air, just barely above the concrete runway. He let the nose back down, holding the plane just above the ground, using the ground effect to stay airborne until the airspeed increased. Drifting far to the left, they finally reached rotation speed, and he pulled up hard on the yoke.

"Eagle Three Three, Tower. Immediate left turn heading zero seven zero to avoid incoming heavy."

Jones pulled hard on the yoke, trying to clear the area as the C-141 passed just below the ALL on the right.

"What next?" Jones asked no one in particular. "Just once I'd like to make a normal takeoff in this thing."

"I hate to tell you this, Colonel," Chief Warren said, "but you're going to have to make a normal landing before you get a chance to try a normal take-off. I don't like the way the nose gear hung up on the roll out. It doesn't look good. May have something to do with that hydraulic fluid leak."

"I thought you said you couldn't find anything?"

"I said we didn't find anything, not that we couldn't. The strut itself may be bent. We wouldn't be able to determine that unless we pulled the entire gear."

"All right, all right. Let's take care of the mission, then we'll worry about getting this thing back down. Red, contact Eagle Escort, get 'em airborne."

USS Nimitz

Adkins sat in the lead bird on Ready Five, five minutes to launch when they got the word. He was flying one of the standard Prowlers, loaded with an ALQ-99 electronic jammer and two HARMs, High Speed Anti-Radiation Missiles. His lieutenant manned the primary Electronic Counter Measures Officer position, ECMO One, on his immediate right. The lieutenant junior grade manned ECMO Two in the back. ECMO Three was empty—no sense risking another crew member when the threat they would encounter was rather well known. The Syrian surface-to-air systems were well understood, Soviet export equipment much like what they had faced in Iraq. ECMO Two had also loaded the Israeli radar parameters into the threat computer, just in case the corridor closed before they got through. Adkins had pooh-poohed the idea at first, but let the lieutenant

JG do what he thought was best. Now he was glad the lieutenant had the threat data loaded. They were already an hour late, and the Israelis were noted for promptness. Even if they made it through the corridor on the way in, there was little chance they would get back through before it closed up again. There were just too many little things that could go wrong, things that would cost precious extra minutes.

"Ready Five, prepare to launch."

Finally. "Roger," Adkins replied.

Adkins throttled up the engines. The airplane strained under the force of the engines. They didn't have long to wait, the launch officer slapped the ground, and time stopped. It always stopped. The launcher had to build up enough pressure before it could hurtle the plane forward, sometimes taking up to four seconds to do so. Then the world went flashing by, the plane accelerating to over one hundred fifty knots in less than three hundred feet.

The KA-6 tanker was already flying overhead. Adkins would top off and wait for the others to get airborne. This was his own Prowler strike force, all four EA-6Bs in the carrier were in his strike package.

"Wizard Alpha, this is Wizard Bravo, airborne and on our way."

Wizard bravo was the other conventional Prowler. The others, Wizard Charlie and Wizard Delta were armed with Sidewinders in placed of their HARMs. Adkins could imagine the looks of the fighter jocks on Vulture's Row, the lookout on the bridge of the ship, and every other fighter pilot's expression when word got around there were two Prowlers armed with air-to-air missiles. They'd be screaming at the Air Wing commander to tell them why they hadn't gone on the mission. After all, it was their job to take care of the air-to-air missions.

Too bad for them, Adkins smiled. Something as simple as a gold coating on the Prowlers windscreens had made the mission his, a coating originally designed to protect them from the powerful electromagnetic radiation from the jamming pods. Now it would be used to protect them from the blinding laser energy.

In less than fifteen minutes his strike package was formed around him. Adkins led them away to the east, looking for the big Air Force bird he'd seen in the hangar on Cypress.

16

D-Day minus One
Above the Mediterranean, outside Israeli airspace

"Eagle Three Three, this is Wizard Alpha. Do you copy?"

"Roger, Wizard Alpha. Copy. State your location." Jones would be the one coordinating the air battle. Kirk would manage the operation of the laser from the back of the plane.

"Eagle Escort is now six miles to your rear. We have you on radar and will rendezvous in three minutes."

"Roger, Wizard Alpha. Anticipate your approach and will begin descent as soon as you've formed up."

Jones switched to the test crew net. "Mission, did you copy the transmission from Eagle Escort?"

"Roger. We're ready."

Ready. Right. We still haven't been able to re-create the anomaly with the auto-track system, Lance thought. I wouldn't call that ready.

"How's the laser?" Kirk asked, walking up behind them just like he used to do in the old days, dragging his interphone cord along.

"Nominal," Dixie said. "The heaters are up to temperature, and the cavity pressure is right on line. We won't have any trouble with the laser; we'll be running it slightly below its maximum capability. That shouldn't stress it much as long as we don't have to run it too long. If some of the modules fail, we can always bring one of the spares on line."

"Beam control?"

"Everything looks okay," Lance said. "We still haven't seen a repeat of the problem. We seem to be ready."

"Why don't you look for the EA-6Bs, see if you can validate the auto-track performance against flying targets."

"Good idea. They should be right behind us." Lance thumbed a switch, dropping the eyelid, then used the joystick to turn the turret directly aft. It didn't take long for him to spot them, four hot, closely spaced targets flying an intercepting course. He selected one and punched the auto-track setting on the touch screen, then let go of the stick.

"Looks good," Kirk said.

"So far," Lance agreed. The tracker followed the selected target, signaling the beam director to turn slightly as the Prowler approached. The tracker continued to follow it as the four heat sources split up.

Two passed to the left and two passed to the right, closing at over one hundred knots.

The beam director followed the target precisely as it passed the ALL, exceeding the design specifications on angular slew rate in the process.

"Wow," Lance exclaimed as the exhaust plume of the jet engine saturated the infrared tracker. The electronic circuitry diminished the signal so the auto-track algorithm could maintain its lock.

"One of my additions," Dixie said, proud to show off some of the improvements she'd made to the system. "It's got seven decades of dynamic range now."

"That's terrific. It used to have only four. The original algorithm would have lost its lunch if it saw a signal change that quickly."

Lance, Dixie, and Kirk studied the image as the tracker continued to follow the target. The four birds split in two directions, two to the left and two to the right, coming around to form up on the ALL. The Prowlers moved into position, two off each wing.

"The video is amazing," Jones called from the front of the plane. He was watching on one of the video monitors the engineers had installed in the cockpit when the plane was in Dayton. "It's almost as good as watching TV."

Lance took control of the joystick again. "Let's try an aim-point correction," he said. A quick click of the thumb switch, and the image of the Prowler was frozen on the screen. "The system is still tracking the target, as you can see in the infrared display," he explained to Kirk as he worked, pointing at the left-hand monitor. "What I'm doing now is telling the computer to offset the aim point from the hot part of the target."

A small white cursor in the shape of a "+" appeared just behind the tail of the plane, the hot part of the exhaust the infrared system had used to track the Prowler. Using the joystick, Lance moved the cursor forward, toward the cockpit. When Lance had it positioned properly, he flipped the thumb switch again, releasing the tracker to the computer. The pilot of the Prowler, Commander Adkins, was centered in the middle of the screen.

"Perfect," Kirk passed judgment. "I think it works fine." Kirk flipped over to the aircrew net. "Let's go for it!"

"Roger," Jones replied over the interphone. Next he keyed his radio: "Eagle Escort. We're a go. I'm heading for the deck, you guys follow me in. Stay tight. I want to avoid the urban areas and follow the preplanned ingress route."

"Wilco, Strike Leader," Adkins replied. "You understand the corridor will now be closed when we get there?"

Shit. Jones hadn't realized they were so late already. He pointed the nose down and trimmed the elevator to hold it there. "Roger," he answered Adkins. "We'll just have to open it back up. From now on, all comm will be over the secure net."

"Going secure," Adkins called from Wizard Alpha.

ECMO One in all four Prowlers engaged the crypto gear, sending the voice communications secure.

Red did the same in Eagle Three Three.

"Any chance you can get those guys in the back to quit pointing that big eyeball at me?" Adkins asked over the secure net. "It feels like the gaze of one of Medusa's serpents . . . Spooky."

"Going off-line," Warren said over the interphone.

"Make it quick," Jones said. "Give everyone in back a chance to take a leak before we get in close."

Warren gave him the thumbs-up as he stepped away from the navigator's console. He wouldn't be able to stay connected to the interphone as he walked through the laser compartment, the bulkhead doors wouldn't let him. He opened the front bulkhead and stepped through, closing the door behind him. As he walked through the device compartment, he took a quick look around for anything that might affect the airplane's flight worthiness. The main thing he noticed was the temperature, much hotter than it had been in there before. The heaters, that was it. Jones had told him the laser's heating elements would be hot enough to melt gold. Warren hoped that was all the heaters melted. They hadn't really gotten approval for those systems to be aboard, probably couldn't have gotten it if they tried. Of course, this wouldn't be the first time they had bent the rules to get an experiment in the air.

By the time he got the aft bulkhead door shut behind him, his flight suit was soaked with sweat. He brushed behind Kirk as he passed down the aisle to the urinal in the back of the plane. He plugged into an extra interphone net before he stepped behind the canvas hanging from the ceiling, a modification installed in deference to their female crew member. He listened to Jones as he drilled their escort.

". . . and make damn sure they stay up."

"Aye, aye, sir. The shades will stay up. Makes it tough to see out the front though. Mind telling us why?"

"Because the gold coating only covers the aft section of your canopy, the front sections are bare. The laser beam would slice through if the front wasn't covered. There wouldn't be much left of your eyes if you took a direct hit."

"How are you guys going to be protected?" Adkins asked.

"Special goggles, got 'em out of the lab at Wright-Patt when they put the laser aboard. We'd have sent some back with you when you came to Cypress, but I don't think you could have used them. They're big bulky things, would have interfered with your helmets. We're going to stay on cabin air as long as possible, hopefully for the entire mission. The guys in the back will just keep the windows covered, they don't really need to see out."

"Five thousand feet, boss," Red warned.

"Beginning round out," Jones said over the radio, pulling back slightly on the yoke. "We'll level off at seven five zero feet."

"Fifty miles from the Air Defense Identification Zone," Chief Warren said, now back from his pit stop.

"How's everything look back there?" Jones asked.

"Looks okay. The test crew is all huddled around that one screen, pointing the beam director back and forth between the escorts, like they're playing some kind of video game."

"I heard that," Kirk said over the intercom, letting them know he was still patched into the aircrew circuit.

Warren smiled.

"All right, sailors, tighten up. Wizard Alpha, you're way too far out. I want it to look like we're one big target if we get picked up by a surveillance radar. And shut down your radar altimeters, and any other emitters you have on. We'll rely on my sensors alone."

"Twenty miles," Chief Warren said.

"Radio silence until we're engaged or someone picks up a threat," Jones ordered. "If we're lucky, we'll get through Israeli airspace without getting tagged."

Two brief clicks in his headset was enough to confirm the message had been received and understood.

Everyone got quiet. Even in the back Lance could sense the tension building. He used the time to search the area, using the laser beam director as his eyes. There was little to see, navigation lights from an airliner departing the Tel Aviv airport, but that plane was departing to the south, moving away from them. A quick check to the north revealed nothing.

Lance continued to survey the area, Dixie watching over his shoulder. Kirk was sitting in his own chair, watching the radar altimeter display on his test director's console, waiting for the abrupt rise that would indicate they were over land.

"Wizard Alpha, this is Wizard Charlie. I have a radar warning. Surveillance."

"Copy, Six. Strike leader, did you hear that?"

So much for staying silent. Jones hadn't really expected them to be off the radio for long, this wasn't the kind of mission that could be performed without adequate command and control, and that meant emanating comm signals.

If the game wasn't up now, it would be soon, Jones knew. If the surveillance radar picked them up, the Israeli air defense systems would come up to greet them, and it was a formidable defense, fighters, anti-aircraft artillery, and the most lethal threat—surface-to-air missiles.

"That's a roger, Wizard Alpha. L-Band surveillance radar at one six five. Must be the HAWK battery at Afula. I doubt if we're in their range at this point." Jones hoped. Fortunately, their RAW gear, used for radar warning, would pick up the emanations from the acquisition radar long before they were close enough to the threat radar to be seen. "Watch for a Patriot radar, though. There are still a few of them out here in the desert. They're directed toward Iraq, but the radar coverage extends in this direction."

"Feet dry!" Adkins called from Wizard Alpha.

Jones pulled back on the yoke, climbing to maintain one thousand feet AGL, one thousand feet above the ground. The four Prowlers were right on his wing tips, hanging tight through the maneuver. That was good. If there was one thing he didn't want to worry about, it was having to keep tabs on his escorts.

"Punch up 4265 on the commercial transponder and set it to standby," Jones told Chief Warren. It was part of the agreement he'd made with the Israeli general in Cypress. In case something went wrong, he was to flash that code on his transponder, a device used by air traffic controllers to keep track of all the planes in the area. In normal operation the transponder would not even emit until an air traffic interrogated it, but they had come up with a solution for that problem as well.

When his particular code appeared, the Israelis were to let them through. He hoped. Unfortunately, he was well aware that in operations like this, operations that weren't well publicized, the men who made the difference often didn't get the information in time. In this case the men who counted were the ones in the air defense batteries, manning the HAWKs and the Patriots, their fingers poised over the master fire switches.

"I've got a new signal," ECMO Two called from the backseat of Adkins' plane.

Adkins could tell ECMO Two's voice was strained, a bit higher in pitch than normal.

"High sweep rate, like a Patriot phased array

radar. Yeah, right frequency, too. Looks like the colonel was right. It came up quick, strong. I think it's still in search mode, though."

"What do you mean you *think*?" Adkins almost lost his temper. He didn't like to hear about "possible" threats. "Is it searching or tracking?"

"It's hard to tell sometimes," ECMO One jumped in, defending his buddy in the back. "That phased array radar can scan so damn fast it's unbelievable. It can track several targets while continuing to scan its entire sector looking for more. There aren't any moving parts, the radar beams are electronically steered. From our sensors it can look like one of the old scanning missiles has us in track mode, even though it's just the phased array doing its routine mission, looking for targets.

"Watch the time history of the power level," ECMO One instructed the lieutenant JG in the back. "A big jump in power is a good indication the phased array has dedicated more of the amplifier tubes in our direction, using less for the surveillance. That's the only indication he's got us."

ECMO One barely got the instructions out when ECMO Two saw the signal jump off the screen. He had to turn the gain control on the display down a factor of ten just to bring the signal back into measurable levels. "Consider us got!" he called over the intercom, then got busy loading the parameters into the jammer computer.

"Line of bearing?" Adkins asked.

"Straight off our port side, slowly moving aft."

"Strike leader! Strike leader, this is Wizard Alpha! We have a Patriot fire control off our port wing. He's targeting us now."

"Copy," Jones said. He turned off his radio and punched the intercom. "Hit IDENT! Now!"

Chief Warren reached up to where they had moved the transponder and turned the rotary switch from STANDBY to ON. Then he pushed the silver button that protruded from the panel. A small green light flashed, indicating the system was emitting.

"I hope to hell this works," Jones said to no one in particular as he keyed the radio on again. "Wizard Alpha, are they still tracking?"

"Affirmative."

"Power up the jammers on both birds and get ready to turn the music on. On my mark," Jones ordered. That would be a last resort. Hopefully, one of the air traffic control centers knew what was going on. The ones that didn't would be pissed, he was sure of that. When the IDENT button was pushed, every ATC radar in the local area got an immediate, bright mark on their displays, indicating the location of a special military mission. At the least they would route all civilian traffic out of the area. Hopefully, at least one of them would identify the special code and get word through to the Air Defense Battery, and would tell them to stand down.

* * *

"We're at their optimum launch range . . . now," ECMO Two informed Adkins.

"Steady," Adkins warned him, sensing the rising tension in the lieutenant's voice. He pulled over on the stick to move in closer to the big plane, a difficult proposition at best, even in good weather over this kind of terrain. With the wind they were fighting, he was surprised they hadn't already bumped into the converted tanker.

"I have a launch," ECMO Two screamed into his mike. "Negative, two launches, two SAMs heading this way."

"Wizard Alpha reporting bogies inbound. Two birds at six miles. Request permission to start the music."

"Negative. Just hold on. Wait till they're closer," Jones said, sounding calmer than he really felt. He knew that if they turned their jammers on now, the whole world, including the Syrians, would know where they were. That was something he didn't want to advertise until the last possible minute.

"Three minutes to impact," ECMO Two began the countdown. "They still have track."

"Reduce altitude to five hundred feet," Jones ordered.

"In these clouds?" Adkins asked himself. "Jones is an idiot," he thought, following the big bird down.

"Is he trying to hide in the rocks?" ECMO One asked, gripping the edge of his seat as tight as he could.

"One slip and he'll be wearing rocks," Adkins answered back, trying to hold his plane steady.

"SAM track is becoming intermittent," ECMO Two called, the continuous high-pitched warning tone screaming in his ears was now punctuated with brief periods of silence. The quiet moments became more frequent, lasted longer and longer. He breathed a sigh of relief when the tone stopped completely.

Then the wailing in his ears returned, louder than before.

17

"They've handed off to another radar!" ECMO Two screamed into his mike. "The new radar is off to our right, damn near right under us. It's got a direct line of sight, no way we can hide from it. Estimate twenty seconds to missile impact."

"We've got to turn the music on *now*!" ECMO One warned.

"Strike lead," Adkins called. "New radar set has us. Fifteen seconds to missile impact."

"Jammers free! Light 'em up," Jones called, wishing upon anything he didn't have to. Now the Israelis were going to really think they were under attack.

ECMO One reached forward to energize the emitter in the underwing pod. In seconds the pod would send false signals to the missile, very powerful jamming signals. They were in a microwave oven. The thin gold coating on the windscreen was all that protected them from the radiation.

There would be one substantial difference between the pod's emission and the real radar reflection, a phase change in the beam of electromagnetic energy would cause the missile to misinterpret the direction to the target. The missile would fly by harmlessly. At least that's what the Russian missiles would do. Would the Patriot?

ECMO One had the safety cover up and was touching the switch when the howling in ECMO Two's ears went silent.

"STOP!" ECMO Two yelled, simultaneously reaching down to pop the circuit breaker.

"The radar's off," ECMO Two informed the pilot, giving his reason for countermanding the order to illuminate the missiles with the jammers, it would do no good now. "They're going ballistic, it's going to be close."

"Radar went down on its own, missiles are ballistic," Adkins relayed the information to Jones.

"Thank God," Jones whispered under his breath. "The ATC guys figured it out."

Two bright flashes, almost close enough to touch, appeared right in front of his plane.

"Pull up!" he yelled into the radio as he pulled the yoke back and pushed the throttles full forward.

The Prowlers were right with him as he climbed, the flames and debris passing mostly below them.

"The Patriot crew must have commanded the missiles to self-destruct," Red said once the airplane was level again.

"Yeah," Jones agreed, "but the cure was almost worse than the disease," he said, repeating a thought he'd had at least a hundred times when Jenny was undergoing radiation treatment for her cancer.

"Lead, this is Wizard Charlie," Jones heard one of the other Prowlers call.

"Go," Adkins answered.

"Exhaust gas temperature shot way up on number two when he went through that flame. It dropped some after we were clear, but not all the way to normal. Now it's climbing again."

"Damn!" Adkins said, slamming his fist onto the dash. He was afraid something like that might have happened. An exhaust gas temperature, EGT, problem was a mandatory mission abort according to the NATOPS safety directives.

"Strike lead, this is Wizard Alpha. I've got a down bird. He's got to abort, and I'll have to send someone with him. You still want to try this with only two Prowlers as escorts?"

Jones cursed under his breath. He'd wanted more support just in case something like this happened. Too bad there were only four Prowlers in the *Nimitz's* Air Wing. No matter. There was no turning back now.

"You know the U.S. Air Force, we'll try anything once. We'll proceed with the mission."

"Roger, Strike lead. Wizard Charlie, that's a go home call. Wizard Bravo, you escort Charlie. Think you can make it back to the ship?"

"Maybe. May have to shut number two down and try to limp in on one engine."

"It's been done before. Try to make it back. If you can't, be sure to dump those missiles before you land anywhere else."

"Aye-aye, Skipper."

The two Prowlers on the south side of the Airborne Laser Laboratory peeled away, breaking right. Their navigation lights disappeared quickly in the low clouds.

"What do you think our chances are of pulling this off?" ECMO One asked quietly over the intercom.

"Hell if I know," Adkins answered, "but you know the Air Force motto: They'd rather be dead than look bad. I think Jones is taking it seriously."

"Watch our engines," Jones told his copilot, thinking about what just happened. "If we ingested any of that crap, we've had it, too, and so has the mission."

"I hate flying into the sun," Jones said quietly over the interphone as he pulled the sunglasses out of his pocket.

The weather had broken just after the two Prowlers turned back. The sky ahead was clear blue, still undisturbed by the front approaching from the west.

"Try these," Warren handed a pair of the laser goggles to the pilot.

Jones reached back over his shoulder, taking the huge goggles from Chief Warren. He pulled the elastic strap over his head, over the interphone set's wire harness and around behind his ears. Dropping the bulky optical protectors over his eyes, he marveled at how much the sunlight was reduced. He didn't even have to squint now, even as the sun broke above the horizon. There was one problem with the goggles, though, he couldn't read the lights on his instruments. How was he going to fly if he couldn't read the gauges? He pulled the goggles off and handed them back to the crew chief.

"No, thanks, I'll save them for later. How's it going in the back, Mission?"

"Everything is nominal," Kirk answered, reverting to his use of the one word that said everything, and nothing.

"We've had a few minor glitches in some of the less important subsystems, but they've all cleared up," Kirk informed the pilot.

"Good," Jones replied, caring little. All he wanted to know was if they were ready to fight. "We're still flying on the deck, and we'll stay down here for about thirty more minutes. I'm going to assume the Israeli air defense will ignore us now, considering they've been told to open the corridor back up, and even if they haven't, we'll be flying the wrong direction to be a threat. When we hit the border we'll pop up, try to spook the Syrians. If everything works right, they'll bring the laser plane up against us. Then we'll take him out. Wizard Delta is our only shooter now," Jones continued, going over the plan they all knew would have to be improvised as the action unfolded, "so we're going to have to get it right the first time. I'll give you a five-minute warning before we climb out. Questions? From anyone?"

Lance shook his head, as did Dixie.

"None," Kirk called back, though he knew there was one question they were all asking themselves: *Am I going to get out of this alive?*

"Golan Heights, dead ahead," warned Chief Warren, looking over the heads of the pilot and copilot.

"Yeah." Jones pulled the yoke back to climb up to the plateau. "How far to the border?"

Warren punched the coordinates into the navigation computer. "Twelve minutes."

"Mission, this is pilot. Estimate twelve minutes to the border. We're nearing the Golan Heights now. Think that radar of yours can see anything?"

"Maybe," Kirk replied. "Depends on the terrain masking."

"Go ahead and fire it up. If they haven't seen us yet, it's a good time to let 'em know we're here. We'll continue climbing after we clear the ridge. I guess it's time to go to work." Jones was sweating profusely now. Flying the big overloaded plane so low to the ground was exhausting. He looked forward to a normal climb out for a change.

"Wizard Alpha," Jones called to Adkins, "after clearing the ridge we'll continue to climb to ten thousand feet. Put your thinking caps on and don't make any mistakes. We'll probably only get one shot at this. Let's make it good."

"Roger, Strike lead. Wizard Delta, stay with me in a loose deuce. We'll try to stay hidden from the laser plane by using the 135 as a screen. When we get word the Syrian is blind, we'll go in. Make your shots count, with only two missiles you have to be on target."

"Wizard Delta. Copy."

Adkins wished he was carrying the missiles. With only his jammer and his HARMs, he was useless against the flying platform.

Jones unzipped his pocket and pulled a single sheet of paper out. He handed it back to Warren.

"Turn to that frequency and read the number below it three times in succession. When someone calls back with the bottom number, let me know."

Chief Warren was confused, didn't really know why he was transmitting this strange message, but the procedure was simple, nothing he couldn't handle. He did it, and got an answer on the first try.

"Done," he told Jones.

"Good. That was to let our Israeli friends know we're in position. They'll launch their fighters now, get them airborne and waiting for our signal. As soon as we're done, they'll go in and take out every surface-to-air site they can get to. The Syrians will think the Six Day War was a practice drill before the Israelis get finished with them. I hope they get the chemical missiles first. If they don't, it might get very bad on the Israeli side of the fence."

Eastern Syria

"Another one's leaving," Conner warned.

Gurion crawled up beside him, putting his own

binoculars up to his eyes. He could see the dim head-lights of the transport pull through the gate of the barbed-wire encircled compound. "That makes three."

"Yeah," Conner agreed, "but did any of them leave before we got here?"

"I hope not. Did you see where this one was parked before it left?"

"Just to the left of the building. It was on the end of the first row."

"They seem to be pulling out in sequence, and I don't think there was another row. We probably haven't missed any. Now that the sun is coming out, you can clearly see the tracks of those that have already left. There are only three sets." Gurion turned back to send another pair of his men off in pursuit of the vehicle.

Conner was definitely glad he hadn't been asked to move out and follow any of the trucks. His feet were killing him, he had blisters on top of blisters. It had been a grueling road march. Fortunately, the trucks that had already left hadn't moved far, and had proceeded slowly. That wasn't surprising, the cargo was extremely hazardous, especially since the rockets were already filled with the volatile liquid propellants.

"How much longer?" Conner asked.

"Should have already happened," Gurion told him, checking his watch.

"I hope we don't have to wait much longer. The more of these rockets we have to follow, the greater chance we'll lose one."

"And losing even one is too many."

"I still don't understand why they're staying so close," Conner wondered out loud. "If it were me, I'd disperse as far away as possible. They've seen how quickly the Coalition forces were able to zero in on the mobile launch sites during the war with Iraq. Surely they learned something from that."

"Maybe they don't intend to try and force us to concede by firing on civilian targets, shooting one or two missiles each night," Gurion argued. "Perhaps they're planning an all-out offensive. They don't need to disperse if they intend to fire all their missiles."

"Surely they'll keep some in reserve," Conner countered.

"That would make sense," Gurion agreed. "What if . . . ?" Gurion panned his binoculars to the largest building in the facility, one he had noticed earlier in the night. The building was near the back fence and stood two floors high, but that wasn't what caught Gurion's attention. Next to the building was a tall tower, with a microwave dish near the top. He hadn't seen it in the darkness. Were the missiles staying close to make sure of the microwave link for communications? Did they depend on that system for launch instructions? More importantly, could he destroy it before the orders were sent? That would give the air force more time to find the deployed SCUDs, to destroy them before the deadly missiles were launched.

Gurion needed two men, two good men for this mission. He didn't have many left to choose from.

He would have to send Reitman, but who else? Gurion's eyes locked on the American. The Ranger.

The Airborne Laser Lab

The High Energy Laser Radar Acquisition and Targeting System, known in the early days by its acronym HELRATS, had never been used during the Laser Lab test series. Funding was cut before it could be implemented. This was going to be its first test. A prototype test, developmental test, installation checkout, and operational test, all under combat conditions. If it didn't work, they would have to rely on the optical acquisition device, the monocular back by the door. The OAD was a fine system as long as you knew where the shooter was going to be, like in the preplanned experiments held over the California desert. Here in the desert they had no idea where the target was, would have to rely on visual cueing to slave the OAD to the target, to turn the airplane if necessary to put the target in the OAD's field of view. Not the best way to go into battle.

In the forward fairing, the aerodynamic enclosure on top of the plane that diverted the four-hundred-knot winds around the laser turret, the HELRATS antenna began to rotate. Within the aft fairing, designed to recombine the air that was flowing around the turret into a stable air mass, the electronic brain of the radar device began to look for a return. When it got a signal, the HELRATS computer would translate the target's radar coordinates to a number the beam director could understand, telling it where to find the target. At least that's how it was supposed to work. The problem had yielded a simple analytical solution, but the Air Force engineers charged with developing the hardware quickly found out how difficult the solution was to implement.

Lance reached over and flipped a switch on a panel installed in the console next to his own. The HEL-RATS radar energized quickly, illuminating the area to the left of the airplane with lethal doses of radar frequency energy, only slightly less potent than what came out of the jamming pod on the Prowlers.

"Looks like I've got a contact," Lance called out as soon as they topped the rise and climbed above the Israeli occupied Golan Heights. "Better tell the guys up front they need to put on their goggles."

"Straight flush radar at nine o'clock," ECMO Two called, studying the indications on the radar display. A second light lit up farther ahead. "And another at ten o'clock. They're all over the place."

"Let me know if any of them get a lock," Adkins told him, then relayed the information to Jones.

"We'll stay along here," Jones answered Adkins, "make a pass on the Israeli side of the border to see what we're up against. Look for the best hole. Then we'll make a one eighty and come back. When we get to the hole, we'll turn in."

"What if there isn't a hole?" Adkins asked.

"Then we'll make one." Jones pulled his goggles up slightly to look under them at his airspeed indicator.

"Roger," Adkins answered, watching the other Prowler bouncing around, dangerously close to his left wing. "Find us a hole, ECMO Two, one we can all fit through."

The lieutenant was feverishly plotting his intercepts. He griped under his breath at having to do the work of two men, wondered why they hadn't let ECMO Three come along. They worked well together, were a good team. He was on his own now, though, marking up the airspace chart he held on his knees.

At first there were only a couple of radar indications, but now a solid mass of radar energy appeared on the scope. Each time one radar moved out of the display, another replaced it, a continuous, never-ending picket fence of electronic sentries. Yet it wasn't really the radar that could do them harm, it was the surface-to-air missiles they supported, directed to the targets—to them. And the lieutenant knew that for every radar he spotted, there were four batteries of the deadly missiles.

Jones was level at fifteen thousand feet. Kirk had told him the aerodynamic design of the pointer/tracker had been optimized for best performance at that altitude. Any lower and the vibrations were too much for the system to reject. Any higher and the air wouldn't recombine properly after it passed the aft fairing and would induce even more jitter into the structure. It was also an optimum altitude to get picked up on the Syrian air defense radar system. They were sitting ducks. All they had to protect them was a single Prowler with its ALQ-99 jammer pods and two HARM missiles. And Jones didn't have much confidence in either of them.

"Is he still out there?" Jones called to the back.

"Affirmative." Kirk was still standing over Lance's shoulder. From there he could see the HELRATS tactical display clearly. The Syrian airplane was still there, continuing its circular orbit at twenty-one thousand feet.

"It's almost like he wants everyone to know what he's doing," Dixie said.

"If you didn't already know what he was doing, you would probably never guess," Lance said.

"True," she agreed. "Is that the best picture we can get?" She stared at a small speck in the TV monitor, a speck she assumed was the laser plane.

Lance reached up and selected the menu for the video tracker. The touch-sensitive screen switched to a different display. Lance touched and held the block marked "MAGNIFICATION." A message flashed at the bottom of the screen: MAGNIFICATION AT MAXIMUM SETTING.

"I guess it is," Dixie answered her own question.

"Yeah. We're just too far out to see him in the video camera. Probably at least fifty miles. He's playing it safe, staying well out of range of the Israeli SAMs. You can't really see the target on the normal video, but he shows up well in the infrared. Take a look."

Dixie craned her head to get a look at the other screen. The heat from the plane's engines stood out remarkably well against the cold air. "Is he moving away?"

"Yes. Pointing his two turbojets right at us. Now you can see him start his turn back to the north. Watch the infrared signature go way down."

The infrared image changed drastically as the plane's engines pointed away from the ALL's infrared camera.

"Now watch for a flash in the video," Lance told her.

Dixie turned her attention back to the small speck in the other monitor.

"There!" Lance called. "Did you see it?"

Dixie nodded her head. "Sun glint?"

"Exactly. As he turns back to begin his westerly run, the sun reflects off the airframe, scattering the light into our video camera. When he rounds south, we'll start to pick up his engines on the FLIR again."

"I still wish we could see him better on the video. How many people do you think are on the plane?"

"I don't have any idea, don't even know how many passengers the transport version of the Coaler holds."

"The AN-74 has four crew and eight passengers,"

Kirk answered, "but I doubt if this one carries that many people. The laser has to take up a lot of the weight and space. By the way, Jones says he thinks the Syrians have their entire defense network up now. Doesn't look like we'll be able to sneak in without being seen, so stay alert."

"Okay," Lance answered. "Let's go over the check . . . What was that?"

The video screen bloomed white. For an instant nothing could be seen, then the picture slowly began to reappear. Before Lance could make out much detail in the image, the monitor saturated again.

"It's the laser—the Syrian's turned his on," Dixie said. "Look at the infrared monitor, it's not affected. The laser wavelength isn't in the FLIR pass band, but it's right in the middle of the video camera's detector curve. There it goes again. He's in some kind of surveillance mode, tagging us about every five seconds. It's saturating the camera."

"Will it damage it?" Kirk asked.

"I don't think so," she replied. "The camera is pretty rugged, we'll have to turn it off before we get much closer, though. If it were our eyes, we'd be in big trouble."

"Better warn the others, TD," Lance called to Kirk.

Kirk nodded. "Pilot, Mission Director. The Syrian has fired up his laser, keep those goggles on!"

Jones was waiting for things to come back to normal. When the flash hit him, he was looking beneath his goggles again, checking the altimeter. It was a good thing they were flying at this altitude, not down in the rocks like before. Now he could see little, like someone had set a flashbulb off right in front of his face.

"Roger." He confirmed Kirk's warning had been received. A little late but Jones didn't mention that. Then he passed word to the Prowlers.

"It's probably in response to our presence," ECMO Two told his pilot. "We just veered closer to their border."

"Eagle Three Three, this is Argus Three Five."

"Go."

"We have indications of fighter aircraft launches at An Siriyah and Sayqual airfields. Looks like they're coming after you. Recommend you initiate your mission as soon as possible."

"Understood, Argus," Jones replied, glad the surveillance plane was finally back up. He didn't really expect this support, not after the call he got that morning. The Argus pilot had warned him they might not be able to fly due to an engine problem. "Wizard Alpha, did you copy?"

"Affirmative. Stand By."

"Where's the best hole?" Adkins asked his back seater.

"There is no hole" was the answer. "The Syrians have every inch of their border covered by a radar net. Not surprising."

"True," Adkins said. It was the answer he had

dreaded, but that he had expected just the same. With Israel as a mortal enemy and the renowned capability of the Israeli Air Force, it was no surprise the border was bristling with antiaircraft defenses. "Any suggestions on where we should go in?"

The lieutenant contemplated an answer. Since there was no way to get between the radar coverage, that left only one possible decision. "How about an end run? South end?"

"We can't go into Jordan," Adkins reminded him.

"No. Not around the end. Through it!"

"Through it? What will that buy us?"

"We'll have to take out at least one radar. That's a given. If we try to go through the middle, they might be able to use adjacent radar to guide the missiles. If we take out the bottom radar, then go as far south as we can, the next radar in the line to the north probably won't be able to reach us. They rely on Jordanian radar to provide the next area of coverage, but we know they don't communicate well with each other."

Adkins thought it over briefly. The lieutenant's plan made about as much sense as anything else. Too bad they couldn't get back down on the deck to use the terrain for cover.

"Strike lead, this is Wizard Alpha. Recommend you fly as far south as possible before crossing the border. We'll take out the radar, then continue to escort you in."

"Roger. Begin left turn to one eighty now." Jones

twisted the yoke to the left, heading away from the Syrian border. He hoped the radar operators would relax if they saw him make the turn away, but seriously doubted they would. There were now over one hundred Israeli fighters taking on fuel to the west of their position, and Jones was confident the Syrians knew the Israeli's were airborne.

"Is the laser still up?" Kirk asked.

"Yeah, pinging away," Dixie confirmed as she watched the video screen flare up again. "We'll have to turn the video off before we get in too close. Even turned off it might still get damaged, but it has a better chance of surviving if we turn off the voltage to the detector."

"Let's wait until we cross the border," Lance instructed. "Until then we'll monitor the camera to verify the laser's still up. How far till the turn?"

"About three minutes," Kirk answered.

"All right," Lance said. "We're still tracking. Why don't you bring the laser up now, Dixie. We'll keep the shutters closed until we get within range. Thirty miles."

"We have to get that close?" Kirk asked.

"Yeah. Any farther out and we won't be able to blind it. And we have to keep to that distance fairly accurately. If we get too close, his laser may heat our FLIR enough to cause the thermal background to rise too much. If that happens we may lose track." Lance punched up one of the digital displays on the HEL-

RATS. It read one hundred ten, their target was just over one hundred miles away.

Dixie started flipping switches, lined up in a long row on a relatively sophisticated panel that had replaced a portion of the old device operator's console. As she turned on each of the laser modules, the lights above the switches went from red to green, indicating the lasers were operating per their prescribed parameters.

"All set," she said.

The device compartment heated up even more as the inefficient lasers deposited their waste heat into the air via the cooling vanes formed onto the laser covers. The orange beams escaped the modules, fanning out in a series of pencil beams that rushed toward the beam director. A specially designed, multifaceted mirror combined the beams into a single, larger diameter stick of light. The thick, four-inch beam was blocked by a retractable mirror at the bottom entrance of the beam director. The mirror redirected the laser into a beam dump, a metal device whose temperature began to rise as the laser light was absorbed.

"Wizard Alpha beginning descent," Adkins called. The jammer would work best if he could get closer to the radar, one of those laws of physics that made driving a Prowler so dangerous.

"Weapons free," Jones responded, authorizing Adkins to use any of his systems to clear the way for the bigger airplane to get through.

"Roger that," Adkins replied, pulling his stick back and hard over to his right. He rolled inverted, and dived through the thin layer of clouds that had formed just below their fifteen-thousand-foot cruising altitude. Wizard Delta was right on his wing.

The dive for the ground lasted a very short time. They rolled back over and leveled off at the treetops, banking right again to put them on a direct course with the radar. Adkins grunted as the positive g forces tried to drain the blood from his head. He tightened his stomach and legs to force the blood back to his brain.

"We've got a launch," Dixie called out, reaching over to reset the switch for the missile launch detect system. "Must be a SAM. Can you slew toward the ground, Lance?"

"Okay," he answered, reaching over to disable the auto-track on the computer.

"Negative," Kirk ordered. "Keep tracking the target. There's nothing we can do about the missile, and I don't want to risk losing our own target. Let's leave the missile problem to our escorts."

"Bullshit," Jones thought to himself when he heard what Kirk was saying. He wasn't about to leave the safety of his plane entirely in the hands of the naval aviators. He turned to his right and gave his copilot an order. "Get ready to launch chaff rounds."

Skimming along at fifty feet, Adkins waited for ECMO Two to call the bogey and start the music.

"Parameters loaded," ECMO Two called out, louder than necessary into the microphone. "Six seconds to music."

Adkins knew the missile would take at least twenty seconds to get to the 135. He hoped the music would be enough to throw the SAM off course.

"Time to go: twelve seconds," Red called out as he watched the modified AN/AVR-47 missile warning receiver.

"Launch chaff," Jones ordered.

Red reached behind his seat and toggled the switch that controlled the chaff release mechanism.

At the rear of the airplane, shotgun shells fired within the special dispensers. In the air behind the plane bits of metal foil were released, reflecting the guidance radar and presenting false radar returns to the missile seeker.

The missiles, modified SA-3s, initiated a counter-countermeasure electronic circuit and ignored the false target returns. The objective, the ALL, remained squarely centered in the missile's electronic sights!

18

Adkins silently counted down the seconds. Three . . . two . . . one, then felt the tingling sensation he always got whenever the high-power emitters came on. He had never been able to figure out if the feeling was real, or just some psychosomatic reaction to the knowledge of what the jammer was doing, how much popcorn-popping energy it was pumping into the air below him.

BAM—Everyone aboard felt the jolt as the beam director broke track and slammed into the mechanical stops.

"Shit!" Lance exclaimed, trying to recover control of the beam director.

"What happened?" Kirk asked, his usual calm self.

"Same as in Cypress," Lance answered, "but worse, I can't get it to come back under control."

Kirk stood up and watched as Lance fought to make the telescope do what he demanded. He wasn't being successful.

After several attempts, Lance reached up and flipped the power switch. "I'm going to try shutting it down and powering it back up. Maybe that will work."

"Status?" Adkins called again into his intercom, screaming this time. Had ECMO Two gone to sleep or what?

"No change," ECMO Two responded, shaken out of his intense focus on the display by the pilot's tone of voice. "The radar's still up, missile is still guiding on the 135. I'll try bumping up the power, see if we can shake the missile off course."

"Screw that. Load HARM One!" Adkins countermanded.

"I still can't get control," Lance said. "None of the transducers are reading out the correct gimbal position, and the signals that get to the gimbals aren't being received correctly."

ECMO One loaded the parameters of the emitting radar into the radar-seeking missile via the data link to the wing station.

"Loaded. And verified," ECMO One said after the green clear light came on, confirming the targeting information was correctly loaded into the missile's memory.

Adkins pulled back on the stick, climbing as hard as the old airframe would allow. When he reached three thousand feet he rolled over and dived for the ground again, using his electronic sensors to search the area below him for his target.

"Twelve degrees port," ECMO One said, calmly repeating what the direction-finding equipment reported.

Adkins tugged the stick to the left, still diving and picking up speed, the earth rapidly approaching above them.

"Secure the music," Adkins ordered.

ECMO Two reached down to shut off the switch, cutting off power to the transformers in the jamming pod.

"Still firing," Red confirmed, checking the display on the automatic chaff dispenser, watching the enunciator count the rounds as they were jettisoned from the magazine.

"Eight seconds to impact," Chief Warren warned, monitoring the missile-warning system.

"Keep calling it. Give me the side it's on at two," Jones instructed him. "Kirk, have your people hang on."

"Seven seconds."

"Centered!" ECMO One yelled when the sensors on both sides of the plane indicated they were receiving approximately the same amount of signal.

Adkins pulled the FIRE trigger on the stick and felt

a kick as the number one HARM screamed off the left rail.

"Magnum-Magnum-Magnum," he yelled into the radio to inform the others he had fired the HARM. All three men watched as the thin trail of smoke from the rocket's solid fuel motor traced a path to the ground.

"It's back up," Lance yelled with delight, grabbing the stick to hunt for his target.

Lance saw the image of the missile streaking toward them, fuzzy due to its close proximity, and locked onto it.

They watched the video monitor in terror as the missile approached their right wing. Lance checked the gimbal positions, the angular rates were at the maximum, the missile was going to pass right next to the plane!

"Two. Right side."

Jones pulled the yoke hard to the left and shoved it forward, attemping to get the missile to miss them high and go ballistic.

Red looked as far over his right shoulder as he could. He watched the huge, fireball-driven javelin of death come streaking up toward them. He put his own hand on the yoke, trying to help Jones turn the plane on its side. It did no good. Jones already had the yoke against the stops. Sweat beaded on Red's brow.

* * *

It took less than three seconds for the HARM to find the emitting radar, marked by a puff of smoke from the HARM's small warhead. Adkins rolled the Prowler upright and headed to the east.

The missile seemed to slow as it got closer to the Airborne Laser Lab, veering toward them. Then, at the last second it began to turn away, as if it had lost its sense of direction. It passed them, missing just aft of the right wing, traveled a few hundred meters, then exploded as its proximity fuse kicked in.

Fortunately, the missile was far enough away and traveling so fast that most of the blast was directed away from the plane. There was no damage, except to the nerves of those who knew how close the missile had come.

Jones rotated the yoke back to center, simultaneously pulling the nose up to bleed off some of the excess airspeed they had accumulated.

"That was too damn close," Red complained, wiping his forehead with the back of his green flight gloves.

"No arguments from me," Jones agreed. "Give me a heading, Chief."

"Looks like zero five zero to bring us back to the original course to the target area. As soon as the guys in the back spot our target, we'll have a better idea which way to go."

"All right. We'll take on a northeast heading and

climb out." They were at seven thousand feet, well below the optimum engagement altitude as specified by Kirk's engineers. At least they were finally in Syria, the enemy's backyard.

Time for a status check: "Kirk, what's it look like back there?"

"Strike lead, this is Argus," called their support aircraft.

"Strike lead," Jones said in response, wondering where their surveillance support was now.

"Argus notes two weapon detonations, one on the ground and one in the air. Two fighters from the group that launched earlier have left their formations and are now heading in your direction. What is your status?"

"Two detonations. I wonder where those came from?" Red asked sarcastically, his mouth screwed up into a frown.

"Yeah," Jones agreed before answering the radio. "The jets aren't very good news, though. Must be interceptors. Kirk, what's your status back there?"

"We're back on line. We had a glitch a few minutes ago, but we're fully mission capable now."

"Argus, this is Strike lead. We are FMC and inbound to the target area. Please keep us informed as to the status of the air defense fighters."

"Strike lead, Wizard Alpha. FMC and inbound as escort. Straight Flush radar is down, courtesy of one U.S. Navy HARM. We'll rejoin you in two minutes."

*   *   *

A glitch? That's what Kirk called it. Lance was more concerned than ever, not only about the system but also about Kirk's seeming lack of concern regarding the problem. If it cropped up while they were trying to take the laser plane out, they might never survive the mission. They would be susceptible to laser-guided missiles fired from the ground or from the inbound fighters. He was certain any aircraft sent to intercept them now would use the laser-guided missiles instead of the traditional radar-guided ones, like the Syrians kept at their borders.

Lance continued to search the air around them with the infrared set, hunting for the target. The laser beam control system and the infrared tracker were functioning properly, but the HELRATS acquisition radar was still down.

"Try cycling it," Lance told Dixie. "If we can't get it up, we'll have to back up a step and use the old optical acquisition device, and it'll be tough to see the target at this range."

Dixie reached up and flicked the power switch to off, waited for all the lights to fade, then turned it back on.

They all watched as the radar display slowly came to life, its amber screen glowing in the relative darkness of the plane.

"What's that?" Dixie asked, pointing to two strong returns coming up behind them.

"Must be the Prowlers," Kirk decided, considering their range and direction of approach.

"Then that must be the target," Lance pointed out, indicating a relatively strong return off the nose of the plane, just outside the sixty-nautical-mile ring. Lance noted the coordinates and steered the beam control system for the target. He was intently studying the FLIR and didn't notice a second pair of radar blips that appeared when the slowly rotating sweep passed their right side.

"Uh-oh," Dixie said in a subdued voice.

"Strike lead, Argus. You have two bandits at one two zero, eighty miles. Looks like the first of the interceptors."

"Strike lead copies," Jones responded.

"No way," Red disagreed. "Those two must have been airborne already, Combat Air Patrol. The fighters launching from Sayqal couldn't get there that fast."

"Agreed. Let's hope they're the only fighter CAP airborne in this area. You copy that, Kirk?"

"Affirmative. We have them on the radar. They're coming in pretty fast, heading for an intercept between here and our target. We'll never get to the laser plane before they get to us."

"Understood," Jones answered, busily searching his mind for an answer to the situation he faced. If only the other two Prowlers were still with them. There just weren't enough assets left. Yet if they didn't get within range of the laser plane they were doomed anyhow, not to mention the mission.

"Wizard Alpha, this is Strike lead. We've got a small problem. Two interceptors closing on our course."

"Copy, Strike lead. We'll run interference," Adkins replied, immediately understanding their situation. "Give me a vector."

"Target bearing now one zero zero," Kirk jumped in. "Make for zero seven five and expect intercept at thirty miles."

"Roger. Wizard Delta, stay with me." Adkins pulled the stick slightly to the right and shoved the throttles full forward.

Both birds flew by the ALL, off to do battle.

"Hope they make it," Red said.

"Yeah, for our sake," Jones agreed.

"Ain't this a hell of a deal," Adkins asked his crew. "Two Prowlers against two MiGs, probably Fulcrums. What kind of odds would you give that?"

No one said anything. Dead silence. That was answer enough.

"Wizard Delta, stick close. You've got both of the air-to-air missiles so we'll have to rely on your firepower. We just need to keep them occupied long enough for Strike lead to get within laser range of the real target. Then we'll shake these guys and engage the laser plane."

Sounds good, Adkins thought. If it will only work. They were flying two attack planes, no, two electronic warfare escort planes, against two high-performance air-to-air fighters. Good luck.

"Bandit at twelve o'clock," ECMO Two called. "High."

Just like the movie. Adkins searched the airspace in front of his plane. The covered windowpanes in front of him didn't leave a lot of visibility, another deficiency he faced if he were to engage the fighters. Not surprisingly, he saw nothing. How was he going to fight if he couldn't even see?

"How are they doing?" Lance asked Dixie.

She studied the radar display before she replied. "Okay so far. The interceptors held back. Now the Prowlers are closing on them, but they're also almost within range of the laser plane. Once inside they'll be susceptible to the targeting algorithms all the other planes have fallen prey to."

"Good point," Kirk interjected from his usual place watching over their shoulders. He had wondered himself why the interceptors were staying back before. Now he knew: they were baiting the Prowlers, sucking them into a trap.

"I've got a launch detection," Wizard Alpha called over the radio.

"What the he . . . Fulcrums don't have a frontal attack capability," Adkins complained to no one in particular. No time to try and figure it out now. "Break right," he screamed into the radio, jerking his own stick hard over.

"Fire up the laser," Kirk ordered.

"What?" asked Lance.

"Bring it to bear on the Prowlers. Those missiles are laser-guided, we'll use our own laser as a jammer, try to disrupt their guidance."

"I need a target," Lance said, diverting from his main target and searching the huge volume of air where the HELRATS radar indicated the Prowlers were supposed to be.

"A little more to the right," Dixie called, taking over the duty of watching the HELRATS display and allowing Lance to concentrate on the infrared monitor. "Lasers are up and nominal," she added.

"There," Lance nearly yelled, excitement ringing in his voice. "Going auto-track," he added, keying the button.

"Beam on!" Kirk ordered as soon as he was sure the tracker was locked on the target.

Lance squeezed the trigger, dumping the pneumatic gases to flip the blocking mirror out of the way. The orange laser beams leaped out of the beam director and sliced through the air to their targets.

Both Prowlers rolled into a hard turn, trying to dodge the rapidly approaching missiles.

Without being ordered to, ECMO Two slapped the

jammer on, hoping to divert the threat. "Music on," he said, in his excitement keying the radio instead of the intercom. The jammer didn't seem to do a lot of good as the missile engines left a smoky trail of impending death that pointed right at Wizard Alpha.

"Damn it!" Lance yelled as the beam control system broke lock again, the laser light scattering all over the area as the beam traced erratic paths through the air. "We've lost track again. The position transducers are sending back incorrect readings, and the command data is going nuts before it gets to the gimbals. It's as if we were in a huge electrical storm."

"We *are* in a huge electrical storm," Kirk said, thinking about the high-power jammer on the Prowler.

"Wizard Alpha," Kirk got on the radio, bypassing Jones, who was supposed to be in charge of the mission. There was no time. "Shut down the music. Repeat—Shut down the music."

The smoke trails were still reaching forward, barely moving on the windscreen. That was a sure indication they were homing in on one of the two Prowlers. It was obvious to Adkins the jammer was again ineffective. "Shut it off!" he screamed.

ECMO Two reached up with a shaking finger and flipped the switch, shutting off the high-power emitters, their only defense.

* * *

"Got it!" Lance called, returning the beam director to the same coordinates it was in when the system broke lock. The Prowlers were bright on the screen, their engines at full military power and hot.

"Lasers are still up," Dixie reported. "All modules are on line."

"It's going to be close," Kirk said.

The smoke trails, smoothly tracking toward the Prowlers until now, became erratic. Adkins could tell the missiles were having trouble tracking their targets.

"Wizard Delta, get ready for endgame maneuver on my mark." It was a standard, practiced technique.

"Now!" Adkins jerked his plane left, while Wizard Delta pulled hard to the right.

The missiles, confused by the change in target signature and jammed by the laser from the Airborne Laser Lab, flew past both Prowlers and detonated well beyond. There was no damage from the missiles, but the Fulcrums reacted aggressively, vectoring for the Prowlers and diving for the ground when they were close enough to determine the aircraft they faced weren't fighters.

The Prowlers regrouped, Wizard Delta forming up on the right wing of Wizard Alpha.

"They're still coming," the pilot of Wizard Delta warned.

"I know, I know." Adkins guessed the Syrians still

had something up their sleeve, but what was it? Then the answer dawned on him.

"Watch it," Adkins warned his wingman. "They aren't going to use the laser-guided missiles this time. They must have standard AA-10s or AA-11s on board. They'll try to get a lock on us from behind."

Adkins strained his neck to look behind his plane, but his view was obscured by the plane itself. "Where are they?" he called to ECMO Two.

"Don't have a clue." ECMO Two frantically switched from sensor to sensor to find the Fulcrums. "They're totally silent. No radar, no radio emissions. Nothing."

That in itself was a clue, Adkins knew. "Watch for a tail shot," he called over the radio. "They're coming in silent. That means an infrared-guided missile."

"Wizard Alpha, Three Three," Dixie called the lead Prowler. "Our radar has them at your six and low, just coming out of the ground clutter. Range approximately ten miles." She struggled to keep track of the different airplanes on the HELRATS display. Not trained in controlling airborne targets or directing intercepts, she found the job almost impossible. All the blips looked the same, merging, tangling, eventually becoming hopelessly confused.

"Roger, Three Three. Is that laser of yours still up?"

"Affirmative," Kirk replied. "It won't do you any good, though. If they're going to use standard infrared missiles, the laser won't jam them."

Adkins racked his brain, searching for a way out

of this mess. He tried to sound calm, not wanting to let his men know he was out of ideas. He made a quick inventory of his assets. Two EA-6B Prowlers, one with two air-to-air missiles and one with a single HARM and a radar jammer. Not much to work with when faced with two of the best Soviet fighters built, armed with guns and probably at least two heat-seeking missiles each. The jammer was useless, as was the HARM. That left only the Sidewinders, but they were supposed to be used to take out the Syrian laser plane.

Adkins finally conceded, putting the entire problem into perspective. If both Prowlers got shot down, there would be no way they could do anything about the Syrian laser. Better to use the Sidewinders now and figure out what to do with the primary target later. After all, there was always the possibility of ramming it.

"Wizard Delta, this is Alpha. What did the armaments technician say about a frontal shot with the Sidewinders?"

"His recommendation was to shoot from the rear, to get as much signature as possible before lighting them off. Why?"

"I sat in on a briefing on the new Sidewinder seekers before we deployed. I remember them saying there was a good probability of success with a frontal shot when the target is hot and small, small so it wouldn't mask the infrared signature of the engine exhaust. Are those the new missiles?"

"The armaments tech didn't say. There's only one way to find out."

"Yeah," Adkins was thinking the same thing. "Let's try it before we run out of time. Break left and roll out low."

Both planes dived for the earth below, negative G forces trying to throw the crew out of their seats. Only the harnesses kept them tightly pinned. The dive continued until they were at the minimum altitude to roll out. Adkins continued to push the stick forward, rolling out of the dive inverted, then snapped the stick over hard to whip the plane into an aileron roll, popping the Prowler upright.

"Got 'em. Three o'clock," ECMO Two yelled into the radio.

The Fulcrums hadn't seen the Prowlers go into their dive. They had been flying without their radar on and had been heading into the sun, following a dead reckoning course straight for the spot where they had last seen the lumbering attack airplanes.

"They're pretty low," Adkins replied. "About two thousand feet. Let's climb up to five thousand, that should put us right in the sun."

The Prowlers climbed up, then turned into the oncoming flight path of the Syrian Fulcrums. The Syrians were still flying blind, searching for their targets.

"Weapon's free when you've got a lock." Adkins crossed his fingers.

*   *   *

Inside Wizard Delta, the right seater swung into action. Hanging the Sidewinders on their plane had been a daring idea, and an engineering nightmare. Instead of being mounted on the wingtips as they were designed, the missiles hung below the inboard wing station on a specially modified pod stanchion. The feedback circuit, used to tell the pilot when the missile had enough signal to fly a high probability of intercept course, was normally fed into the internal communication system and signaled the pilot with a steady tone in his headset. There was no time to integrate that type of signal into the EA-6Bs. The old comm system had already been extensively modified, was already fed by a variety of signals and warning systems, none of which it was originally designed to handle.

Instead, a special display, normally used in the A-6 attack version of the Prowler, had been installed to give the right seater a visual indication when the missile had the target locked on.

"No signal yet," the right seater called.

"I have a green on the missile," the pilot replied coolly, unruffled by the risk of what they were about to try. "The system is powered up and hunting. Let me know as soon as you get a return."

The right seater continued to stare into the scope, looking for some indication the missile had seen the target.

*   *   *

"I have a visual." Adkins could now see a minuscule spot centered on his windscreen. It was the Fulcrums. The spot didn't move, indicating they were on a collision course. Their combined speed would exceed nine hundred knots, less than two minutes before they would reach each other. He hoped there would be little left of the Fulcrums when it came time to fly by them, else their guns could wreak havoc with the aging Navy aircraft.

The pilot of the number two Prowler absentmindedly toyed with the launch button on his stick, wondering when he would get the signal to fire.

"There's a hit," the right seater said, his head forced far into the hood covering the display. "And another. It comes and goes. We have to stay lined up on him better."

"I'm doing the best I can at this range, the target's just a little dot," the pilot justified his technique. Just as he said it, the target grew rapidly in his windscreen. Now it was easy to keep the plane centered.

"Got it—target is locked on!"

The pilot toggled the switch and the Sidewinder burst off the rail, screaming off in search of its victim. Quickly, the pilot reached up and armed his other Sidewinder, simultaneously tipping the nose of the plane to the right, centering the other Fulcrum.

"Target locked!"

The pilot launched his other missile.

The crews of the Prowlers watched in horror as

the first missile missed its target. The Fulcrum pulled a horrendous turn at the last instant to dodge the projectile. The MiG continued its turn, veering away from the approaching airplanes.

The second Fulcrum wasn't as lucky, didn't have enough time to avoid the Sidewinder. The image of the Fulcrum expanded greatly in Wizard Delta's windscreen as it got closer, then exploded in a ball of fire as the missile ripped through the interceptor's titanium skin.

With no chance to avoid it, Wizard Delta flew right into the maelstrom. The Prowler ingested flame into its own jet turbines. The flames pre-lit the onboard JP-4 fuel, sending a fireball back out of the front of the engine. The engine ripped itself apart. Tiny, superheated metal remnants of the turbine blade shredded the starboard fuel cell and the plane exploded.

"Damn it," Adkins howled as he pulled up hard. Any closer to Wizard Delta and his plane would have been destroyed as well. His crew hunkered down as the hard G pull forced them into their seats.

He rolled out of the turn and began to look for the other Fulcrum.

"Wizard Delta is down," he reported back to the others. "We have no air-to-air capability now." Might as well remind them of the obvious.

"We've got a bandit coming right at us!" Dixie yelled into the interphone, her voice rising in pitch as the threat of death grew near.

"Where?" Kirk rushed over to look at the HEL-RATS display.

"From the left. It must have overshot the Prowler and decided to try and take us out. It's climbing."

They watched the indicator light change color as the three-dimensional radar tracked the target.

Kirk reached over her seat and turned the interphone dial to the aircrew net, then keyed his own mike: "Pilot, Kirk. We've got trouble, looks like a MiG made it through the Prowlers and is headed our way. Dixie is on your net and she'll call the bogey. Go ahead Dixie, give them the status."

"He's still climbing. It looks like he'll pass below us and turn for a tail shot. My guess is he'll approach from our eight o'clock."

"Roger," Jones replied. "Is there any way you can give us a heads up if he fires a missile?"

"Sure can."

"Good. The warning receiver up here is giving erratic readings. Kirk, we've got enough flares to try and survive one pass. More than that and we're going to be in a world of hurt."

"Understand. Lance, Dixie, I want both of you to get into your seats and strap in. Make sure your chutes are tightened up and put on your helmets. If we take a hit we may have to bail out."

Great, Lance thought to himself. Jumping out of an airplane hadn't been high on his list of things to do during this little reserve tour. He hoped he could remember what they taught him in the survival course.

"Okay, he's turning now," Dixie warned. "He's passed below us and is at about seven o'clock."

"Get ready on the flares, Red," Jones said. "What's the missile-warning receiver saying?"

"It's a constant alarm." Red hit the display with his fist again, trying to get the amber warning light to go out. It was unnerving to look down and see the missile alert illuminated all the time.

"Ignore it," Jones said. "Just listen to Dixie and pop the flares when she calls the missile."

Dixie studied the display vigilantly, sharing her time between the radar and the MISSILE LAUNCH DETECT light on the beam control panel. She was well aware that any mistake, no matter how small, might very well doom the entire crew.

The Fulcrum was still climbing and had not yet pulled onto their trail when the missile launch detect flashed on.

"We've got missile launch," Kirk yelled into his mike.

Red heard the alert. His finger, already positioned just above the switch, stabbed the button home and in a spit second the flares began to fire out of the dispenser.

"Negative." Dixie interpreted the light as a false alarm. She knew the MiG couldn't have been in position to shoot yet.

Red looked up, unsure of what to do.

"Shut it off!" Jones ordered. "We don't have any flares to spare."

Red flicked the switch back. The counters now read six cartridges in the right dispenser and five in the left. Hardly enough to sustain a continuous counter-measure.

"Less than a dozen left," Red reported.

"Shit." Until now Jones thought they stood a chance. Their chances were dwindling as fast as the pursuing MiG closed the distance between them. "We'll have to wait until just before the missile gets to us. Otherwise, we'll run out of flares before the missile is diverted."

"Roger." Red's hand was starting to shake slightly. He looked at his hand in dismay, willing it to stop.

"Dixie," Jones said. "If you can, give us the time to impact when you see the missile fire."

"That'll be tough." Dixie was still concentrating on the radar display.

"There's nothing here to give us that information," Kirk explained to Jones.

And there was no time to figure out a way to get it: "We've got a launch," Dixie said. "Eight miles and closing."

Red began counting out loud, having already cal-culated how long he thought the missile would take to cover the distance to them. Red let the missile get as close as he dared, then launched the final flares.

"It's veering," Dixie called out, relieved.

The missile, a modified version of the Soviet AA-8

APHID, more sophisticated than the standard export model, indeed appeared to veer as the missile's infrared counter-counter measures kicked in. In actuality the missile was leading the plane, waiting for the flare to fall away before reengaging its prime target.

Once the last flare fell away the missile tried to turn back into the plane, but the angle between the missile's flight path and that of the ALL was too great. The missile couldn't make up the difference.

Red watched in horror as the missile screamed over the right wing. His eyes grew wide as the proximity fuse detonated the warhead just outside his cockpit window.

19

A cloud formed in front of Jones's face, a stabbing pain seared into his ears. Those were his first indications something was wrong, terribly wrong. A piece of paper rushed past his face. Jones followed its path, watched as it was sucked out of a hole that had been blown in the right side of the plane. The roar of the engines was now apparent, no longer the muted, muffled sound heard only when listened for.

The temperature of the air in the cockpit plummeted as the air pressure dropped to balance with the outside. Jones held the yoke tightly to keep the plane under control, swallowed hard to relieve the pressure in his ears that had resulted from the rapid decompression. He noticed an unusual amount of pressure on the rudder pedals. They weren't as responsive as before. He started to tell his copilot to make a damage assessment but stopped when he looked in Red's direction. Red's head was hanging unnaturally to one side, blood covered his flight suit from a wound on his neck.

He looked back at Chief Warren, also slumped in his seat.

"Chief, can you hear me?" Jones asked repeatedly. Silence.

Jones held onto the yoke and collected his wits. First thing was to check for the MiG. He searched his side of the plane but could see nothing. On the other side of the cockpit several window panels had been blown out, and there were some large holes in the cockpit itself. Fortunately, nothing was on fire.

The lights in the newly installed instruments, the ones they had taken time to upgrade while in the hangar at Wright Patterson, flickered, leading Jones to wonder how many of them were still reliable, wondered which ones he could trust to give him correct data. The older gauges, the ones they hadn't had time to replace, seemed to be functional.

He checked the engines, especially the power readings. Three appeared to be operating within limits. The fourth, the inboard engine on the right side, closest to where the missile detonated, was reading extremely erratic. Jones listened intently, pulling his headset away from his ear so he could hear better. It was difficult to make out any of the normal engine sounds with the wind blasting through the holes in the cockpit, but it didn't sound as if the engine was operating as the display indicated. Hopefully, it was just the instrument. That assessment was further reinforced as the digital display flickered again, went off for a long second, then flashed back on.

* * *

In the back of the plane, the crew heard an explosion just after the missile flew by. Then nothing. Back at the safety console, powered up automatically while the beam control system was on, a red light flashed on. The pressure drop in the forward section of the plane sent a warning message to the display. The light came on and stayed bright red. The readings for the other two compartments, the laser device and test crew areas, remained green.

Their first indication of the extent of the damage came when Jones called over the intercom.

"Kirk, I'm going to need some help up here," Jones told them calmly, only a slight indication of worry in his voice, most of which was masked by the extraneous noise from the wind blasting past the holes in the airplane.

"What happened?" Kirk asked.

Jones explained. ". . . and I think Red's dead. Don't know about Chief Warren, I can't get him to answer. I need you to come up and help me fly this thing!"

"On my way," Kirk answered, unstrapping from his seat.

"Bring a walk-around bottle, and your flight jacket. We don't have pressure integrity and we've leveled off at fifteen thousand. It's cold, too."

"Roger," Kirk answered pulling on his coat when he stood up. He grabbed one of the portable oxygen bottles and plugged the hose from his mask into the device. He started to move forward, but stopped. He

moved quickly back to the safety console and
checked the pressure in the device compartment. He
came back to his seat and plugged into the intercom
to give Lance and Dixie some instructions before he
left for the cockpit.

"The pressure held in the laser compartment, so I
don't think anything's happened in there. Shrapnel
couldn't have damaged any of the equipment without penetrating the skin of the plane first. I'll have
to bleed the pressure out of the device compartment
before I can open the bulkhead door leading to the
cockpit. That shouldn't affect any of the systems, but
I'm not positive. Once forward, I'll try to repressurize
the laser compartment, but there's no guarantee I'll
be able to. Keep on your toes back here, this thing
is far from over. Dixie, find that Fulcrum. Lance, I
want you to figure out how we can take out that
laser plane." Kirk disconnected his interphone cable
and moved forward.

Kirk opened the bulkhead door and entered the
device compartment, now a sweltering one hundred
twenty degrees. He looked around as he moved up
the narrow passageway along the left wall of the
plane, carrying the small oxygen bottle in his hand.
He remembered they were only good for about ten
minutes, long enough to get back to a safe altitude
if there were a sudden loss of pressure. Jones had
decided to stay up at fifteen thousand, not overly
high, but high enough to cause oxygen starvation—
hypoxia. Kirk didn't want to suck on the bottle any

longer than necessary, wanted to get hooked back into the aircraft's oxygen system as quickly as possible.

Reaching the forward bulkhead door, Kirk bent down and looked through the small glass window to check for anything that might block his way. The window was fogged up, and he wiped it with his gloved hand. It didn't help, the fog was on the other side. Kirk set his oxygen bottle on the floor and pulled the long, metal lever to the side. It was tight, and he had to use all his strength to get it to budge. Once the bolt cleared the door frame, the small, metal door slammed open about an inch, stopped by two safety bolts installed for that exact reason. Kirk held himself away from the small crack around the door as the air in the device compartment was sucked into the partial vacuum of the cockpit.

The other sensation, drop in temperature, was not as great as it had been in the cockpit when the missile blew out the windows. The heaters for the lasers kept the device compartment fairly warm and dry, also decreasing the amount of smokelike fog that appeared in the chamber. Kirk looked back and checked on several of the highly polished mirrors, making sure there was no condensation on their surfaces. He was relieved when that didn't occur, knowing water on any one of the mirrors would reduce their reflectivity and cripple the beam control system.

Kirk released the safety latches and pushed the door the rest of the way open. He picked up his oxygen bottle and crouched down to pass through the small portal. Once through, he closed and secured the bulkhead door.

The mission director turned forward, his jacket blasted by the wind coming in through several large holes in the cockpit, holes Jones probably hadn't even seen from where he sat. Kirk looked down at the limp figure of Chief Warren, his head slumped over, his body held upright only by the restraints that pinned him to his chair at the navigator's console. He reached down to touch Warren's neck, feeling for a pulse. There was none. Warren's skin was cold and clammy, even though he had died only minutes earlier.

Kirk moved forward again, up to the pilot and the copilot. Or at least what was left of the copilot. Kirk grabbed Jones' shoulder to let him know he was there, then reached over to check for a pulse from Red. He pulled his hand back in revulsion, feeling a huge hole in the side of Red's neck. His hand was red with blood.

Jones pointed at Red, then aimed his thumb toward the back of the cockpit.

Kirk understood. He was to pull Red's body out of the copilot's seat. He disconnected the restraint harness that held Red in his seat, then searched for a footing in the cramped cockpit. In the best position he could find, Kirk grabbed Red under his arms and pulled. Nothing happened. Kirk pulled again, harder this time, but with the same results. Something was holding the body in place.

The rudder pedals tugged at Jones' feet each time Kirk pulled to extract Red's body. He realized Red's feet were caught in the controls, so he released the yoke long enough to hit Kirk on the shoulder, then point down between the dead copilot's feet.

Kirk reached beneath the glare shield and jerked both of Red's feet free, then wrestled his body out of the seat.

As soon as Kirk had Red free, Jones felt the rudders become responsive again. He began a slow right turn to keep them in the area, scanning the skies for the MiG.

Red's body was heavy, limp, and slippery with blood. It was difficult to get him up out of the hole created by the seat, glare shield, and center console, but Kirk finally managed, dragging the body back to the navigator's console. He wiped most of the blood from his flight gloves and moved forward to climb into the copilot's position. The wind continued to beat him after he was in the seat. Finally, he connected the hose from his mask to the oxygen system, pausing long enough to take a long drag of the cool air. Next he made the electrical connection to the intercom.

"How do you read me?" Kirk asked, looking over at Jones.

"Loud and clear. How's Warren?"

"Dead."

Jones' spirits sank lower than he thought possible, a familiar feeling of grief settling in the pit of his stomach. Losing Red was one thing. It hurt, but Red was single. Warren had three kids. What was he going to say to them when he got back? Who was he kidding. What he meant was *if* he got back.

"Where's the MiG?" Kirk asked, hoping to bring Jones back to the problem at hand.

"Not a sign. I haven't seen anything since we got hit, not even the Syrian laser plane."

Kirk flipped the copilot's interphone to "TEST CREW." "Dixie, where's the MiG?"

"He bugged out, sir." She was still intently studying the radar display. "Must not have had any missiles left, or he would have stayed around to finish us off. It's not over yet, though. I'm just now picking up the fighters out of Sayqal, must be the ones Argus warned us about. They're about a hundred miles out."

"How long before they're in range to launch?" Jones asked.

"Considering how far the other MiGs were from the Prowlers when they fired, I'd guess about sixty miles, maybe eight to ten minutes."

"That doesn't leave us a lot of time, does it?" Jones asked Kirk.

Kirk didn't answer, wondering how they were going to get rid of the Syrian laser plane with what little they had left. An answer wasn't readily apparent.

"Wizard Alpha, on your starboard wing." Adkins pulled in alongside to make a damage assessment. "Looks like you've taken a bad hit. I see several small holes just in front of the wing, plus the broken windows."

Kirk looked out one busted window as the Prowler dropped low to inspect for further damage. The Prowler fell out of sight, then reappeared on the left side of the plane. It rolled around them, coming into formation again on the right side, just outside Kirk's window. He could see the three helmets, each straining to look at the damaged Laser Laboratory.

"Looks like you lucked out," Adkins called. "I don't see any fluid leaks, and the engines are all turning."

Lucky? Right. Jones shook his head, guiding the plane through the air as if it were second nature. Let the damned sailor tell Red and Warren how lucky they were. Let him be the one to tell Warren's family, his kids. Jones was sinking deeper and deeper into the depths of depression, his conscious thoughts clouding with images of a time before, to another period when self-pity almost overcame him.

Then, another image appeared inside his tormented head, an image of his lost mate. She wore a flowing white dress, brighter than anything he had ever seen. She held her hand out, and he took it, knowing he would be with her again someday. Her touch gave him courage, he felt a surge of energy course through his body. The image faded, and he sat up straight. How could he ever go to her, how could he face her if he didn't do whatever he could to make this mission a success. There were others, many others, who risked as much as he did on the outcome of this fight. It was up to him to live up to their trust.

"What now?" Jones asked himself, wondering if anyone knew.

"What now?" Lance pondered the same question, racking his brain for the answer. Intuitively he knew there was an answer. The parts to the solution were all there, waiting, floating around inside his head. All he had to do was put them together. Disgusted, he hammered his fist on the console.

Dixie, still watching the approaching fighters in the radar display, jerked upright, startled.

"Lance," she asked, her own fear starting to assert itself, "What is it?"

Lance turned back to the infrared monitor, ignoring her. The Syrian plane sat there under the cursor, seemingly invulnerable. It was taunting him. Challenging him.

Lance glanced back at the radar display, then back to the infrared monitor. There was a similarity. Was that the answer? He smiled, confident he had solved the puzzle.

"Kirk, this is Lance," he called forward. "I think I know how we can take him out!"

20

"Well, speak up. We don't have much time," Kirk said.

"Pass these parameters to Wizard Alpha and have him load them into the HARM. Nine point two gigahertz with a pulse repetition frequency of one four two kilohertz."

Dixie looked up at him as Kirk relayed the information to the Prowler. She smiled, a look of understanding crossed her face. "Those are the HELRATS radar parameters."

"Yeah. Time to turn the tables on the Syrian. How close are the fighters?"

"Only about five minutes out. We'll have to hurry."

"My guess is they'll come for us this time. That'll free the Prowler to get closer to the laser plane. Give him a vector to intercept that takes him away from the fighter's flight path."

"Okay."

Dixie passed the vector to Kirk, who relayed it to Adkins.

*   *   *

"Roger." Adkins understood what he was supposed to do. He shoved the throttles full forward and pulled away from the ALL, heading on a circular route toward the Syrian laser platform, avoiding the approaching jets.

"Let me know when you have the parameters loaded," Adkins instructed the lieutenant in the backseat.

"Aye-aye, sir, but I really don't see what this is going to buy us. Besides, we're nearly BINGO fuel."

"Just shut up and do it!" Adkins yelled, admonishing the back seater. He was getting tired of the unnecessary feedback, knew they were almost to the limits of their fuel. Hell, if necessary he'd drop to the five-minute-reserve criteria before breaking away to meet the tanker over the Med.

"Can you override the surveillance mode on the HELRATS?" Lance asked Dixie.

"We don't have to. Just let the laser break track, then the radar will go back into target acquisition mode. It'll focus the radar beam on the Syrian plane and wait for you to tell it you have the laser boresighed—but don't hit the button. Then we'll have both the radar *and* the laser focused on the plane. Our laser will continue to jam the Syrian laser, rendering all the missiles with laser seekers impotent, and the HELRATS will illuminate it with the radar, giving the HARM something to track on."

"The only problem is we'll be blind." Lance tried to think through each contingency. "With all of our systems directed at the Syrian laser plane, we won't be able to see what the Syrian fighters are doing, where they're at."

"That's true," Dixie agreed, "but if this doesn't work, what the Syrian jets do won't make a whole hell of a lot of difference."

"True enough. Let's go for it!"

"Let me get one last look at the jets. There. Got it. They're still about four minutes out. Go ahead and break track."

Lance thumbed the trigger on the joystick and watched the image of the Syrian laser plane wobble slightly as he used the manual control to keep the target under the crosshairs. "Let me know when the radar is stabilized."

Dixie watched the display stop circling. The radar centered on one of the two jet fighters coming up to intercept them. "Hit it again," she instructed Lance.

Lance clicked the thumb trigger again to release the HELRATS, forcing it to continue its search.

Dixie's display stopped again, this time settling over the correct target. "Got it!"

Lance reached up to trigger the manual auto-track, forcing the HELRATS to continue illuminating the target with radar energy while allowing the infrared tracker to stay on the target as well. He moved the cursor slightly aft on the image of the Syrian plane, then punched up the auto-tracker again, forcing it to move closer to the center of the plane, back to where the laser was emitting.

"Now we just wait until the Prowler gets within range," Lance said, keeping his hand on the joystick in case something went wrong.

"What the hell are you waiting on?" Adkins asked the lieutenant, trying to keep his temper under control.

"The signal's real shitty," the lieutenant tried to explain. "It's not like shooting at a real emitter. The radar bounces off the plane in a dozen different places, and varies when we maneuver. I'm having a real problem getting a signal that doesn't wander around, and it's going to have to be solid if we hope to have a chance at hitting this thing."

"It'd help if we didn't maneuver as much," ECMO One said, trying to act as a mediator.

"All right, goddamn it. I'm gonna fly right up his ass." Adkins brought the plane into straight and level flight. "Lock onto him, Lieutenant. That's an order!"

"What are they waiting for?" Dixie asked, subconsciously pulling her seat harness tighter. She felt better now that she wasn't having to constantly watch the radar display for new targets. She glanced over at it occasionally, just to make sure the Syrian laser plane was still being illuminated. She was getting anxious, knew the other Syrian fighters were getting close, almost close enough to fire. "What's taking so long?"

"I don't know," Lance said, still holding his hand close to the joystick, ready to grab it if the auto-tracker broke lock. "I know the radar return is breaking up when it bounces off the plane, but they should have had a strong enough signal to fire by now. Maybe they . . ." Lance stopped short when he saw a red light start to flash in the corner of his eye.

Dixie sucked in her breath and reached up to shut down the rest of the laser before the overheated modules fed parasites back into the amplifiers and caused the whole thing to blow up. "This isn't good," she said, understanding the magnitude of the problem.

A high-pitched tone pierced the background noise, causing Lance's back muscles to tighten: "And that's worse!" he said, reaching over to turn off the missile launch detect audio alarm.

"Kirk, this is Lance. We've got big problems," he warned over the intercom, not sure what title to use now that things were so screwed up.

"What is it?"

Lance could hear the howl of wind blowing into the front section of the airplane whenever Kirk keyed his microphone, knew it must be miserable up there.

"We've had to shut down the laser. Seven of the modules overheated and dropped off-line. Most of the others were about to go as well. We never expected to have to run them this long. Plus, we've got a missile launch detect from one or both of the Syrian jets. We don't have any way to determine how many missiles they fired. My guess is when our laser shut down they got a good lock and let go with everything."

"How long before you can fire the laser back up?" Kirk asked, taking a look at what was left of the missile warning set in the space between the two seats. There was no image, the glass over the video display was broken. The digital numbers were still illuminated, but registered all 8s. Kirk hit the reset switch and waited for the system to cycle through its self test.

Dixie held up one finger.

"One minute or less," Lance answered.

Kirk cycled through the time to impact readout on the missile warning receiver. The first number came up as thirty seconds, the closest threat. There were three other numbers, thirty-six, thirty-eight, and forty-three. A total of four missiles inbound. "You better get that laser back up in less than twenty seconds, or we've all had it. Missile is now twenty-four seconds out."

"But it could blow," Dixie argued, pointing at the temperature reading above the two hottest modules. They were cooling off slowly, would never be at a safe temperature before the missiles reached them.

"Bring the extra modules on line," Lance said. "We'll use them exclusively. If the Syrian is tracking us now, that means his optical system is looking right at us. It shouldn't take all of the modules to start up a parasitic in his laser."

Dixie pushed the appropriate areas of the touch-sensitive screen, bringing the standby laser modules up to operating status. Mechanical mirrors flipped into the beam path and redirected the laser beams into the main beam channel, into the input port of the beam director.

"Fifteen seconds," Kirk called.

"Just hold it steady," Lance told him while he checked the position of the laser plane's image in the display. He used the joystick to move the cross hairs to a spot just over the target airplane's wing, to where he thought he could see the laser port.

"If we direct our beam right back into his beam director, it won't cause a parasitic," Dixie reminded him. "We'll have to be slightly off to the side."

"Or we can dither our beam."

"Right," Dixie agreed, having forgotten one of the basic tenets of control-system design. "We can use the conical scan algorithm."

"Exactly." Lance reached up to call the appropriate menu from the computer, selecting the old algorithm he had used years ago when they shot down the missiles in the Laser Lab tests.

"I'm glad I didn't delete that piece of code," Dixie said. "I was tempted at times, but it was still useful for doing some calibration work."

Lance got a green light, indicating the code was loaded into the beam control computer, then keyed the thumb switch on the joystick. They both watched as the image of the laser plane began a rapid nutation, spiraling around in the video display as the conical scan moved their laser beam in tight circles about the target.

"Five seconds," Kirk called.

"Nothing to do now but wait and hope," Lance said, crossing his arms in front of him.

"Three . . . Two . . . One . . ."

Dixie gripped the armrests of her chair tightly, waiting for the lethal missile to come blasting through the thin skin of their old airplane. A loud squeal in her ears made her jump, her heart stuck in her throat.

"There it goes!" Jones yelled over the interphone as the first missile passed well below them, diving for the earth.

"And there are the other three!" Kirk pointed at three other trails of smoke, also below them and heading for the ground. "Must have a fail safe that directs them toward the ground if they lose signal."

"Tone!" ECMO Two called.

"MAGNUM, MAGNUM, MAGNUM," Adkins called as he got the same signal in his headset and pickled off his only remaining HARM.

"Another missile launch?" Lance reached up to reset the missile warning sensor. Why launch more missiles now? The laser was still jammed, they couldn't possibly have a lock.

* * *

"Damn!" Adkins exclaimed as he realized he had keyed the intercom instead of the radio when he called the missile launch. He punched up the radio and repeated his call just as the HARM impacted the Syrian transport. It passed straight through the fuselage before detonating and igniting the vaporized fuel. Their enemy was instantly obliterated, leaving no doubt they had made their first air-to-air kill with an air-to-surface missile.

Lance saw the missile streak into the left side of the video display a split second before the Syrian laser plane went up in a ball of fire.

"Target is down!" he called forward to let the two colonels know they had succeeded.

"Switch the HELRATS back into search," Kirk ordered from the front. "Find the other MiGs!"

Dixie did as she was told, redirecting the radar to scan the area for any other returns. The original two MiGs were fleeing, having disposed of all their ordinance, but there were several large returns that appeared to the north. She waited, then switched to high-resolution mode on the display. The large radar return broke up into about two dozen smaller blips. Dixie sucked in her breath—there were at least two squadrons of fighters headed their way. She was about to tell Kirk what she saw coming when the entire formation began to turn away.

"It looks like about two squadrons of fighters were about to come greet us, but when we took out their targeting system they turned for home," Dixie informed Kirk, relief and pride filling her voice.

"Copy," Kirk replied. "Sounds like something we should do ourselves. Keep your eyes peeled back there."

Dixie felt the plane begin to turn to the south, headed back the same way they came.

"Warlord Bravo, this is Eagle Three Three," Jones made the call over the special radio the Israelis had installed while they were in Cypress.

"Eagle Three Three, this is Warlord Bravo. We read you."

"You are cleared in. Code is . . ." Jones checked the little note card the Israeli general had given him in Cypress. ". . . Zulu . . . Echo . . . One. Repeat . . . Zulu . . . Echo . . . One. Over."

The Israeli commander verified the special code, and Jones turned off the radio. There was to be no further contact with the Israelis. No one was supposed to know the Americans had even been in Syria, although Jones had no idea how the State Department was going to explain the wreckage of a U.S. Navy EA-6B in the Syrian desert.

"Let's drop to ten thousand," Jones told Kirk. "That way we'll be relatively safe if the pressurization system craps out. It's been working awfully hard the last fifteen minutes. We'll still be well above the Israelis. They should have about two hundred fighters blasting through the Syrian defenses any second now."

"I just hope they're in time."

"Yeah. We've done our part. If the guys on the ground don't come through, the Syrians will still have a first-strike option with the chemical warheads. It wouldn't surprise me in the least if they exercised it."

"Yeah, but like you say, we've done our part," Kirk said. "Not much else we can do. Head out the same way we came in?"

"Sure."

"How's our fuel?"

"I'm not sure, Warren was tracking it back there," Jones used his thumb to point over his shoulder. "My guess was we were past the point of no return about ten minutes ago."

"We don't have enough to make it back to Cypress?" Kirk asked, his elation turning sour.

"We don't have enough fuel to make it back anywhere."

21

"There goes another flight." Jones looked down again. "Six planes. F-16s."

"Yeah. The Syrians are in for a hell of a surprise. You'd think they would have learned something from the last war. They must have gotten overconfident from their experience in Desert Storm. From everything I heard, the Syrians fought better than any of the other Arab forces in the Coalition."

"But there weren't any Israelis in the Coalition," Jones said. "If there were, the Syrians would have learned another lesson, one that would save them from the grief they're about to face."

Kirk thought about that for a moment, wondered if the Israelis would use their nuclear weapons if they couldn't successfully take out the chemically armed SCUDs. Probably. There was one thing he was certain about—the Israelis would go to any means necessary to preserve their State.

"Looks like we're feet wet again," Jones interrupted Kirk's thoughts.

Kirk looked out through the broken window. From ten thousand feet he could barely make out the Israeli shoreline below. Normally the site would have been beautiful, but not today. Other images plagued Kirk's thoughts, images of the ALL crashing into the sea.

"What do you think?" Kirk asked Jones.

"It's no good," Jones replied. "There's even a head wind, unusual in this area. We've burned more fuel than I expected. Too bad this thing isn't rigged for refueling. There must be a couple of dozen tankers down there pumping up the fighters. We're out of luck, we'll have to ditch."

Kirk felt his stomach churn. This old plane probably wouldn't survive a ditching, would break up when it hit. No one would survive. He watched without feeling as Jones reached over and pulled the throttles back on both outboard engines, then trimmed the nose down slightly to maintain airspeed.

"Don't sweat it, Colonel," Jones noticed the look on his new copilot's face. "I doubt if we'd been able to land anyhow, the nose gear's trashed. Warren told me about it right after we landed in Cypress, said he didn't think we should try to land it again."

"Then how the hell did you expect us to get out?" Kirk asked angrily. Had Jones committed them to a death sentence?

Jones used his thumb to point to the back of the plane. "Back door," he said.

"Bail out?" Kirk asked, a look of shock creeping

into his eyes. "Do you know what the odds of surviving that are? And who's going to fly the plane?"

"The odds of jumping out are better than sticking with this thing. And I'm going to fly the plane."

Jones looked at Kirk. "I don't have anything to go back to, John. This is the only way for me to go out."

Kirk thought about that. He didn't have anything to go back to, either, and there was no way Jones could fly the damaged plane by himself.

Eastern Syria

Stupid. That was the only word to describe what he was doing. Conner was worried he had let this gung-ho shit go to his head, had forgotten how long it had been since he worked with this kind of soldier, how long since he had been an air liaison officer attached to the Third Battalion, Airborne Rangers.

Conner scurried after Reitman, staying low. They stopped and hid just outside the compound, watching warily as the foot patrol passed by. It was now or never. Reitman rushed up to the fence, his desert camouflage uniform blending well with their stark surroundings. Conner was close on his heels, sensing that his green flight suit made him stick out like a sore thumb. It would have made a lot more sense to let one of the Israelis come on this mission, but there weren't a lot of them left, barely enough to man the target-designating system for the fighters. If the fighters ever came, they were already two hours late.

Reitman quickly clipped the chain-link fence, pulling up the lower part to let Conner crawl through. Conner fell on his back and fought his way through the small opening, then pulled his pack after him. After he held the wire for Reitman, they pulled it back down, disguising the fact they had trespassed into the facility. Hopefully they would be finished before the patrol passed by again.

Conner and Reitman raced to the nearest cover, a truck at the end of the row. They slowly made their way down the long line, heading for the antenna tower near the main building. It was easy going. The sun was up now but still low enough to cast long shadows. The two men used the shadows, hiding in them.

They were near the smaller of the two buildings when Reitman froze, holding his hand back and down, signaling Conner to be quiet. Something was wrong. Conner hadn't seen anything, hadn't heard anything. He had no idea what held Reitman's attention. Both men dropped lower as a loud piercing squeal shattered the peaceful silence. Rusted hinges. Conner looked carefully between the trailer and its long, cylindrical cargo, watched as men started pouring out of the small building.

"Must be a barracks," Conner whispered as the Syrian soldiers formed up. Neither man was impressed, the Syrians were disheveled, unkempt. Even the officer. The only things that looked well cared for were the AK-74s each soldier held, and held properly.

"Correct," Reitman said quietly. "All the Syrian barracks look the same. These men must be the guards they send out with the missiles. It looks like they are about ready to deploy most of the launchers. We better get busy."

They moved out again, slower this time, taking extra care not to be seen. Their only weapon was Reitman's UZI, Conner didn't even have a handgun. They passed the small barracks and were approaching the larger command post. Reitman stopped them again, moving to hide between two of the trucks. This time Conner could see exactly what the problem was. The patrol had finished its check of the perimeter and was now inspecting the line of vehicles, moving toward where the two intruders were hidden. Peering around the corner of the trailer, Conner could see one guard walking slowly down the row while another checked between the trucks. They even took turns stooping down to look beneath the vehicles. Conner waved at Reitman, checking near the cab of the truck. They met back at the center.

"Same thing on this end," Reitman said after Conner explained what he saw.

"What now?" Conner asked, worried there was no way out. He knew if they were captured, they would surely die. Either at the hands of the Syrians, or from the Israeli bombs that would soon decimate the facility.

Reitman looked around, searching for an escape. He tapped Conner on the shoulder, not wanting to risk being overheard. The guards were getting closer. Reitman smiled, pointed up with his thumb.

Conner peered over the edge of the door window, searching for the guards. Once again, there was good news and there was bad news.

"The guards are two vehicles away now, they didn't hear us," Conner whispered.

"Good, we'll wait until they're a little farther away and then climb down."

"No time," Conner finished with the bad news, "the guys we saw come out of the building are heading this way, getting in the trucks. We've got to move out."

"Let's do it, then." Reitman slowly pushed the door open. He cringed when the dented metal popped against the fender. They both waited, holding their breath, fearing the guards would come. They didn't.

Conner followed Reitman down from the cab of the truck, not bothering to close the door completely. They moved over to the next line of trucks, taking advantage of the carelessness the Syrian soldiers were showing. They obviously had no need to be careful, these trucks had already been inspected. At the last truck, Conner looked out and checked in both directions. The area was clear. He was surprised at how little activity there was near the command building.

They had no problem getting to the tower, hiding in the shadow of the building as they moved. Conner stood guard with Reitman's UZI while the Israeli commando placed the charge. The American looked around continuously, his nerves on end. Then a thought hit him, it was going to be impossible to get back out the way they came in. The Syrians, by manning the vehicles, had effectively cut off that avenue of escape. The alternative was to make a run for the nearest section of fence, directly across from the communications tower. Not an attractive idea. It was at least seventy-five yards to the fence, open terrain. Then there was another fifty yards to the closest cover on the outside. A feeling of dread began to fall over Conner. Was this it?

"How long should I set the timer?" Reitman asked quietly, breaking Conner's train of thought.

"Huh, I don't . . ."

Operated from somewhere inside the building, a generator next to the tower started up. Both men jumped.

"I think they're getting serious," Conner answered loudly, his voice masked by the noisy generator. "There are power lines so they've got power coming into the building, but apparently they don't want to depend on it for their mission. They're using the generator as primary source. We better set the timer to give us just enough time to get to the fence, through it, and over to their cover. Maybe three minutes."

"You're faster than that," Reitman argued, setting the timer for two minutes. He hit the start button. "GO!"

Reitman grabbed the rifle from Conner and sprinted for the fence.

Conner's lungs stung as he tried to keep up with the Israeli. He had run the hundred-yard dash in high school, and even though that had been many years ago he was still fast. It was hard to tell, though, as Reitman stopped at the fence a good ten yards in front of him. Reitman pulled out the cutters and began to snip away at the wire.

Both men ducked as the satchel charge exploded loudly behind them. They watched the microwave tower fall to the ground. Success. Then the Syrian guards at the far end of the row of missiles spotted them and came charging forward.

Reitman resumed his work with added enthusiasm. The sand near them puffed twice as Conner bent over to lend a hand. The sound of the rifle cracks followed almost immediately accompanied by outraged yells from the Syrians.

"Hurry!" Conner urged, knowing that it would take the guards only a little time to close in on them.

Reitman didn't need any urging, the rifle fire had done that for him. In seconds he had cut a hole in the fence. Big enough this time for them to get through easily. He held it back and let Conner go first.

Once through, Conner held the wire up for Reitman, instinctively ducking as more rifles fired in the background. He pulled on Reitman's arm to help him through and felt a jolt. A dark round circle appeared on Reitman's chest, blood seeped from the wound.

Reitman slowed, his strength waning. Conner could tell Reitman wouldn't be able to make it through on his own. A hail of metal fell around them. Conner pulled harder on Reitman's arm. He couldn't pull the Israeli through the fence and hold the wire at the same time. He would have to stand and pull with both hands. He would be an easy target.

"What the hell," he said, raising to one knee as he got ready to pull Reitman through.

In the background, beyond the firing of the rifles, he heard the distinct sound of a KFIR engine slice through the air.

Conner heard the plane scream overhead, crossing from left to right. It was high, moving fast, gone before the first concussion blasted Conner to the ground. He guessed it was a five-hundred pounder. The inferno that ensued was hellish, liquid-fueled canisters exploded in succession, like dominoes tumbling down the line. They lit up the early morning sky for miles around, made Conner and Reitman even easier targets. Fortunately, there was no one left to shoot at them. The Syrian guards had been instantly annihilated when the missiles cooked off. Conner stood and pulled Reitman through the fence.

Conner fell back on the ground when he had the Israeli through, resting and catching his breath. The flames grew brighter as more fuel tanks exploded. Conner felt the heat lash out toward them, felt the hair on his exposed hands burn away. He grabbed Reitman and lifted, pulling one of the injured soldier's arms around his shoulder. He half carried, half dragged the Israeli away. To his credit, the Israeli commando struggled to help, his pain, obviously excruciating, apparent only in his expression.

At the edge of the clearing two other men appeared. Thinking they were Syrians, Conner dropped to the ground, knowing it was too late to escape. He caught his breath when they moved closer, then breathed easier when he recognized them as Israelis. The commandos dropped to the ground beside him as they heard two other explosions several thousand yards away. They all looked west, watched as another fire leaped into the sky. One of the other SCUDs, Conner decided.

"Let's move," one of the Israelis ordered.

Conner stood back as they each grabbed one of Reitman's arms and pulled him away.

Ten minutes later they stumbled into a clearing, moved to the north side, and stopped in the low brush. The Israelis laid Reitman down slowly, then one began to tend to his wounds. Two other Israelis appeared in less than a minute—one was Gurion.

"How is he?" Gurion asked.

Conner started to answer, but was interrupted by the Israeli who had been working on Reitman.

"Not too bad. Lost some blood, has at least one broken rib, and may have a collapsed lung. Fortunately, it looks like the bullet went clean through."

"He'll make it?" Gurion asked.

"Sure, he's going to be in a lot of pain, though."

"We'll give him something when the chopper gets here. Should be ten minutes."

Chopper. That was the best word Conner had heard in the last four days. He'd almost given up on ever getting out of this thing alive. Now it looked like they stood a fair chance.

Conner sat back and rested, waiting for the chopper to arrive, trying to stay out of the way. In pairs, the other Israelis showed up. In all there were sixteen. No losses. But how many were successful? How many SCUDs were launched before the fighters could destroy them? He went over to ask Gurion.

"We got them all. Thanks in part to your knocking out that communications tower, I'm sure. The Syrians are under heavy centralized control. Two of the missiles weren't destroyed until at least five minutes after the initial strike. If they'd been able to communicate, I'm positive they would have launched the others. One launch crew just fled when they found they couldn't make contact with their commander. The State of Israel owes you a great debt."

"I'll settle for a ride home."

"I think I hear your ride now," Gurion said as he looked toward the south.

In a couple of seconds Conner could hear it, too, the unmistakable thumping of a helo's rotors.

The helicopter, guided in by infrared beacons placed around the perimeter of the clearing, touched down tactical, its rotors churning the air into a sandstorm. Conner shielded his eyes as the sand pounded away at his already raw skin. The commandos, four of them, carried Reitman aboard first, then the others began to mount up. Conner pulled up the rear, followed only by Gurion.

Conner dived into the chopper, then turned to wait in the door. His lungs refused to let him breathe the sand saturated air. Shielding his eyes with one hand, Conner held his other out to the Israeli officer.

"Rangers lead the way, sir!" Conner screamed above the pounding of the rotor.

"All the way, Ranger!" Gurion yelled back as Conner dragged him aboard.

Aboard the ALL

"We better get the kids out," Kirk said.

"Yeah, here close to the coast. That'll increase their chances of getting picked up. They know not to say anything?"

"Yeah." Kirk flipped to the test crew net. "Lance, Dixie, you two better get ready to bail out!"

Lance's face drew taut when he heard Kirk's in-

structions. He looked over at Dixie. She wasn't smiling, but she didn't seem all that concerned, either.

"Did you hear what he said?" Lance asked.

"Yeah. We get to jump." Dixie pulled the straps
tight on her parachute. She released the seat restraint
and started to stand up when Lance reached out to
grab her forearm.

"Doesn't that bother you?" he asked.

"No, not really. This will be number ninety-two
for me. Sky diving is one of my hobbies, remember.
Of course, I've never jumped out of one of these
planes before, but it shouldn't be a big deal. We better get ready. Pull your straps tight and make sure
your helmet is on secure."

Lance pulled the straps until he could feel pressure
in his crotch. He unhooked his own seat restraint
and stood up. Too quickly. The pain reminded him
the chute made it difficult to stand up straight when
it was properly tightened. The straps between his
legs pulled him back down until he was bent slightly
at the waist. The pain subsided. Lance disconnected
the headset cord from his helmet.

Dixie led the way back to the escape chute. Lance
could see her reading the instructions on its operation, remembering what he was supposed to do from
his own egress training over a decade earlier. He
wished now there had been enough time to review
some of the procedures during the last few weeks.
There hadn't. He hadn't considered it important,

thinking Chief Warren would be there to show him what to do if something went wrong.

Dixie pulled down a faded red bar, inserting the free end into a bracket designed to support it.

Air rushed up as a panel below them blew out. Lance jumped back, surprised. His ears plugged, and he had to swallow to clear them. The roar of wind replaced the normally muffled sounds of the engines. He looked down through the grate at his feet, startled to see water far below.

He tugged at Dixie's sleeve, then yelled to be heard over the rushing wind, pointing down: "Look's like we're over water!"

Dixie nodded. She walked back to the tail of the plane and returned dragging a green canvas bag, nearly a meter in diameter.

Lance read the white stenciled lettering: SURVIVAL KIT, WATER, 1 EA. Great.

"Just relax," Dixie yelled at him. "Don't look down, concentrate on the horizon. As soon as you hit the water get out from under the canopy. Nothing to it. Let's tell Kirk we're ready."

They both grabbed one of the interphone cords from the old instrumentation console and plugged in.

"Colonel Kirk, this is Dixie. We're all set."

"Good, we're already down to four thousand feet so you better get going. Good luck."

"What about you two?" Lance asked.

"We'll have to stay with it, the autopilot is screwed up from the missile hit. Now, go. That's an order!"

Dixie unplugged her interphone cord and tugged at Lance's sleeve, urging him to do the same.

Lance wanted to do something to help his old friend up front, but quickly realized there was nothing he could do. Lance reluctantly pulled his interphone cord free.

Dixie pulled up the metal grate that covered the now-open hole in the plane's lower fuselage, securing it with a latch. She dragged the survival kit over to the edge of the hatch and pulled one end of a cord from the canvas bag, hooked it to a snap ring in the floor of the plane. "We'll have to go out right after I drop this, so we'll land close to it. It should automatically inflate when it hits the water."

Lance took a deep breath and nodded, then watched as Dixie kicked the bag into the hole.

It dropped about eight feet and then stopped, stuck in the shaft.

"Shit!" Dixie dropped to her knees to stare into the hole, trying to see what the survival kit was hung on.

Lance joined her, peering into the darkness. He couldn't see an obstruction, decided the bag was just a little too big for the hole.

Dixie stood up. There wasn't anything long enough to push the bag through the shaft.

"Just do what I do," she yelled. "Make sure you know where your D-ring is." Dixie grabbed her own rip cord in her right hand to show him. "We're low enough now, just pull it when you clear the plane."

Lance watched as she grabbed the bar and stepped

over the hole, hanging for a second. She held her legs against the side of shaft to stop her swaying, then let go of the bar.

That was all it took. Her feet knocked the canvas bag free and her momentum carried her down and away, following the life raft out of the plane.

Lance was alone now. His hands were covered with sweat. He wiped them on his flight suit and grabbed the bar, then lowered himself slowly into the hole. The wind coming up through the hole blew him back and forth. He tried to use his legs to stabilize himself as Dixie had, but it did no good. He was sweating profusely now, the salty liquid was running down into his eyes, burning them. He knew he was going to have to drop, but he was having a hard time convincing his hands to let go.

The ALL, the place where he had completed some of the most fascinating work in his entire life, seemed to sense his hesitation. It hit a down draft, then popped back up. The snap forced his wet hands to slip from the bar and he dropped into the void. A huge gust of wind greeted him when he cleared the belly of the plane, blowing him toward the tail of the 135. Lance grabbed for the D-ring.

Lance drifted lazily beneath the canopy. It was fully open; that was one thing he remembered from his early training, to make sure the parachute cords hadn't gotten tangled above him. Lance had hoped Jones would be able to pull off some kind of flying miracle, the kind he had shown them so many times during the last three weeks. That hope faded as soon as he cleared the phone, when he heard the engines die, starved of fuel. As he spun to face the west, he watched the ALL descending in the distance. It was extremely low now, only slightly above the water.

He barely saw the splash when the ALL hit, wondered what it must have felt like. It was hard to believe Kirk was still in there, still flying his beloved Airborne Laser Laboratory.

Lance looked below him now, saw Dixie hit the water, then her chute fall on top of her. The orange raft was already starting to inflate nearby. He estimated he would land fairly close to them, a short swim. He glanced to the east and watched a small boat change course and head in Dixie's direction. A reception committee already. Now all they had to do was figure out what to tell them.

EPILOGUE

D-Day plus Fourteen
The new Syrian border

Colonel Robert Gabriel sat in the back of the four-door Mercedes as it bounced to a stop. His thoughts careened back to that fateful night when he had watched "Pervert" bail out of his RF-117. He had been helpless to come to his aid.

"Snake" Gabriel looked out the window. The image was blurred, even with the heavy prescription lenses he now had to wear. In spite of the aberrations, he could see the distinctive marks of a recent battle. The deep excavations made by two-thousand pounders were unmistakable.

"How are you doing, Colonel?" the major, a doctor, asked him.

"About as well as can be expected." Gabriel fought back the self-pity that threatened to overpower him. Even the promotion hadn't done much to help him overlook the misery he felt, hadn't helped him fight back the fear that struck him each time they told him his eyes weren't getting better. The last prognosis was fifty/fifty, a fifty-percent chance he wouldn't be permanently blind by this time next year. Zero chance he would ever be able to see with any clarity. Goddamned Syrians. The type of laser they used for their targeting had a lasting effect. Crueler than death.

"They're here," the major said. "Think you can get out?"

"Of course," Gabriel replied, his spirits lifted. He looked forward to greeting the Pervert, thankful to the Israelis for making his release a requirement in Syria's terms of surrender. He felt for the door handle and opened it, recoiling as the desert heat blasted him. Brushing it off, he stepped outside the car, glimpsing shadows as they moved past, hearing the distinct sounds of metal, guns. Israeli guards.

Gabriel leaned against the car, waiting.

"He's coming, sir," the major told him. Then whispered: "It doesn't look good, Colonel. His eyes are bandaged. He'll need your support."

Gabriel's heart sank. He waited, fighting back the tears. Words were spoken, in Hebrew and Arabic. Then people walking away, the blur of bodies as the guards pulled back. Someone stopped in front of him.

"Johnny?" Gabriel asked, quietly.

"That you, Snake?" came the always exuberant voice.

"Yeah. How are you, Johnny."

"Okay. Except I can't see for shit."

"Yeah. Me, too."

D-Day plus Forty-two
Santa Barbara, California

Lance turned down the hill and headed for home, picking up the pace a little. Sweat dripped from his hair, not yet as long as Mandy liked it, but much longer than he had worn it while he was working for Kirk. He thought back to over a month ago, remembering Colonel Kirk. Hell of a guy. Jones, too.

The mid-afternoon sun was pleasant; the sea breeze made it cooler than the few weeks he had spent in Israel. It all seemed so long ago, so far away. Maybe that was good, there was death there.

Lance had settled back into the old routine, a delay of the space shuttle even gave him a chance to work out a few of the little problems on the project he'd left before joining Kirk's team. After straightening up the last little software glitch, he had given himself the rest of the day off, deciding to jog home. Mandy could take him back to get the car later.

Lance walked the last hundred yards, then went around to the back of the house when he found the front door locked. Mandy was there, laying on her stomach beside the pool, wearing the bikini he had bought her when he got back from Israel. It was the kind of bikini that was good for getting almost a complete tan, barely covering the essentials.

Running up quietly he jumped into the pool, showering her with water. Mandy let out a squeal and sat up, holding the top of her bikini against her chest with her arms, the straps hanging loosely to her sides.

"You dweeb," she yelled, reaching back to reattach her straps.

"I love you, too, dear," Lance said, swimming to the side of the pool.

Mandy came and sat on the edge, dangling her legs into the water. "What are you doing home so early?"

"Missed you," Lance answered, climbing out to sit beside her. "I decided to run home. Now I need a shower, want to join me?"

"I'd love to. The kids won't be home for another two hours. There's something you need to look at first, though, it came special delivery. I'll go get it."

Lance watched Mandy walk to the back door. She looked great, more like a twenty-year-old than her thirty-three years. He got up himself and sat in one of the pool chairs. Letting the California sun dry him, he wondered what the government wanted now. It had to be something from the Air Force. They kept sending more and more forms for him to fill out about his short tour of duty. Everything from pay information to something about credit toward retirement. It was probably going to cost them as much to fill out the paperwork as they paid him in salary for the six weeks he had been in uniform. And to think he had seriously considered going back into the reserves while he was working on the ALL. It was a lot of fun, much more than he had anticipated, but now the paperwork came. He decided Kirk must have been shielding him from most of it while he was working on the plane. Now Kirk wasn't there to take care of it for him.

The back door slammed, and Mandy returned with a large envelope.

"More Air Force stuff." She handed it to him.

Lance looked at the return address. It was from the judge advocate, Wright-Patterson AFB.

"It's from the legal office," Lance said, confused. Why would they be sending something to him? He opened it.

There was a cover letter.

Major Lance Brandon:
    During a recent review of Colonel John Kirk's (USAF, deceased) personal belongings, we discovered this package addressed to you. In compliance with his request, we did not open the package and have shipped it to you in its entirety. Should you have any questions, please direct them to our action officer, Captain Laura Young, phone number listed above.

Lance shook his head, he hated the stilted bureaucratic language the government used. He handed the cover letter to Mandy and ripped the top off the smaller envelope, wondering what Kirk would have sent him. He turned the envelope upside down and two small, silver oak leaves, insignia for a lieutenant colonel, fell out. There was also a letter. It was handwritten and bore the date they left for Cypress.

Dear Lance,

I don't know where to begin this, Lance. I want to tell you this in person as soon as we get back, but I have this strange feeling. Call it a premonition. Whatever. The bottom line is if you're reading this, you made it home, and I didn't. I hope like hell you make it back, because I got you into this.

What I want to tell you is that you belong in the Air Force. I know why you got out, I still remember those long talks we had back in Albuquerque, and I'll be the first to admit the facts haven't changed appreciably. The pilots still make more money, and the bureaucrats still make life hell for scientists. But I think you can see when we're done that the real payoff can't be seen on a Leave and Earnings Statement.

If we're successful, and I have no doubt that we will be, we will have taken away the enemy's ability to wage war. We will have saved countless lives, and we will have preserved freedom. If all of America's technical capability were to reside in the civilian community, we would not have been able to develop the ALL, would not have had the tools to usurp war before its total fury were unleashed. That's why we need you, and others like you, in the military, in the Air Force. I hope you will stay with us.

I've enclosed a small token with this letter. It's been said the Air Force is too new to have much in the way of tradition, but there are a few. These insignia were pinned on my shoulders by Colonel Weimer at my promotion. He received them from Colonel Riser, a former prisoner of war in Vietnam. They were given to him by Colonel James Benjamin, who received them from Hap Arnold himself.

It is my hope that you will continue the tradition.

Your friend,

James Kirk, Colonel, USAF

Lance studied the silver oak leaves. They were solid, heavier than the gold ones he had bought at the Base Exchange in Dayton. They were well used, too, he could tell from the many small, fine scratches. But they hadn't lost their luster.

"Mandy, what would you say if I decided to join the reserves?"